WHEN

I AM

THROUGH

WITH

YOU

WHEN
I AM
THROUGH
WITH
YOU

STEPHANIE KUEHN

Dutton Books

DUTTON BOOKS
An imprint of Penguin Random House LLC
375 Hudson Street
New York, NY 10014

Copyright © 2017 by Stephanie Kuehn.

Library of Congress Cataloging-in-Publication Data

Names: Kuehn, Stephanie, author.
Title: When I am through with you / Stephanie Kuehn.
Description: New York, NY : Dutton Books, [2017]
Identifiers: LCCN 2016040902| ISBN 9781101994733 (hardcover) | ISBN
    9781101994740 (epub)
Subjects: | CYAC: Survival—Fiction. | Hiking—Fiction.
Classification: LCC PZ7.K94872 Wh 2017 | DDC [Fic]—dc23 LC record available
at https://lccn.loc.gov/2016040902

Printed in the United States of America

10 9 8 7 6 5 4 3 2 1

Design by Anna Booth
Text set in Arno Pro

For Tessa, whose heart belongs to the wild

Long had I loved you; why I know not.
—Vladimir Nabokov, "Beneficence"

BEFORE

1.

I DIDN'T PICK ROSE, BY THE WAY, IF THAT'S WHAT YOU'RE WONDERING. I didn't choose anything about her. No doubt that says more about me than it does about her, but she was the one who approached me at the school theater that morning, sometime in the early fall of our sophomore year. I used to study every day before classes in the theater lobby, on that dusty stone floor amid the mottled mix of shadow and sun falling through the plate-glass windows.

She knew I sat there, I guess. She knew a lot of things about me before we even met. In fact, the first words she ever spoke to me were, "Where were you yesterday?"

I'd looked up, startled, from the messy stack of papers surrounding me, to see a girl with bright eyes and brown skin and very short hair staring back at me. "I was sick," I told her and not all that nicely, if we're being honest. Something in her tone felt like an accusation. Like I'd done her wrong by not meeting her expectations.

"And now you're not sick?" she asked, and she bounced on her feet a bit. She was a small girl, I realized, all bones and empty space.

I scowled at her question. "Why do you care?"

"I care, because you're the only one who's ever here this early, and you've missed four days this semester already. When you're gone, I'm alone. Who knows what might happen?"

Do you see how that might sound? How I might interpret her words to mean she relied on my presence to keep her safe?

"I get migraines," I told her, which was true, but not the only truth.

At this the girl shrugged. She flopped beside me and chewed her nails, watching while I did my homework. I was frantic, really. Forty minutes to first period and my essay on *Lord of the Flies* remained unfinished. I was attempting to say something pithy about anarchy and fascism really being two sides of the same coin—both because I believed I was clever and because I believed my cleverness made me who I was.

"I'm Rose," she said after a moment.

"I know." I didn't bother looking up this time. Brash, pixie-like Rosemarie Augustine was the new girl, relatively speaking. Her parents were the ones who'd taken over the historic Eel River Inn, and the whole Augustine family had moved up to Teyber from San Francisco three months prior. In our sleepy, dead-end Humboldt County town with a population of fewer than 2,500, it would've been hard *not* to know who she was, even if we hadn't yet been formally introduced.

"Aren't you going to tell me your name?" she asked. "It's Ben Gibson, I know, but the rules of proper discourse require you to tell me."

"I'm Ben Gibson," I told her.

"You're a sophomore like me, right? And your birthday is in April and you live with your mother."

"That's right."

"Do you have a girlfriend, Ben?"

I still didn't look up. "I have homework to do."

"This book's shit, you know." She reached into my lap to tap the cover of my school-loaned paperback—it was the one with the drawing of a crown of leaves tied to a boy I supposed was Ralph but longed to believe was Jack. "It doesn't say anything about humanity. All it does is give boys an excuse to be assholes when it suits them."

"Okay," I said because I liked the book. I liked to imagine what it would be like to be trapped on that island, far from home, desperate and competing for survival—although I knew I'd never have the charisma or strength to lead anyone anywhere, not even into darkness. Besides, if boys really were assholes when it suited them, didn't that mean the book was right?

"Do you have a girlfriend?" Rose asked again.

"No," I said.

"Well, now you do."

So that's how we met. And while I wasn't sure whether to take her seriously, I figured if Rose wanted me to be her boyfriend, then that's what I would be. Fighting the force of other people's wills might be something I fantasized about, but it wasn't anything I ever did in real life. What would be the point? It wasn't until I found Rose leaning against my locker after school that I realized just how serious she was.

"Take me somewhere," she said.

"Why?" I asked.

"Because that's what boyfriends do."

True as that might've been, I couldn't imagine where I might take her. I'd never been a boyfriend. Plus, my house wasn't an option.

I hedged. "Well, where do you want to go?"

"No," she said firmly. "You decide."

"But I don't like deciding."

"You don't like it or you're not good at it?"

"Both."

"Fine." She grabbed my hand. Yanked me through the crowded hallway in a way that was less pixie and more bull shark. "I'll choose. But let's get out of here. This place is making me sick."

I'm not sure what else to say about Rose. If you know me at all, then I doubt that's surprising. I suppose I could tell you more about how we got to know each other. How she took me to the inn that afternoon, where we sat outside in the shade of the redwood trees, and I told her how much I liked her shoes—they were made of this bright camel-brown leather and were shinier than anything I'd ever seen. Rose smiled when I said this, pleasing me that I'd pleased her. Plus, she was pretty like her shoes—shiny and rare and right in front of me; I was entranced, watching feverishly as her lips moved and her legs crossed while she rambled on about life with her French-Peruvian parents and dour-faced twin brother, who, she hinted, in a provocative voice, had *serious issues* of some mysterious nature.

I could tell you how she pined daily for the city she'd left behind. The people. The music. The food. The culture. Being able to see a first-run movie every now and then. Owning the inn might've been her parents' dream, but Rose thought for sure she was going to leave this place someday. The town of Teyber was just a way station on her march to Somewhere, and I supposed I was, too. Rose had plans for college. Graduate school. To be special. Be the best. That's one way we were different. From my vantage point, there was no hope for escape; I'd reached my zenith, a dim, low-slung, fatherless arc, and had long stopped believing in more.

I could also tell you how, in the two years we dated, Rose was my first everything. First kiss, first touch, first girl to see me naked and lustful without bursting into laughter (although she was the first to do that, too). We did more eventually. We did everything. Whatever she wanted. Rose dictated the rhyme and rhythm of our sexual awakening, and I loved that. I never had to make up my mind when I was with her.

By the way, I have no problem admitting I was nervous as hell the first time we actually did it—both of us offering up our so-called innocence during an awkward Thanksgiving Day fumbling that happened on the floor of the locked linen closet at the inn. For an awful moment, right before, as I hovered above her on the very edge of a promise, I feared I wouldn't be able to—my ambivalence runs deep—but Rose stayed calm. In her steady, guiding voice, she told me what to do and just how to do it. I was eager to listen. I was eager to be what she needed.

I don't know. There's more to say, of course, much more. Two years is a long time in a short life, especially when you're in high school. But that's not the Rose anybody wants to read about, is it? Tragedy is infinitely more interesting than bliss. That's the allure of self-destruction. Or so I've found.

But I'll end with this: I miss Rose. I'm even glad I met her, despite what happened on that mountain. There were bad parts, yes; if I had my own days of darkness and suffering and pain-imposed sensory deprivation on account of my headaches, then in between her moments of verve and brashness, Rose had her own kind of darkness—bleak and savage, like a circling wildcat waiting to eat her up. What she needed during those times was for me to keep her alive, and for two years, that's exactly what I did. And whether I did it by making her laugh or making her come or shielding her from her fears of tomorrow by giving her all my todays, I did it because she told me to and because I loved her. Truly.

So why'd I kill her?

2.

IT STARTED LIKE THIS: THE SUMMER BEFORE OUR SENIOR YEAR, ROSE
and her twin brother, Tomás, were supposed to spend six weeks in Peru
with their grandparents. It was their first time traveling to South America alone, and honestly, the trip sounded fucking awesome—even if
Tomás had to be there (he was a real dick—a total snob about all things
Teyber, and as much as I hated the place, I hated the way he hated it
more). But Rose didn't want to go and I didn't understand this and my
not understanding made her not want to go even more.

"You won't miss me," she growled, as we lay face-to-face on her
queen-size four-poster bed. "You want me gone."

I winced at what I could tell was the first tightening surge of an oncoming migraine. "What are you talking about? I'll miss you. Of course
I'll miss you. More than anything."

"You promise?"

"I promise."

"Things will be different when I get back."

"Why will they be different?"

Rose kicked her legs. Her bare heels made smudges on the wall.
"Because we'll be different people then. We won't be who we are now."

"We'll be different tomorrow, too," I said. "That's the way it always
is. You can't count on anything to stay the same."

"Well, six weeks is a lot of different."

She was right, of course—plenty of small differences had a way of
adding up to something largely unknown—but it seemed to me Rose

was the one who would be doing most of the changing. I'd seen her photographs from her previous trips to Lima, vistas awash with sandy beaches and sparkling water. It would be winter there, but other than the frigid Humboldt current swirling up from the south, their winter consisted of foggy days and occasionally having to wear a sweatshirt at night. Not to mention Rose would be spending most of her time at the university where her grandfather was a linguistics professor. That did give me pause. I could easily picture all the Peruvian college men she'd meet, the handsome ones with perfect hair and dark eyes, who'd smoke unfiltered cigarettes and speak with her in Spanish and take her out for coffee, then maybe drinks, then dinner, then—

You can understand my concern.

Still, I thought, as my migraine settled in and really began to take hold, I'd never been anywhere outside of the county, much less the States, a fact unlikely to change anytime soon. To encourage Rose to stay here, in a town she hated, just to be with me while I went nowhere was foolish. Selfish, even.

Still, I thought, maybe some separation would be good for us, a learning experience. After all, Rose would be going off to college the following summer. The promise of her future was bright, dazzling, while mine, on the other hand, consisted of staying in Teyber and taking care of my mother. Rose hated talking about it, but the fact of the matter was the boyfriend she'd picked out of her high school lobby was not only broke as hell but also bound by blood—and worse—to a woman who wasn't her. So we needed to get used to being apart, to see if the long-distance thing would work.

Still, I thought, maybe I just needed some goddamn time alone. For once.

I thought a lot of things that day, I guess. But what I said was this: "*Go.*"

My mother got into a car accident two days after Rose left. It's tempting to see that as an omen of some sort, proof of the intervening hand of fate, but it's hard to read too much into something that's happened before and is almost sure to happen again. This time she missed a turn on the interstate at around one in the morning and ended up twenty feet down the hillside embankment with the Ford's front end smashed in. She, however, had nothing worse to show for it other than a broken wrist, a bad attitude, and cuts from the glass.

I was mad at her for the accident. I remember that. There were no skid marks and my guess was she'd fallen asleep while drunk, although she insisted she'd swerved to avoid hitting a fox that had run into the road. She didn't deny the drinking; the grim daughter of even grimmer Estonian immigrants, my mother learned young that the most effective form of rebuttal was silence. Regardless, the car she'd ruined wasn't just hers but mine, and I knew I'd have to work two jobs to pay to fix it.

After she'd taken a cab home from the hospital and gotten herself settled in bed with her bottle of Vicodin—all while willfully ignoring the ruined Ford I'd had towed that now sat in the street leaking antifreeze in front of our sagging bungalow—I slouched my way down to the auto repair shop on Bloomington to see if they would work with me on a payment plan or barter of some kind. I could do oil changes, at least. Rotate tires. Take out the trash.

When I got there, Avery Diaz, the owner's daughter, was standing behind the counter. I'd known Avery since elementary school; we'd been in most of the same classes. She was smart. We were friendly. Seeing her got my hopes up and I explained my plight as humbly as I could.

Avery listened to me, her dark eyes warm, but reached to squeeze my hand when I'd finished talking. "Sorry, Ben. My dad won't work that way."

I nodded and thanked her, then left the shop. That night I stayed out late, alone. It wasn't like me, but I didn't tell my mom where I was going and refused to answer any of her texts when she tried contacting me. Instead I walked through the woods to the empty cliffs above the Eel River. In good years, when the water ran high, people would party there, diving from those cliffs to knife the glassy surface below. But the cliffs were empty. The water hadn't been high for a long time.

I sat and watched the moon, the starry vastness of the sky. I was lonely, I suppose. But I wasn't thinking of my girlfriend and all the ways I missed her. I was thinking of my mom. Of a fox caught in her headlights. My father had abandoned us both when I was two, never to return, and now she'd crashed our car on the only road heading out of town.

Where had she been going without me?

3.

ROSE WAS RIGHT, BY THE WAY. THINGS *WERE* DIFFERENT WHEN SHE got back. At first I thought it was me. I got food poisoning the night before she returned and missed her texts when she landed at San Francisco International the following morning. I saw them when I crawled out of bed to call in sick to work around noon. Figuring the last thing she'd want to hear about was how I'd spent the last twelve hours unable to eat, writhing in pain, running to the bathroom, and praying I got my pants down in time, I texted back: *Can't wait to see you.*

Her response: *Dinner tonight at ERI. 8 pm. Dress nice.*

I felt like trash, but ERI was the Eel River Inn and *dress nice* meant we'd be eating in the inn's restaurant with her parents. So I wrote: *I'll be there.*

There's this mood I can get into sometimes. It's hard to explain, but it can strike after a bout of sickness or hours spent dozing in the heat; after jacking off too many times in one day or staying up too late to watch the sunrise. I don't know how to describe it other than to say I feel sort of dead—faded, really, or reduced, like there's less of me or I'm not as much of myself. It's as if I've forgotten who I am or who I'm meant to be or if I'm really even anything or anyone at all.

That was the way I felt walking across town that August night. It was ten to eight, the bottoms of my feet hurt, and I was sweating like crazy in my dress shirt and tie. The air was dog-day hot—it reeked of far-off fires—but the corners of the sky had begun to darken. A betrayal of sorts: summer days growing shorter as if they'd lost their will.

It's Rose, I told myself, trying to snap out of my apathy. *You're going to see her. Finally.* And I wanted to see her, I did. But something was wrong. Despite six weeks of loneliness, there was no spark of desire. Not in my gut, my heart. Not anywhere. It was as if that part of me had vanished, and now I was going through the motions of seeing my girl-friend because that's what I was supposed to do.

I chalked it up to illness, my mood, the god-awful heat, and fingered the box rattling around in the pocket of my pants. It was a gift I'd gotten for Rose while she was gone—a vintage pair of pink-stone earrings I'd found in one of the local antique shops. The store owner had traded them for an old driftwood side table my lost artist father had made and left behind.

I really had missed her.

That's what I told myself, anyway.

I reached the inn at last—a rambling three-story Victorian on the outskirts of town and set on eight acres of redwood groves and fern-lined trails. The renowned on-site restaurant resided in what had originally been the carriage house. Apparently it had even earned a Michelin star back in the eighties, but like most good things in Teyber, that star was long gone.

Shoulders hunched, I made my way down the pea-gravel drive toward the dining entrance. My legs were tired and everything smelled like lilies. I was late already—I should've left earlier—and that meant everyone would be waiting for me, and that meant Rose would be disappointed before she even laid eyes on my sweat stains. But there was nothing I could do to fix any of that.

The front porch light was on. I walked up the steps and opened the door.

After cruising the length of the half-empty restaurant, I found Rose seated at a table by the fireplace, which roared and crackled every night of the year, no matter the season. No matter the heat. Her hair was longer, prettier, and she wore a black tank top and jeans. My stomach started hurting again at the sight of her, although I couldn't have said why.

"You look pale," she said after I kissed her cheek.

"I've been sick," I told her.

"Migraine?"

"Food poisoning, I think."

"That happens," she said.

I nodded. It did, didn't it? I wanted to say something about her, something good. But the truth was, if I looked pale, she looked . . . exhausted? That wasn't the word, not quite, but she didn't look how I remembered her. She didn't look like Rose.

"Where's your family?" I asked, sliding into the chair across from her. The table was set for two.

"It's just us tonight."

"It is?" I glanced down at my clothes. The ones I'd dressed nice in.

Rose lifted an eyebrow. "Isn't it better this way?"

"I missed you," I said quickly.

She stared at me. She stared for a long time without saying anything. Rose had returned tan, despite the whole winter thing, but she had raccoon rings around her eyes from her sunglasses. Or something. I loosened my tie and shifted around under the weight of her gaze. Calculated the distance to the bathroom.

"That color looks good on you," Rose offered, nodding at my shirt, right as I reached to unbutton my collar.

I paused mid-fumble, trying to discern what it was she wanted from me. When no further commentary came, I left the button alone.

"I missed you, too," she said finally, like she'd just figured it out. "Tell me about your summer."

We spent the next hour engaged in the type of stilted conversation that happens between old acquaintances or new strangers. I told Rose about my mother's car accident and how I'd picked up extra hours at the market in order to get it fixed. Rose told me about Peru, but it was clear she didn't want to. Her descriptions were superficial: what food she ate and the weight she gained and how much she hated spending time with her two teenage cousins. She didn't once mention her brother.

"But I thought you liked them," I said, referring to the cousins.

Rose waved a hand. "Those idiots want to come here for college. Have you ever heard anything so stupid?"

"You mean to the States?" I was confused. "Aren't you going to college here?"

"But I have to. It's not like I have a choice."

I took a sip of ice water. Rose had always been excited about college. Had her heart set on Stanford, in all its Left Coast glory. She also knew my choice was not getting to go at all. "I'm going to be working with the orienteering club this fall," I said.

Her eyes narrowed. "Working how?"

"Don't know exactly, but Mr. Howe asked if I'd be interested in being his assistant for the year. It pays. Not a lot, but you know. Better than bagging groceries."

"What do you know about orienteering?"

My cheeks warmed. The fact was, I'd been reading all I could on the topic, because what I actually knew was nothing. "I'm learning."

"And your mom's letting you do this?"

"Yeah, well, we need the money. She can't exactly say no."

Rose nodded but looked bored. I was sweating again and asked if we could go outside for some fresh air. She brought her coffee with her, and we stood on the back porch that cantilevered over the river. Our shoulders touched, but I didn't feel any closer to her than I had when she'd been in a different hemisphere.

"Don't you ever wonder what the point of all this is?" she asked me.

I stared at the water below, at the way it went around some of the rocks but ran over the tops of others. "The point of what?"

"Our lives. The things we do."

"You and me?"

"No. I mean everything. All the things we're meant to accomplish. Going to school. Finding a job. Falling in love. I mean, we're *supposed* to do these things just because some other people did them first, but what if they're not the things that will make us happy?"

"Well, what would make you happy?" I asked, although what I wanted to say was, *haven't you already fallen in love?*

"That's just it," Rose said. "I don't know. But I don't want to close any doors before I've had a chance to walk through them."

I flashed a smile. "You can't walk through them all, you know. Not everything's a choice."

"That's depressing, Ben."

"Sorry."

"It's more than depressing. Thinking like that makes me want to die already and get it over with."

"Sounds like you've been spending too much time with Tomás," I said, which was an attempt to make her laugh. Rose's brother had been in my English class the year prior, and he was the dreariest thing, prone to idolizing all those soppy dead poets, like Thomas Chatterton, who'd killed himself when he was seventeen by swilling arsenic. I had no clue what Tomás saw in him, whether he felt a kinship with the guy's name or his morbid gloom or the fact that he was a fraud, but on more than one occasion, I'd caught him scribbling down some of Chatterton's worst lines in his notebook. I mean, just awful stuff, like "the sickness of my soul declare."

Rose turned then and grabbed for my tie, pulling me closer in the process, which seemed to catch her off guard. Her fingers stroked silk before letting me go. "You know, Ben," she said. "If anything happened between you and anyone else while I was gone, it's fine. You can tell me. I'll forgive you."

This startled me, to say the least. "Seriously?"

"Seriously."

"Yeah, well, nothing happened," I said, and that was the truth. Nothing had even come close to happening. My summer had been one long drift of dissocial malaise; endless nights spent streaming porn, reading Murakami; days spent oversleeping, forgetting to eat, and doing my best to lose my mother's Vicodin prescription. I mean, I hadn't even *talked* to any girls my age, much less hooked up with one.

Rose sighed at my response, a sad sigh, and perhaps I was meant to tell her that if she'd done anything while she'd been in Peru, I'd forgive her, too. But I didn't.

We kept standing there. The sun abandoned the sky, leaving behind nothing but a glimmer of blue and purple, a hint of bruising along the tree line, and I wanted to hold Rose or kiss her or make her laugh, but it was like I'd forgotten how.

The earrings, I remembered. *I should give her those.* I reached in my pocket just as Rose knocked her coffee mug off the deck railing. It shattered at her feet. I bent to pick up the ceramic shards, and when I stood again, Rose pointed at my hand. I looked; blood was dripping everywhere—I'd sliced myself good on a piece of the mug—and I stared wide-eyed at the wound, unable to tear my gaze from the way my skin was just kind of hanging open, letting everything inside slip out.

The strangest thing happened then: The longer I stared at the blood rushing to leave my body, the more I grew light-headed and hot all over. It felt like I was melting or on the verge of bursting into flames. But before I could say anything or find a place to sit my melting ass down, my ears began to buzz, my vision went grainy, and I guess I passed out cold.

I woke to quite the scene. People were crowded around me. My tie was off, my shirt open, my bare chest exposed for all to see. A waiter

17

was trying to pour water down my throat, and another wrapped a towel around my cut hand. Annoyed, I pushed them away and sat up. Rose had managed to drag a doctor she knew out of the dining room, although thank God no one called an ambulance or anything.

The doctor crouched beside me. She insisted on listening to my heart, feeling my pulse, and asking me questions about what medications I was taking and if I was prone to panic attacks. I answered honestly but must've been too much of a dick to deal with because as soon as she figured out I wasn't dying, she stood again, started talking to Rose.

"I see this a lot, you know," the doctor said. "People fainting at the sight of blood. It's very common."

"Hmm," Rose said.

"Does your boyfriend have any underlying medical conditions?"

"He gets migraines from an accident he had as a kid. They're pretty bad. And he said he was sick last night. Food poisoning."

"All the more reason for resting. And water. If he's not feeling better in a day or two, he should see someone."

"Hmm," Rose said again.

They talked more, but I tuned them out. The crowd drifted away, and I sat on that porch beneath the glowing late summer moon, and worked to regain my bearings. I'd been sick, yes, and was probably dehydrated. It was also true I got migraines and blood could make me queasy. But I knew for a fact those weren't the reasons I'd lost consciousness. Because while I was sure there were plenty of guys out there eager for their girlfriends to absolve them of their sins, there was nothing in Rose's offer of forgiveness that had felt anything like a gift.

Not at all.

Not to me.

4.

BACK IN TENTH GRADE, MR. HOWE HAD BEEN MY U.S. HISTORY TEACHER.
That was the year we studied the Revolutionary War, the Civil War, the
Spanish-American War, and probably a whole bunch of other wars I
can't be bothered to remember. I do know we ended the year learning
about the start of the First World War, which, as far as my understanding of it went, had begun for pretty much no reason at all.

Mr. Howe had been easygoing with us then, funny, laid-back, and I
liked him a lot, even though history was the one subject I'd never taken
to. In my mind, the past was something we were destined to repeat
whether we learned about it or not. But I'd always liked the way Mr.
Howe could go from smiling and joking to intense and focused when he
lectured. And if I didn't care all that much for the things he was talking
about, it was still kind of neat that he did.

Caring about his job, by the way, was a good thing, seeing as Mr.
Howe had been teaching at Teyber Union for forever. He was also married, owned a nice house in the country, but as far as everyone knew,
Mr. Howe's true passion was mountain climbing. Built like a Saint Bernard, which was to say barrel-chested, red-cheeked, and with a massive
beard, he always managed to return from each spring, summer, and
winter break having reached some new height or achieved some personal accomplishment. It was a world I knew nothing about, but the
walls of his classroom were covered in photographs of peaks he'd mas-
tered: Mount Whitney, Mount Hood, Pikes Peak. Even Denali. Everest

and Kilimanjaro were on his bucket list, and I was sure he'd conquer them in his lifetime. Or else die trying.

I guess what I want to say is that I always respected Mr. Howe's ambition, even if I didn't understand it. That was a big part of the reason I accepted his offer to help with the school's orienteering club in the first place, although it wasn't the only reason. There was also the money I knew he knew I needed. And the way I craved almost anything that would help me feel in control of my life.

Beyond that, though, there was something in the way Mr. Howe asked that made it seem as if I were being offered more than mere employment. He didn't just call me up on the phone. Instead, sometime near the start of summer, he invited me over to his place for lunch. Obedient, as always, I'd ridden my bike across town to his sprawling farmhouse, not knowing what he wanted, only to be greeted at the door by his wife.

Her, I'd never met, but it turned out Mrs. Howe, who was elegant and bare-shouldered and had black hair that fell to her waist, was the sort of person who could look you in the eye and make you feel as if she'd give you everything she had, if that's what was needed. I was smitten. Heart pounding, I followed her through the house to their giant kitchen, where she waved for me to sit at this fancy marble island that looked as if it could seat ten people. And that wasn't even the dining room. That was somewhere else. "Kyle had to run to the store," she told me. "He'll be back in a minute."

"Oh, okay."

"I'm Lucia," she said. "But you can call me Lucy."

"I'm Ben."

"Would you like some tea, Ben? It's herbal."

"Uh, sure," I said, wiping my hands on my shorts. I didn't care to be in strange homes, much less alone with my teacher's pretty, bare-shouldered wife. All I knew about her was that she traveled a lot and that she wasn't from Teyber originally.

Lucy set about making the tea. She was quiet while she worked, which I liked. So different from my mom and her constant, frenetic need to ask questions and demand answers. Moments later a glazed ceramic mug appeared in front of me. Steam wafted from it, smelling of ginger and honey.

"Thank you."

She sat across from me with her own mug. "My pleasure."

"So do you work in, like, sales or something?" I asked.

Lucy's brows knitted. "Sales?"

"Is that why you travel?"

"Oh," she said. "No. Thank God. I don't think I'd be very good at that."

"Then what do you do?"

"I'm a psychologist."

At this, I perked up. "Oh, yeah? I read a lot about psychology."

She smiled. "What do you like to read about?

"Lots of things. Theories about how our personalities are developed. Or why people say one thing and do another."

"Where does this interest come from?"

"I don't know. My mom, I guess. She's not a very happy person."

Lucy watched while I blew at my tea. "That's sad."

"It's weak." I felt guilty the minute the words left my mouth, so I added, "But I'm weak, too."

"Why do you say that?"

"Because I can't make people happy. I keep trying, but I'm always screwing up."

"Does your mom tell you this?"

"My girlfriend mostly. She gets embarrassed for me a lot. I don't blame her. I mean, I do a lot of dumb stuff."

"I'm sorry to hear that."

I looked up at her. "Your clients must like you, huh? You listen really well."

Lucy reached to pat my arm. "That's nice of you. But I don't have any clients. My work is in public policy and research around mental health. It's why I'm away in DC so often. I've been gone for the past two weeks. Just got back yesterday, in fact."

"How was it?"

"Well, I missed the cherry blossoms again, despite my best efforts. But there's hope for the future, I suppose. Spring'll come around next year."

I melted a little. Her words pleased me, even if the sentiment was sort of ridiculous. And maybe it was something in the way she listened or the way she waited for me to speak, but Lucy was having the strangest effect on me. My mind raced, and I couldn't stop talking. "So, uh, are you and Mr. Howe going to have kids someday?"

Her eyes sparkled. "Oh, we wanted to once. Very much. But it's too late now. We're old."

"Really?" I didn't actually know about these things, but I also didn't know how old Mr. Howe and Lucy were. If I had to guess I would have put them in their early forties, but that seemed like there was still time. "How long have you been married?"

"Kyle and I met twenty-four years ago this month. We've been married for eighteen."

"So what happened? Jesus, I'm sorry. I know I'm asking a lot of questions."

"It's fine." Lucy tipped her head to one side, letting her long hair fall even farther down her back and exposing her neck. "Well, first we moved around a lot. When I was finally done with school, we decided to come back to Teyber—Kyle grew up here. That's when we really started trying. I always knew I wanted a large family. I'm the youngest of seven. Kyle's the oldest of five. We thought we'd thrive on chaos."

"But . . ."

"But it never happened for us. The doctors ran all sorts of tests. But . . . nothing."

I stared at her. "That's it? I thought there were all sorts of ways to have a kid. In vitro or surrogacy or egg donors. Something." I would have tried them all, I thought. Every last one, if that's what the woman I'd married had her heart set on.

Lucy seemed to have a window into my head. "I didn't want to triumph over nature. Neither of us did. It's not that we didn't want a family. But once you put yourself in a war with what's meant to be . . . well, I can only speak for myself. It would change the way I looked at everything. I couldn't give that up."

I could. I knew I would in an instant, given the chance.

"Ben!" I jumped and turned to see Mr. Howe walking into the kitchen, with his arms full of groceries and a huge grin stretched across his face, visible even beneath his beard. "So glad you could make it. You've met Lucia, I see."

I leapt up to help and Lucy did, too, and later we ate lunch together on the screened porch, looking out at their yard. The food was good and they were funny and kind, and they both said they hoped I'd come over again. I told them I would. I didn't want to leave.

After dessert, Mr. Howe took me into his book-lined study and showed me some of his climbing photos. I liked looking at those, to see places I'd never go. It was like looking at photos of a moon landing. He also showed me a ladder-backed chair he said my father had made. I didn't believe him at first, the detailing was too delicate, but sure enough, when he flipped it over I saw the initials carved into the wood on the bottom of the seat: *GG*, for Gus Gibson.

"Did you know him?" I asked. "My father?"

"I sure did. We met when Lucia and I first moved back here. We used to surf together in the mornings before school. Gus loved the ocean the way I love the mountains."

"Oh," I said.

"Do you talk to him?"

"No."

"Never?"

"I mean, he writes sometimes and sends money. He's a doctor now, lives in Connecticut. But I don't think my mother would want me, you know, having a relationship with him. After what he did."

Mr. Howe frowned but didn't mention my father again. Instead he asked for my help with the orienteering club that fall, and I can see now how maybe that sounds weird, the way I'm describing it. Like, here was this guy who knew I was fatherless and wanted to get too close. But it wasn't that way, and after talking with Lucy, I got why. Everyone needs things they can't have. So despite knowing absolutely nothing about orienteering or reading maps or even how to survive outside of my own stupid head, I said I'd help. Because Mr. Howe needed a son. And what I needed, above all else, was to succeed in making other people feel good about me.

5.

I HOPE IT'S NOT SOUNDING AS IF I HAD NO TRAINING FOR THE JOB I'D been hired to do. I mean, I didn't at first, but that changed in the weeks before school started. Mr. Howe had me take a CPR certification class as well as a first aid course, and I also completed an online wilderness safety training module. That was all in addition to the hours I spent on my own, poring over the International Orienteering Federation's official rulebook, trying to figure out what I'd gotten myself into. Rose never wanted to hear about any of it—she didn't consider not getting lost a sport—but I was diligent in my studies. I was ready for the challenge.

Well, ready or not, on the first day the club met after school, only four students bothered to show up. That was disappointing. Three guys and one girl. I knew them all, obviously; Teyber Union was only so big.

There was Duncan Strauss, a junior, a well-known pot dealer, and someone who seemed to miss as many school days as I did; Clay Bernard, a clean-cut sophomore with a personality not unlike my own—that is to say, studious, quiet, and somewhat bland; and senior Archie DuPraw, who was kind of a wild card, and while Archie and I tolerated each other in a wary way, I certainly didn't expect to see him in an extracurricular setting like that. Archie never took anything seriously, from what I could tell. He was the type of guy who, at seventeen, still got off on sniffing glue, getting blackout drunk, and doing stupid shit, like mumbly-peg or playing chicken on the train tracks. And not necessarily in that order.

But the real surprise was the girl. It was Avery Diaz, from the auto repair shop. It startled me to see her walk in the classroom on big, dumb Archie DuPraw's arm—I had no idea they were friends, much less anything more.

Not much happened that first afternoon. Mr. Howe and I went over some of the activities we'd be doing: hiking, map reading, learning basic survival skills. There would be two backpacking trips during the year and anyone who went on at least one of those trips would earn PE units, which explained Archie's presence, since rumor had it he wasn't going to have enough units to graduate in the spring. The plan was also to participate in a number of team orienteering competitions throughout the northern part of the state, mostly out in the Sierras, although I got the feeling Mr. Howe didn't approve of racing. "*L'art pour l'art,*" he told me, which I later found out meant "art for art's sake." After I handed out the club permission slips, we let the group go for the day.

I was walking across the parking lot when I heard someone call my name. I turned and squinted into the afternoon sun to see Avery running toward me. Alone. I stopped and waited for her.

"Hey," she said. "I didn't know you were working with Howe."

"Yeah. I just started."

"That's cool."

I didn't say anything. I just stood there and felt awful. Depressed, I guess, and all that, which was stupid seeing as there was nothing wrong. The wind was blowing and Avery's dark hair looked messy—it was sticking out in places. I had the urge to run my fingers through it.

"How's your mom?" she finally asked.

I shrugged. Looked away.

"My dad and her were good friends growing up. Did you know that?"

"I didn't know that."

Avery smiled. "After my mom died, I wanted him to date her. So he wouldn't be lonely. That would've been something, don't you think?"

I put my hands in my pockets. Rocked back on my heels and cleared my throat. "That wouldn't have been such a good idea."

"I know," she said softly. "I'm sorry."

"I gotta go," I told her.

I headed straight for the inn. It was full of autumn visitors, and it took a while to find Rose. She wasn't outside with her brother, who was sitting in the garden reading Proust, of all things, and she didn't answer any of my texts. Turned out she was helping her mother set up a wine tasting for a group of eager guests in that bright wicker-filled space they called the parlor. She took one look at me and dragged me up to her room.

"What's wrong with you?" she demanded.

"Everything," I said, and I felt like a petulant child. My heart was pounding, and blood was rushing to my cheeks. I leaned down and I kissed her. Then I kept kissing her, frantically, eagerly, passion blooming inside me for the first time since she'd come back. In that moment, I couldn't stand it, the way I felt; I had to have her. I pulled her down on to the bed beside me, pawing beneath her clothes and cupping her tits.

Rose kissed me back, but she laughed, too, like my ardor was something humorous. I didn't mind, so long as she was with me, willing to meet me where I was with her own brand of passion. We stayed locked like that for a while, rolling around a bit, with me slobbering on her neck and dry humping her like crazy, but then she was pulling my jeans down, my boxers, too, and I wanted to take her then, push my way on top of her. But Rose had other plans, because she twisted out of my grasp and slid to the floor like a cat to settle between my legs.

I groaned, despite myself. Having her mouth where she put it was the hottest thing, but I couldn't touch her when she was doing that and I wanted to touch her. So even as I loved what she was doing, even as she laughed again before quieting down and allowing the room and space around us to fill with a different sort of sound and the most perfect sort of feeling, a softness and rhythm that pushed me toward a shuddering end I lacked the ability to control, all I could think was, *Oh, Rose, I want this, I do, more than anything. But this isn't how I wanted it.*

I wanted you to want me, too.

6.

TWO MORE STUDENTS SHOWED UP FOR THE NEXT ORIENTEERING CLUB
meeting, lured perhaps by that promise of PE credit. Otherwise I wasn't
sure what had brought them. The first was Shelby Sawyer. I'd known
Shelby since her days as the bucktoothed, blond-haired, overly freckled
girl who cried snotty tears every morning at kindergarten drop-off, but
I had a hard time talking to her now that she'd emerged from puberty
as this sleek, six-foot-tall, volleyball-playing goddess. This was clearly
a personal flaw, because Shelby was friendly with just about anybody.
She'd confided in me once that she preferred spending her time raising
alpacas for 4-H, but that her parents insisted volleyball would look better on college applications. It made me feel bad to hear her say that, but
I also saw their point.

The second person who showed up to the meeting was Tomás,
Rose's snob of a brother. Like I said, they were twins—fraternal,
obviously—but with Rose's short hair, the similarity between them
was overwhelming, Tomás's Y chromosome and crappy personality
notwithstanding. It always startled me to see her bright brown eyes on
him since the expression on his face usually read as if he were seconds
away from throwing himself in front of a train.

It would've been easy, by the way, to believe Tomás had come to
the meeting because of Shelby, only he'd never been anything but completely open about the fact his interests lay elsewhere. And yeah, sure, I
wish I could say stuff like that didn't matter—to Teyber, to me—but of
course it did. His hating me didn't help much either.

We picked the site of the first backpacking trip together, as a group. I liked that about Mr. Howe. He treated us, if not like equals, then as if it were a given that we would be someday. There's just something about presumed competence that makes you really want to try, you know? We spread a map of Northern California out on Mr. Howe's desk and scoured the acreage for an appropriate locale.

Archie DuPraw immediately homed in on Mount Shasta or Mount Whitney. Both had name recognition and a sense of imminent doom—climbers had perished on those mountains—but Mr. Howe pointed out that taking on a California fourteener as our first mountain was like getting a Mercedes as a first car. What would we have to look forward to?

"Be humble," he told us. "That's the only way to survive out there."

Mount Lassen was in play, in all its volcanic beauty, but we finally decided on Thompson Peak—the tallest summit in the vast Trinity Alps, which felt like an accomplishment all on its own. Our day of departure would be a Friday in the second week of October; school would be closed for administrative development, which was a stroke of good fortune. The trip was soon, Mr. Howe acknowledged, and we had a lot of work ahead of us to prepare. But we wanted to get out there on the mountain well before the storm season hit. At 9,000 feet, Thompson Peak was crusted in permafrost, and there was usually snow piled high well into the summer, making fall the most accessible season. October was the warmest time in Northern California, full of dry heat and crackling with fire danger. The worst weather we might get was a touch of rain. And even that, Mr. Howe told us, was highly unlikely.

Shelby and Tomás needed permission slips, which I hadn't thought to bring, so I had them follow me down to the faculty supply room on the first floor while Mr. Howe took the rest of the group outside. As we walked the empty halls, Tomás's loafers squeaked on the linoleum floor in a way that sounded rude. I wanted to ask why he bothered wearing expensive shoes in such a shitty place, but I already knew the answer: There was nothing Tomás Augustine wouldn't do to remind himself how much better he was than the rest of us.

Once in the supply room I tried using the copy machine, which had detailed instructions laminated and pinned to the wall above. I followed these instructions in precise order only to have the copier promptly jam, making me swear. Tomás rolled his eyes and walked out of the room, phone in hand. I crouched to fix the machine—there were no instructions for *that*—and just ended up pushing a lot of buttons.

"Let me." Shelby elbowed me aside, squatted down, and pulled out the bottom tray, the one with the angry blinking light. She reached her arm in and dug around for the stuck paper. I mumbled a few words of gratitude, before getting up and stepping back to watch her work. I appreciated the help, naturally, but thing was, the farther Shelby reached, the higher the hem of her insanely short shorts went. Not to mention, it appeared she wasn't wearing any underwear. I couldn't help but stare. Already I could see bronzed skin, the sweet pull of tight curves, a hint of shadow and more. I held my breath and felt lucky. Willed Shelby to keep reaching.

And reaching.

"Jesus Christ, Shel," a voice behind me said.

I whipped around at the same time she did, only to see Tomás leaning in the doorway, his jaw tight and his arms folded. He spoke to her while looking directly at me. "Your entire ass is hanging out."

"Is it?" She reached back to pull her shorts down, wiggling her butt while she did it. "Hope you got a good look, Ben."

"I didn't see anything," I said. "I swear."

"Yeah, right." Shelby stuck her arm in the copier again. Groped around for the jammed paper.

I glanced back at Tomás, to gauge his reaction to my lie. The dark look on his haughty face said it all: He hated me more than ever.

7.

PEOPLE LIKE TO ASK IF ROSE WAS A JEALOUS GIRLFRIEND. I'M NOT
sure that it matters, but back then I would've said yes. My answer today
would be different, of course, but I'm allowed to change my mind, just
as much as Rose was allowed to change hers.

It is true that when we were together I was leery of spending time
with other girls. Rose was never the type to make catty remarks or
sharpen her nails at the first sign of competition, but on those rare occasions when I happened to neglect her, it always made her so *sad*. I
couldn't stand it, to know I'd hurt her like that. My mother liked to tell
me I was being manipulated, that girls used their tears as a weapon—
their kindness, too—but she wasn't looking out for my best interest
when she said stuff like that. Just the opposite: She could only conceive
of a girl using me because she saw no value in me in the first place.

My mother, by the way, was the sole female in my life Rose was
ever openly jealous of. That should've been a clue, perhaps, but neglect-
ing Rose to care for my mom didn't make her sad so much as it royally
pissed her off. Tension had smoldered between them from the first day
they met and Rose accidentally called my mother *Mrs. Gibson*.

Admittedly, the name mix-up was my fault. I hadn't had a chance to
tell Rose that my mom had dumped my father's name the minute he'd
dumped her. Later, she'd gone on to take Marcus's *Salvatore* and pushed
me to take that name, too. Insisted, even—apparently it was the *Christian* thing to do, like Jesus wouldn't want people knowing my mom had
ever screwed anyone else. But I refused, mule stubborn, finally growing

so furious with her prodding that I wrapped a piece of cord around my neck and tried to hang myself from my closet door in rebellion. I was only six when I did this and it was stupid; the cord snapped almost immediately, sending me crashing to the floor. But it must've scared my mom because she never mentioned the name-changing thing again.

Anyway, not causing Rose pain was the reason I didn't want Tomás to tell her about catching me staring at Shelby Sawyer's ass. It was also the reason I assumed he would. And maybe it doesn't seem like a big deal in retrospect, but I felt sick over what I'd done, physically sick, which meant I shouldn't have done it.

The strangest thing was, in the days that followed, Rose never once mentioned Shelby or what her brother caught me doing. She didn't say a word about it. Instead, she did the most surprising, yet most Rose-like thing of all—she joined the orienteering club. She didn't tell me she was doing it, either. She simply showed up at the next meeting and jumped into the trip planning with the rest of the group, full of unexplained fervor and verve—the type of energy I hadn't seen her expend since she'd gotten back from Peru. As if spending three days backpacking without electricity or running water was just the rejuvenating opportunity she'd been dying for.

"To spend time with you, Ben," was Rose's coy answer when I asked her why. Those were words I longed to believe, but there was something in the way she said them—with not a trace of sadness or hint of regret— that felt wrong. Disturbingly so, especially in light of her it's-okay-if-you-hooked-up-with-someone-else comment over the summer, which on its own had been enough to make me black out. My Rose, it seemed, had either changed completely, was no longer the girl I knew, or else was biding her time to let me know how she really felt. Both were options that left me beached on the shore of helplessness. I couldn't ask Rose what was wrong because she was acting like everything was fine. But fine can so often be the very worst of feelings.

For me, at least.

Look, I'm going to tell you the rest of what happened now. How we all went up on that mountain and ran into the Preacher and his brother and got some stupid ideas that led to some really bad decisions. I'm going to tell you everything, including what happened to Rose, and exactly why I did what I did.

But there's something I need to say before I get into all that because I don't want my intentions misinterpreted: This isn't meant to be a confession. Not in any spiritual sense of the word. Yes, I'm in jail at the moment. I imagine I'll be here for a long time, considering. But I'm not writing this down for absolution and I'm not seeking forgiveness, not even from myself. Because I'm not sorry for what I did to Rose. I'm just not.

Not for any of it.

DAY ONE

8.

WE LEFT FOR THOMPSON PEAK AT NOON ON FRIDAY ON THE TWELFTH of October. For her part, my mother seemed glad for my departure, which was worrisome. She usually didn't approve of my leaving her alone overnight for reasons I mostly understood; a spinal injury she suffered in the same impact that had damaged my frontal lobe made it hard for her to move or stand for long periods of time—not without assistance.

In truth, she rarely left the house unless it was to hobble down to College Lane, our seedy neighborhood bar. Having grown up in Teyber, she knew everyone at the Lane every night of the week—both a blessing and a curse. Hell, even *I* was welcome at the bar, which made me feel more grown-up than it probably should've considering the place wasn't exactly the pinnacle of maturity.

I guess now would be a good time to tell you that my mother can be unpredictable. It's not just the spine thing. Or the drinking. Life's been hard for her in ways it isn't hard for other people. She's sensitive, I guess. Overly so, and no, I don't know what makes people like that. I also don't know how to fix it.

I do know that when my mother was growing up she didn't have a good relationship with her family. Her dad was kind of a dick, and I gather he liked to take it out on her. Marcus was the same way, really, only he had God on his side, which didn't help matters any. Anyway, the bottom line is you should know that doing normal stuff—like holding a job or going to the store or keeping up the house—it's all too much for her. So those were things that I did. And while I didn't always like it, I also tried not to get too hung up about it. At least she loved me. That wasn't something everyone had, so I tried hard to remember that shit could've always been worse.

That Friday, however, my mom couldn't have cared less about my leaving. I ducked into her bedroom to say my good-byes only to find her in the grips of her bed husband—that's what she called this stained denim pillow with outstretched arms and a pocket for the TV remote—with a beer already in hand, chain-smoking her Camel Lights. Her green eyes, the same watery shade as my own, were bloodshot and droopy. When I tried telling her the details of my trip, like when I'd be back or who to call if she needed something, she cut me off with, "I don't need to know any of that. It's fine, Ben. Go on. Do whatever the hell you want. It's all okay with me."

"It is?"

She waved a hand. "Of course. I can't possibly expect you to take care of me when you have so many other interesting things to do."

After that, I left the house and got down to the school in a hurry. I was scheduled to spend the morning with Mr. Howe before anyone else got there, going over our supplies and maps and timelines.

The plan was for all nine of us to drive out to the remote town of Cecilville, where we'd camp for the night, right on the Salmon River's south fork. In the morning we'd drive to the trailhead and begin the backpacking portion of the trip. The route we'd plotted would have us hiking the steep trail to Hunters Camp, then climbing on toward the thin air and high altitude of Grizzly Meadows. This was where we'd set up camp Saturday night, right at the base of a towering waterfall fed by the looming Grizzly Lake.

The lake itself we intended to reach Sunday morning, taking time to ascend the massive Grizzly Falls and the rocky scramble overlooking the meadow. Trails twisted up from there toward the mountaintop, but it turned out it wasn't possible to climb much higher without ice axes, even in warm weather; Thompson Glacier guarded the peak year-round. But at 7,100 feet, we'd get a full view of the summit. This was also where we planned to spend our Sunday afternoon, practicing map reading, finally packing up before too late, and heading back down for the drive home.

Before everyone else arrived, Mr. Howe and I loaded up his truck with food and gear. I liked working next to him. It was a good kind of effort, both sweaty and silent, and those brief hours ignited me with rare sparks of hope. Got me dreaming that maybe I'd have an aptitude for this physical stuff and I could get a job after high school doing something outdoor related. Be a rafting guide on the Trinity River in the summer. Bring the ice climbers out in the winter and snowshoers in the spring. Teyber would still be home—I didn't have a choice in that—but maybe there could be moments for me elsewhere, in other places, all offering the chance for something bigger in my life, something better, like joy.

All this fantasy vanished fast, though, dissolving easily into despair. Because while it didn't make sense to feel bad about wanting to feel good, I knew well from experience that dreaming too much could often become a helpless sort of thing.

"You sure you'll be okay, Ben?" Mr. Howe asked. He was double-checking the first aid kits and I knew what he meant. Technically the trip was school-sponsored and seeing as he was the adult in charge, we had to give him any medications we might need ahead of time so he could administer them if necessary. He was looking at all the drugs I used to fight my migraines: Zomig in both pill and nasal form; Zofran in case of nausea; and Tylenol 3 for pain. I refused to get a prescription for anything stronger; but when I was younger and my headaches would last for days, I sometimes ended up in the ER getting shots of morphine.

"It's just in case." I slipped the flare gun I was holding into the backpack with the other emergency supplies. "I won't need all that."

"You still get them a lot, your migraines?"

"Not as much. Maybe twice a month now. Or if I'm really stressed." Or if I ate MSG or drank too much coffee or the pressure in the atmosphere changed too quickly. I hated the look on Mr. Howe's face, but all the teachers knew about my headaches, so there was no point avoiding it. They had to know, obviously: how they could come on without warning, in the worst cases leaving me unable to speak or with the sudden need to vomit. But they really were better than they used to be. Right after my injury, I'd gotten them three or four times a week, but they were fading now with distance. Like a memory.

"Shame how that happened," Mr. Howe said.

"I know."

"You deserved better."

I nodded but didn't say anything else. Deserving better meant I hadn't gotten what I deserved, and even then I wasn't so sure that was true.

9.

I'VE READ THAT "TRAVEL IS A STATE OF MIND." BUT AS APPEALING AS the thought is, to me it's always felt a little like proclaiming sex to be overrated to a roomful of virgins. No one wants to hear that about something they haven't had a chance to do. And while most people wouldn't consider driving into the mountains, one county over, to be true travel, in any sense of the word, for me, who had never once left the cool fog and homegrown haze of Humboldt, I might as well have been setting off into the Amazon jungle or the Australian outback.

That's all to say I wasn't filled with any metaphysical bliss or deep philosophical insight as our small caravan departed Teyber sometime around noon. There was nothing profound running through my veins as I stared out the car window and watched the familiar landscape slip away, abandoning the only world I'd ever known: those cool, shaded rivers and wet, fern-lined canyons, that dark earth rooted deep with redwoods, solemn giants whose thick canopies spread wide to fan the forest floor before stretching toward the heavens.

I was nerves and instinct. My bones rattled with each bump and sway of the road as we wound east and upward, moving away from the coast and into land that was drier, hotter. Far more foreign. There was true pain in leaving, I found. It was in the dryness of my throat, the sweat of my palms, the dizzying race of shadows spinning across my forearm.

The miles whipped by, and before long, we approached the county line, prompting me to hold my breath—a superstition I didn't know was in me. Only rather than the expected road sign announcing our entry into rural Trinity—a landlocked county with a single stoplight to its name—I spied a large green placard that had been erected on the shoulder. In the center of it was a yellow circular seal inscribed with twin Xs. The words WELCOME TO JEFFERSON were painted above in black.

My lungs deflated with a whoosh. I knew what that sign meant. If intent mattered more than the law, then we hadn't just left Humboldt County; we'd crossed out of California altogether. The "State of Jefferson" was the name chosen by a group of disenfranchised counties looking to secede from the Golden State in order to become the fifty-first in the Union—all in the name of personal liberty and freedom, which, from what I could tell, mostly involved being able to walk around in public with a loaded gun.

I shifted my gaze forward as the road grew windier, trying to stare through the front windshield and keep a hold on the horizon—no easy task, considering I was sitting in the backseat of Rose's Pathfinder, wedged between Archie DuPraw and Avery Diaz. Not only was it hot and stuffy being stuck in the middle like I was, but I'd begun to feel ill, a situation not helped by Archie, who was sleeping with his mouth open and his head on my shoulder.

That seating arrangement, by the way, was not my doing. Back at school, when we'd been figuring out who would go in what car, I foolishly told Tomás to go ahead and ride shotgun—the Pathfinder was his, too, after all. I assumed Archie and Avery would want to sit together. But after Avery crawled inside, Archie took one look at the middle seat, slapped my back so hard it hurt, and told me to get on in. All six foot two of me. Not to mention, he took up so much space himself that by the time we were all situated, I was practically sitting on top of Avery. But Archie didn't appear to give a rat's ass if my balls were in his girlfriend's lap or if any other part of my anatomy might be touching her. He'd started snoring the minute we got on the road.

Avery poked me in my side. "You okay?" she whispered.

I shot a quick glance up front. Rose had her eyes on the road. Tomás was fiddling with the stereo.

"I don't feel so good," I whispered back.

"Here." She reached into her backpack and pulled out a Ziploc bag.

"What's that?" I asked.

"Ginger candy." She placed one in my hand. "They're good for your stomach on long car rides."

I took the candy and put it in my mouth. I didn't tell her it wasn't the car ride making me feel gross, but a combination of skipping breakfast and being forced to sit next to her boyfriend, who smelled like the Dumpster at work on the days we tossed out expired meats. "Thanks."

"How much longer?" she asked.

I checked my phone. It was one thirty. We'd only been on the road for an hour and a half. "Maybe three more hours?"

Avery popped a ginger candy in her own mouth. We both sucked in silence. It was a soothing silence, not an anxious-making one, and I couldn't help letting my mind wander and wonder how it was someone like her had ended up with Archie. Only when I thought about it more, I realized I knew why it was most guys didn't go for girls like Avery. It wasn't that she wasn't pretty. Or sweet. Or friendly. Or any of those qualities guys valued because they thought they made a girl less likely to say no. Avery's problem was that she was *ordinary*. Forgettably so, unless you really got to know her. That meant that even though she and Rose shared the same brown skin, smoldering eyes, and Latin roots—hell, they were lab partners in AP Bio; they probably shared a brain—what mattered more was Rose's boldness, her family's money, and the fact that her last name was Augustine and not Diaz. All those things added up to make Rose seem exotic and rare, and if that sounds racist or sexist or anything else terrible, that's probably because it is.

"Do you remember my seventh birthday party?" Avery asked in a low voice. "When we rode together to the beach?"

I smiled, because I did remember. Her parents had driven a whole group of us out to the ocean to look for whales, which had been Avery's favorite animal back then. She used to do all her book reports on them. Art projects, too. We'd sat next to each other on that car ride, small thighs pressed close together as soft guitar music spilled from the back speakers—Jobim sang to us in Portuguese. The old Buick's windows had been rolled down the whole way, I remembered that, too, letting in the salt air to fill our heads and pepper our skin.

Once at the beach, while the other kids clambered around and stood on boulders with binoculars, hoping to spy humpbacks on their migration toward the warm waters of Mexico, I did my own thing, preferring to stay on the rocky shore, closer to the waves, walking in circles with my head down to scour the ground for pieces of cobalt sea glass and driftwood in a rare daze of contentment.

Sitting beside Avery now, I realized I recalled that day with such vividness for two reasons: One, our house was scattered with pieces of blue glass and driftwood—long-ago remnants of my father, who'd clearly been enamored by the roiling surf and the gifts of its fathoms—but Avery's birthday was the first time I'd ever actually seen the ocean, despite living no more than fifteen miles from the coast; and two, the peace of that day had been shattered the next when my mother woke me with tears in her eyes and pain in her voice to tell me there'd been a terrible accident at the city pool.

I don't know. Some accidents are more unfair than others. That's what I believe, even though the word itself implies no one meant for it to happen. But on that long-ago morning, Avery's mother, who swam laps every day as the sun rose over the eastern hills, was the first person to arrive at the pool the way she always was. And unlike my father's wild ocean, I like to imagine the water's surface was calm for her the moment she dove in. There was no way she could've known a short circuit from an ungrounded pool light had charged the deep end with hundreds of volts of electricity. No one could've known. And maybe that's the point of tragedy—to remind the living that fate is always waiting, just right around the corner. But if you ask me, dying for that kind of reason seems like the most unfair thing of all.

I glanced over at Avery, still sucking on the ginger candy, and I wondered if she was thinking of the same thing I was. Of her mother's heart stopping from shock and all the misery that followed. Or was she able to isolate that one pure, good moment—riding with me in a car on the day she turned seven, when we were both small and happy and headed toward the beach? I didn't ask, though. Given what I knew of loss and pain, the answer seemed obvious.

My gaze drifted southward. I wasn't looking at Avery's cleavage, which was covered by her T-shirt, but at the gold pendant hanging around her neck. It was an animal of some sort, and it had a sparkling crystal for an eye that glinted in the sunlight. I kept staring and I guess I just assumed the animal must've been a whale, a memory of a time in her life when her mother was still alive to bring her to the water's edge.

But it turned out the pendant wasn't a whale. It took me a minute to figure that out. No, the tiny gold animal resting against Avery's throat wasn't a sea creature at all. It was a fox. A vixen, even.

A beast both cunning and sly.

10.

WE STOPPED IN THE RURAL BLINK-AND-YOU-MISS-IT TOWN OF
Cecilville for gas. I guess I should say Rose and Mr. Howe stopped for
gas, since they were the ones doing the actual driving. Everyone else
just did whatever the hell they wanted. Tomás and Avery went to use
the restroom, Shelby made a phone call, Clay stayed in the truck, reading a book, and Dunc and Archie snuck off behind the nearby saloon
to get high.

Me, I kind of wanted to follow those last two. Not that I liked smoking weed all that much, but I hated being around people who were
stoned when I wasn't. Somehow *I* always ended up feeling like the
dumb one.

But I knew better than to wander. Rose liked me close. So I got
out of the Pathfinder, slid my sunglasses on, and gently closed the
door. Cecilville itself was nothing but a gateway to the mountains—
a mere smattering of buildings. Most of its storefronts were boarded
up and the streets desolate. But I stood and breathed deeply. I'd never
been this close to wilderness—true wilderness, the kind you could get
lost in—and I wanted to savor it all: the rush and roar of the mighty
Salmon River; the bright chatter of birds—a whole chorus of killdeer
and chickadees; the cloying late-day heat; the dust-filled air; and more
than anything, the rich beauty of the Alps, those rocky edges and snow-
capped peaks that filled the vista with their staggering rise and fall,
seemingly stretching on forever.

Rose called my name from where she stood by the pumps, but I didn't answer right away. Then she called for me again.

I turned and pressed a smile on my face as I peered over the top of the Pathfinder. "What's up?"

"Where'd you get those sunglasses?"

I shrugged. I knew the glasses were flashier than what I normally wore—they were these oversize black-and-gold wraparounds—but I'd found them in the break room at work a few days earlier and had no intention of returning them.

"Really, Ben?" she said.

I smiled wider. "Did you need something?"

"Could you get me an iced tea?"

"Yeah, sure." I was happy to be useful. I darted across the pumps and made my way into the market.

An older woman with bleached hair and a septum piercing sat behind the counter watching television at roughly the same volume as a Learjet. The news was on and she was clearly riveted. From what I could gather, two inmates all the way down in Napa had escaped from the state mental hospital and were now on the run from the cops.

"They'd better catch those assholes," the woman muttered as I set Rose's iced tea on the counter in front of her.

"Hope so," I said brightly, although deep down, I hoped the fugitives would get away with it because you know they never do.

"Hey!" the woman barked suddenly, rising out of her chair to yell at someone behind me. "You gotta be eighteen to look at those!"

Twisting to peer over my shoulder, it would be a lie to say I didn't feel a stab of pleasure to spy Tomás cringing in embarrassment near the very back of the store. He had a cardboard box in his hands but I couldn't see what was in it.

"You eighteen, kiddo?" the woman shouted.

Tomás dropped the box and bolted.

"What's in there?" I asked her.

"Porn," she said with a cackle. "But nasty stuff, like pregnant ladies."

"Really?" This was fascinating, to think that's what Tomás had been looking at. A part of me wanted to peek in the box myself and see what else was in there, but I resisted. I wasn't eager to be humiliated.

When I got back outside, Rose wasn't taking in the view or the fresh air or anything. She was staring at the TV screen mounted over the pump, which was showing the same news station as inside, while putting on sunscreen. She rubbed the lotion on her face and arms like a punishment, then checked herself for white spots in the Pathfinder's side mirror. Satisfied, she stepped back and I handed her the iced tea.

"God, it's hot out here," I said because the sun was beating down on us.

"Mmm," Rose said.

"I'm already sweating."

Rose didn't answer. Instead she leaned back against the car and stretched her arms above her head like a Y. She knew I liked the way her back arched when she did that. Feeling a quick pulse of desire, I reached out, put my arms around her waist, and pulled her to me. She was short. I was tall. Her head cupped beneath my chin.

She looked up at me, smiling a lazy smile. It was one I hadn't seen in a while, and I met her gaze eagerly, welcoming bliss.

"That's pretty stupid, don't you think?" she said.

I tipped my head. "What are you talking about?"

Rose pointed behind me. I turned to look. There was a bumper sticker affixed to the back of the silver F-150 parked at the next pump over. Adorned with stars and stripes, the shiny sticker pronounced: FREEDOM ISN'T FREE.

"What's stupid about it?" I asked.

She shrugged. "I mean, *I* didn't have to fight to come here. And I'm never going overseas to fight in some endless war. So for me freedom *is* free. Because, you know, I'm not the one paying."

"Why, I guess that's called a gift, Rose."

"Well, it's not one I asked for."

I raised my eyebrows, more than a little taken aback. Up until that point, I'd always been able to overlook Rose's occasional acts of entitlement for her other, better qualities. Who wouldn't? Girls like Rose didn't come around every day of the week, girls who were pretty and smart, and who just up and decided one day that you were going to be their boyfriend so that you didn't have to do any deciding of your own.

But I mean, *goddamn.*

"Sounds like you've got a lot of things all figured out," I said stiffly.

Rose wriggled around and kissed my cheek, her bright eyes fixed on mine. "Yup."

Then it was time to get back on the road and head for the nearby campground. Mr. Howe hollered for everyone to get in their respective vehicles, and Rose started honking her horn like a wild lady. That got everyone to move their shit, even Tomás, who'd pretty much perfected the art of passive-aggressive slow walking. He didn't dare look at me as he got in the car to sit beside his sister.

Archie and Dunc came sprinting around from the back of the market like a pair of dogs caught digging in the trash. Archie skidded up to the open Pathfinder door, took one look at me, and burst into red-faced laughter.

"What's so funny?" I snapped. My mood had soured, thanks to the stupid bumper sticker thing. I couldn't get it out of my head.

"You," he said, still laughing. "You're funny."

"What's funny about me? Did I say something funny?"

"It's your sunglasses."

I scowled. "What's wrong with my sunglasses?"

"Two words," he said, motioning for me to take the middle seat again. "Lady Gaga."

I flipped him off, but Dunc, who'd been watching us, gave me a goofy grin and a thumbs-up before getting into Mr. Howe's truck.

"I like your glasses, Ben!" he shouted. "I really do!"

At least someone did.

11.

WE SET UP OUR TENTS ON THE VERY EDGE OF THE SALMON RIVER. IT was decadent really, that first campsite, considering what we were in for. That night, we had wood and a fire ring and running water and toilets and pay showers—all things we'd sacrifice the minute we stepped foot on the mountain—not to mention, the campground was basically deserted, which meant we had the run of the place until morning.

Dusk approached. Tomás and the girls wandered down to the riverbank to watch Clay fish. The trout were jumping, sending ripples across the water in the reedy light, and Clay had a thing for fly-fishing; apparently he was some kind of prodigy at it, if you could be called a prodigy for being good at tying a bunch of feathers together and sticking a pole in the water. Dunc and Archie went off walking, and while everyone else was otherwise occupied, Mr. Howe and I sat together at a picnic table to go over the next day's itinerary. I also asked him to check over my contour map and elevation profiles for what felt like the billionth time.

"You seem a little anxious," Mr. Howe said.

I squirmed around on the wooden bench I was sitting on, hard enough to get a splinter to poke my ass through the back of my shorts. "It's just, I've never actually been backpacking. Or overnight camping even."

"You mean, at all? Ever?"

I shook my head.

"And you're worried about what it'll be like once we're out there?"

"I'm worried I'll do something *wrong.*"

Mr. Howe rubbed his beard before answering. "Ben, when have you ever done something wrong?"

I laughed, a strangled sound. "Oh, I can think of one or two times."

"That's not what I meant."

"I know."

Mr. Howe picked up my notes and my maps, folding them all neatly before tucking them into my trail book. "You have nothing to worry about. Trust me, I've never seen anyone this prepared. You're going to be fine. It would be hard not to."

"But what if I'm not?"

"Then I'll help you. We're not climbing Everest, here, kid. Okay?"

I nodded, and we sat there in silence, with darkness coming down and the soft hush of the river echoing off the canyon walls both above and behind us. It wasn't long before the others returned, led by a swaggering Clay who'd managed to snag a decent catch of rainbow trout. He threw his rod down and gutted the fish right there on the table. Fallen scales glimmered in the moonlight.

We ate around the campfire, sprawled on blankets in the heavy warmth and flickering glow. When I finished my food, Mr. Howe urged me to get up in front of the group and explain what we were going to be doing over the next two days. I was nervous, but it turned out when I spoke, everyone listened (for the most part). That was cool, being seen as a voice of authority. I don't know. I felt good at that point in the trip, is what I'm trying to say.

But see, that's the thing about feeling good. It builds you up and makes you care and then you end up feeling like crap when someone or something tears the good thing down, which they inevitably do. That's exactly what happened later that evening; Mr. Howe begged off to bed before the dishes were done and I was supposed to be the one in charge, keeping things under control and making sure people followed the rules and didn't do anything stupid. Instead everyone promptly abandoned me, leaving me to clean up on my own while they snuck into the woods to get piss drunk and make asses of themselves.

For her part, Rose stayed with me, watching as I dried the dishes and sulked by the fire. But she didn't want to. I could tell.

"Come on," she said. "Let's go hang out with everyone. Let's do something."

I glared at her while jabbing at the flames with a crooked marshmallow stick. "Do what exactly? Are you just dying to spend the evening hanging out with Duncan Strauss?"

"*No.*"

"Shelby Sawyer, then?"

"You wish."

"What's that supposed to mean?"

"It means I don't give a damn about Shelby Sawyer."

I jabbed at the fire some more. "You don't?"

"No. The only thing I care about is not sitting here like an asshole."

Well, that was good news about Shelby, I supposed, but I hated the antagonism between us. In that moment, Rose and I were flint and steel, each going for the strike meant to spark the other. But I took a deep breath, jutted my chin toward the woods. "They're the ones who're assholes, you know. They all heard what Mr. Howe said. We've got to get up early tomorrow. He's gonna be pissed if everyone gets trashed."

Rose dug at the ground with heel of her shoe. "I'm pretty sure Mr. H. is well aware of the things high school students are capable of doing when their chaperone goes to sleep. He's not an idiot."

I set my jaw. "Fine. You go, then. I'm staying."

"Are you serious?"

"Why wouldn't I be?"

"You're different, Ben." Rose leaned back as she said this, swaying out of the fire's light, as if trying to get a better look at me.

"Different from what?" I asked.

"Whoever you were."

"Maybe I am." I agreed, but I wanted to tell Rose that *she* was the one who was different—that she'd been different ever since she'd come back from Peru, all distant and moody in ways I couldn't help her with because she didn't want my help—and also, that I really hated what she'd said at the gas station earlier and maybe *that* was the real reason we were sniping at each other. Because nothing in my life had ever been free. Not shelter or safety. Or even self-worth. All of those things, each of them, had come with a cost. And I was the one who'd paid.

Always.

But then Rose went and changed tack. She grew soft suddenly, running her hand down my back, across my thighs, kissing my lips, and whispering in my ear to screw the rest of them, that I was right; they *were* assholes and she wanted to be with me, just me. She also wanted to do it beneath the trees, she said with a grin. Right then. No one would see us or hear us, and anyway, who cared if they did?

I was less than inspired. Nothing felt good or right between us. But she knew what to do: how to touch me, nuzzle me, nip me, convince me. She could make up, if not always my mind, then the rest of me—the parts that were simple and untortured and impossible to ignore. So I did it; I let Rose take me by the hand and lead me from the campground into the woods, where empty beer cans littered the forest floor.

She brought me to a place far from the others, past the run of the river and the hum of the road. It was a spot where the white pines loomed above us. Their limbs tossed and dipped with wind, and Rose was right—those trees never bothered to notice as we tumbled at their feet, twined and gasping, naked and moonstruck.

After, we lay back in the needles and stared up at the heavens. Drowsy and drained, I longed to sleep-drift in the autumn air, right there, with my clothes half off and her head on my chest and my hand on her stomach. I felt closer to her than I had in a long time because sex did that. It made me feel like she loved me and I loved her back. But right then an airplane flew overhead, a slow flicker of lights pulsing across the stark night sky, and Rose turned and asked me what the saddest thing I'd ever read was.

I hesitated. She knew how I was with decisions, how I hated being wrong so much I rarely let myself be right. But after some thought, answers began spilling out of me, lots of them, one after the other, since I didn't like to choose. First I mentioned *Never Let Me Go*, then *The Book Thief* and *Watership Down*, all of which broke my heart in different ways. Then I started in about *Native Son* and *The Sandcastle Girls* and *The Bridge to Terabithia* and that story about the girl in Japan with leukemia who makes all those paper cranes and then dies.

"Oh," I said, "and *Old Yeller*. I bawled like crazy when I read that one in fourth grade. It made everyone in our class cry."

"But you don't cry," Rose said.

"I *can't* cry. That's different. But I read *Old Yeller* before I got hurt."

"Well, that book's not sad anyway."

"It's about a boy who has to shoot his *dog*."

"Because it's the right thing to do."

"That's what makes it so sad!"

Rose shrugged. A careless shiver of shadow and moonlit bone that made me ache. I could taste her on my lips yet felt like I barely knew her.

"Well, what do you think's sad?" I asked.

"Being alive."

"Oh, come on."

"What do you want me to say? Death and loss aren't sad. They're all life is. But most people can't deal with that, so they convince themselves of lies. Like the idea that faith can bring salvation. Or that war can deliver freedom. But those aren't truths. They're just fancy ways of dressing up death."

"Freedom's definitely not a lie," I countered.

"No," she agreed. "It isn't. But that doesn't mean it looks like what we've been told it does. Freedom can take different forms for different people."

"I don't know about that."

Rose reached to touch my chest, fingers tapping against breastbone. "That's because you're sentimental. You believe everything means just what it's supposed to."

"I'm *not* sentimental," I said, and this was a truth I was sure of. From an early age, my existence had been forged by loss and suffering, some of which was circumstance and most of which was my own damn fault. Trust me, there was nothing, not one thing, in my life to be sentimental about.

"Maybe," she conceded. "But I think you want to be."

"Okay."

"Being stuck is sad, too, though. Maybe that's the saddest thing of all."

"Stuck how?"

She frowned. "I don't know how to explain it. Just . . . stuck. Trapped in a place of your own making and not knowing how to change."

Pulling her close, I longed to share Rose's point of view, to see things exactly the way that she saw them. But her words confused me. I knew what it was like to be trapped and how helpless a thing that could be—how it made trying to do anything feel pointless, until inertia was indistinguishable from active revolt. But in my mind, there was no comparison—death and loss were infinitely more frightening than being stuck somewhere I couldn't get myself out of.

I tried explaining this to her, my rambling thoughts, but Rose rolled away from me, right as I was talking, as if she weren't one bit interested in my thoughts on death or stuckness or sadness or anything. But she was listening. I know she was. She listened to every word I said that night, and in hindsight, it's clear that this was the beginning of the end. In hindsight, it's clear I should've known that fate, wild and inescapable, was readying itself to gallop out of the gates after us both.

But back then, on that warm October night, as I lay with my Rose after screwing her for what would be the very last time, beneath the fluttering trees and the glowing swell of the stars above, I swear to God, I had no idea.

DAY TWO

12.

LATER, MUCH LATER, AFTER WE'D DRIFTED AND DREAMED IN SEPA-
rate worlds, Rose and I found our way back to the campsite. Stumbling
around with a flashlight, I took a quick head count, relieved to see that
everyone else had returned safe, if not sober: Tomás, Shelby, and Clay
were all in separate tents, while the rest lay sprawled in sleeping bags
around the darkened fire ring. The wind blew, and pieces of ash fell
softly on their hair like snow. We slid into our own tent. Our own sleeping bags. I held Rose in my arms.

We drifted again.

Then dawn came. Too soon. And it seemed Rose's intuition about
Mr. Howe's awareness of what us teenagers could get up to without him
was right. That went a long way in explaining why he got Archie and
Dunc up at the crack of daybreak—well before anyone else—to start
the fire and get breakfast going.

"Rise and shine, motherfuckers!" Archie crowed, banging a set of
pots together as he marched past our tent. The noise made me jump
and swear, and Rose mumbled something about stringing him up by
his dick, which I was a hundred percent on board with. Cruelty begets
cruelty, I guess, and all that.

I stuck my head out of the tent. "What the hell are you doing?"

"You hungover, too?" He grinned.

"I have *ears*. And Jesus, put a shirt on, already. You look like a fucking monster."

He banged the pots again, right in my face, laughing when I winced. "Move your ass, Gibby. Howe says we're leaving in an hour."

Ducking back into the tent, hackles raised, I began to reevaluate my assessment of Archie. I'd always written him off as harmless, the class clown, but more and more, it appeared he might be a total asshole. Rose, who was brilliantly naked beneath her sleeping bag, rolled over and went back to sleep. I kissed her cheek, then stroked her breast, my fingers brushing along the dark edges of her nipple. I allowed myself to savor a few beats of lust before scrambling to find clothes. I needed to get out of the tent and take charge. Maintain whatever authority I had left from the night before.

By the time I got my shirt, shorts, and shoes on and stepped outside, dawn had come and gone. The sun, still creeping over the bony ridge to our east, was now high enough to bounce off the moving river and strike my eyes like sharp lasers of white-gold light.

I winced again but didn't look away.

It really was time to rise and shine, motherfuckers.

Morning did its thing. Mr. Howe drove out to the ranger's office to get an overnight backpacking permit and inform them of our route, while the rest of us toiled bleary-eyed at breaking down tents and packing our bags and rolling our bedrolls as tight as we could before loading up the cars again.

Then we stood together around the dwindling fire, all eight of us. We clutched mugs of instant coffee and cocoa and slurped bowls of cold cereal and plates of powdered eggs. The river was in the background, that wide, slow wash of green, and Dunc and Archie decided to smoke a bowl right there out in the open, which was pretty par for the course. But they were feeling charitable, I guess, because they passed the pipe around.

Everyone partook, except Tomás, who didn't do that sort of thing, and soon the acrid scent of cheap weed filled the air, filled our lungs—not just with that familiar sweet-skunky pungency, but with the strangest sense of destiny. It's hard to describe without sounding naïve or painfully adolescent, but it was something I felt deep in my bones that day. As if *that* place was where I was meant to be. At *that* moment. With *those* people. Like there was an inevitability to being seventeen and preparing to climb a mountain, and if nothing else in my life ever happened, then I might just be okay with that.

I turned to Rose, stupid shit-eating grin on my face, ready to share my weed-induced profundities and ask whether she thought that if our lives were inevitable did that mean free will was a lie? Only Rose wasn't looking at me. She was gazing deep into the woods, in the direction of the trees we'd fucked beneath. I stared at her while she did this. There was an expression on her face I couldn't read, but she had to be thinking of me or else why would she be looking there? So I kept staring, but I also kept grinning, because in knowing where her mind was, I felt needed, complete. Besides, I liked the way the Trinity sun lit her hair, every strand luminous and bold.

The sun rose higher.

The day grew warmer.

Mr. Howe returned, and we did one last check of our supplies. A sudden burst of nerves spurred me to trim down my backpack load even more, and I encouraged others to do the same. Weight mattered on the mountain, I told them, every ounce. I'd read that in all the trekking and survival books I'd been dragging back and forth from the library over the past few months. As far as basic directives went, packing light was right up there with "cotton kills," "check twice to make sure the fire's out," and "for the love of God, tell someone where you're going and when you'll be back before you leave."

In truth, we weren't setting off on that rugged a trip—this was no Patagonian adventure race leading us to the end of the world—but that knowledge did nothing to soothe my need to ensure everything was *just right*. To not screw up. So I continued to bark panicky orders, insisting that any item not absolutely necessary get left behind. This included extra shoes, clothing, cooking gear. Whatever.

And then we were ready. We had what we needed and not much more: our maps, our compasses, our food, our gear, and although we planned on staying overnight on the mountain, it was October in California; and by the time we'd piled into the cars again, like crayons in a box, and drove to the China Spring staging area, where we parked and put on our packs and our sunscreen and filled our water bottles and locked the car doors, the sun was already hot, so very hot—that in spite of the glacial lake and the snow-white peak we'd be climbing toward— no one, not one of us, ever thought to bring a jacket.

13.

THE CONFLICT STARTED ALMOST IMMEDIATELY, AS WE STOOD HUDDLED
around a carved trailhead marker that read: GRIZZLY TRAIL JUNCTION/
HUNTERS CAMP, 2.1 MILES. No one was stoned anymore, just sulky, and
I held the laminated map close to my eyes, squinting at its topographi-
cal swells and landmarks.

The map-holding thing was a stalling tactic. I was meant to solo lead
this section of the hike—Mr. Howe had already gone ahead to scope
out trail conditions on the way to Grizzly Falls—which would take us
up and out of the Salmon River Valley and straight onto the mountain.
Only there was nothing easy about this first leg; the path we'd chosen
was a shortcut created to give quick access to Thompson Peak, avoiding a long climb in from the south. The trade-off for brevity, however,
meant the trail was insanely steep and more than a little treacherous.
Despite our weeks of preparation, I knew the hike's difficulty wasn't
going to go over well with my peers and found myself torn between the
urge to set reasonable expectations and flat-out lying.

Finally—as always—I took the path of least resistance. "So, uh,
we're just going to hike a little ways up this hill until we get to the junction. Shouldn't take too long. It'll get our blood flowing."

"Thanks, Dad," Archie called out.

I ignored him, clapped my hands together, and tried to sound spir-
ited. "Let's get going, okay?"

"Why does Ben get to do the navigating?" It was Tomás who said
this. And it wasn't his words that pricked me so much as the way he

spat my name. *Ben.* Like I was something gross that had gotten stuck between his teeth.

I shot him what I hoped was a stern look. "I'm doing the navigating because I'm the one who knows the route. We explained this last night."

"But you've never been here before."

"Well, I've studied the map. A lot."

Tomás remained unconvinced. "What if *I* want to practice reading the map? Or someone else?"

I glanced at Rose for support—the last thing I needed was her brother's mutiny—but she stared at her shoes and played with her hair, clearly dead set on saying nothing.

I turned back to Tomás. "You're free to practice whatever the hell you want. You've got your own map. But right now, I'm in charge. Got it?"

He sighed and muttered something under his breath that sounded like *bullshit* but finally nodded. "Fine."

"Good. Let's go, then."

I stood with my backpack on and a dorky sun hat and my weird sunglasses, and I waved everybody onto the path while doling out more of my overprotective dad advice: what to do if a bear crossed our path; how much water we should be drinking and when; reminders about sunscreen and heat exhaustion and staying away from leaves of three.

Nobody cared, of course. They started down the dirt road, talking loudly among themselves, and no one acknowledged my words. Or effort. Not even Rose, who abandoned me to walk alongside her stupid brother and hold his hand. I couldn't help noticing Clay trailing awkwardly behind them with this lost puppy look on his face.

Shoving the map back into my pocket, I consulted the compass once again. It said we were heading southwest, which was absolutely in line with the map coordinates and all my pre-trip GPS plotting, so it wasn't a surprise. But I don't know. Expected or not, it was still a thrill to see science in action like that. I'd never used a compass before in any real-life setting—just practicing with the group at the high school and a few times on my own as I dragged my heels around the empty Teyber streets on those bleak nights when it was too hard to sleep and too hard not to.

It sounds foolish now, I realize, but I marveled at the compass doing exactly what it was supposed to do, and while I'm certainly not a cynic or anything, there's not much in this world that impresses me. So there you go.

Before heading off after the rest of the group, I glanced over my shoulder, startled to find Avery and Archie still with me. They hadn't budged from where they stood by the trail marker, and it was pretty clear they hadn't stayed behind because they were eager to fall in place behind my natural leadership skills, but because they were arguing.

"Put it away," Avery said.

I froze. There was a tone to her voice that stilled me. Not to mention there was something uncomfortable in the way Archie's hulking form loomed over her smaller one. He was more broad than tall, but with the way the sun hit his back, his shadow consumed her entire body.

"Put what away?" I asked.

Neither answered me, but Avery's gaze darted toward something in Archie's hands. I looked. My gut clenched.

He had a gun.

A fucking *gun*.

"Goddamnit." I felt my legs go weak. My relationship with firearms was complicated, to say the least. "Why in the hell do you have that?"

Archie shot me a baleful look, then shrugged. "Protection."

"Protection from what?"

"You never seen *Deliverance*?"

"Arch . . . ," Avery said.

Archie gave a sick grin, letting his wide shoulders slump. "Kidding.

I'm kidding. But, Gibby, weren't you the one warning us about bears and apex predators? I mean, I don't plan on getting mauled out here and dying like an asshole, do you?" That's when Archie swiveled suddenly, his arms pointed straight out, hands held together, the gun aiming for the trees. Avery yelped and stumbled back while he pretended to pull the trigger.

I blinked. Very quickly. A brief flicker of pain pulsed along my jawline before edging higher, toward my left eye.

Shit. My vision blurred. I swayed on my feet a bit.

"You okay?" Avery asked me.

"Just put it away," I told Archie in a low voice. "Put the gun in your bag and leave it there. If you see a fucking bear, then we'll talk."

And that was that. Archie looked pissed, like I had no right telling him what to do, but he put the gun away, stuffing it into his backpack and zipping the whole thing up while engaging in some consummate under-his-breath bitching, which I guess was the effect I had on people. Then he huffed off after the others. As if his sensibilities had been offended. I watched him go.

Well, okay, then.

Blowing air through my cheeks, I turned back toward Avery. It was on the tip of my tongue to snap at her, to ask what the hell she saw in him. The taste of high school guys notwithstanding, surely he wasn't her only option. Abstinence had to be better than that. Archie DuPraw was dick jokes and muscle shirts and beer bongs at eight a.m. Concealed weapons, too, apparently.

"Well, that was interesting." Avery tugged at her long braid, wrapping it around her neck so that it hung just below her shoulder.

"Your boyfriend's a real piece of work," I told her.

"He's not my boyfriend."

I lifted an eyebrow.

"Archie's my cousin," she explained. "His mom's a Diaz. That's his

Mexican half. It's the better half, trust me. The DuPraws are . . . well, they've got problems. He's proof of that."

"Oh."

"But even if he were my boyfriend, it wouldn't be my fault that he's an asshole."

"I didn't say it would be."

"But you were thinking it, weren't you? Everyone always blames women for the things men do. It's why men never learn."

Well, that sounded like something Rose would say, and while I knew better than to argue, I didn't exactly agree with the sentiment. Men could be stubborn, yes, and unreasonable—violent even, in the most destructive of ways. But I also knew there were women in this world equally destructive—ones who did what they did, while all the while making sure they never had to take the blame for their actions, leaving them free to cause more and more pain until everyone within their reach was suffering. But what I said to Avery was, "I'm sorry."

She softened. "Don't be. I shouldn't have said that. I'm just . . . I don't like feeling like I'm his babysitter. It's his fault for needing one."

"Absolutely."

"You did a nice job of dealing with him, you know."

"I did?"

She nodded. "He listened to you and Archie doesn't listen to everybody. Not even me. And he likes me."

"Well, I don't think I did much of anything," I said.

Avery had an easy smile. One that never made me wonder what it was she was thinking. "Always the modest one, aren't you, Ben?"

I tried smiling back—I liked what she'd said, I really did—but I felt unwell all of a sudden. As if the adrenaline from seeing the gun had finally drained from my body, and the remaining grit of guilt and shame was working hard to stir up those memories inside of me I'd tried for so long to forget.

Avery said something else I couldn't hear. I didn't answer her and felt bad about that. Instead I fumbled for my water bottle and took a long swig. Then another.

"Sorry," I gasped.

"Headache?" she asked.

"No." I drank more water, and the dumbest thing was, part of me wished it *were* a headache bothering me, because awful as they were, at least I could explain those to people. With Avery I wouldn't have to do that. She'd seen me sick before. In sixth grade, she'd even helped me to the office once when the left side of my face went numb and didn't make me feel bad when I confided in her how scared I was.

"What is it, then?" she asked.

I glanced up, taking in Avery's easy smile and twinkling eyes, the gold vixen hanging from her neck. In that moment, I ached to tell her how deeply the aftermath of her mother's death remained etched in my mind—not just the funeral or the wake, but all of it. The way her desk in our third-grade classroom had sat empty for weeks, such a vivid symbol of loss; the way that golden haze of syrupy sorrow had enveloped her upon her return, as if she were a queen encased in a hive of her own sadness; and the way I'd watched that sorrow squeeze the brightness out of her, day by day, leaving behind something drab and stale. A flat soda of a girl. I couldn't stand it back then, to see her transformed by an act that couldn't be undone. *Grief*, I guess, was the proper word. I longed to tell Avery all that because I wanted her to know it was the way I felt, too. Every day.

But I didn't. Instead I slid my water bottle back into its strap.

"You ready?" I asked and nodded toward the waiting mountain.

"I'm ready," she said.

And just like that, we were off.

14.

IT DIDN'T TAKE LONG FOR US TO CATCH UP WITH THE REST OF THE group. When we did, I found Rose and took her hand, separating her from her brother. None of us said anything about the gun or what had happened back at the trailhead marker. Not me. Not Avery. Not Archie. It wasn't anything any of us agreed to do, but at that point in time, the gun was gone, hidden, out of sight. There really wasn't much to say. So we moved on.

Then things happened like this:

After the initial walk down the dirt access road, we turned onto the actual China Spring trail, cresting a modest hill, only to be greeted by an open view of Thompson Peak. It was like stepping into paradise; I'd never seen anything like it. The trail flattened, and everywhere everything was green. Lush. Sparkling. Alive. A squirrel perched on a mossy tree stump watched us, then chittered and darted away. Sunlight gilded the meadow, which stood tall with wildflowers, the footpath lined with fiddle ferns.

I was awestruck. Everyone else kept doing what they'd been doing, but my mood soared. To be there, in that place I'd studied for so long but had scarcely allowed myself to believe was real, was the most wondrous thing. Walking alongside me, Rose squeezed my hand, which meant she liked it, too, which made me happy. Above us, to the west, reared the peak itself, that glacial basin riven by shadow. I held my breath and stared. It was more dramatic than any Ansel Adams photograph

I'd seen, and not only because it was real and right in front of me. The mountain was just that goddamn beautiful.

The meadow dipped and we were in the woods again. The mountain vanished from sight, replaced by thick trees and even thicker gloom. We wouldn't catch sight of the summit again until we were almost at the lake. But like the impending elevation profile, I kept that truth a secret. Better for the rest of them to wonder, I thought, than to have no hope.

The trees grew denser the farther we went; the trail steeper, cutting back and forth through the woods as we climbed. Crawling over fallen trees and skirting around dicey sections of the path where the earth had eroded away, we made our way onto the mountain. We passed a pond filled with orange-and-brown salamanders, and the air hung ripe with juniper scent. Mosquitoes and gnats swarmed in thick clouds, and soon we were all swatting and sweating while gasping for air.

At some point along the way, Dunc got a blister.

He started to complain.

Avery said she had some moleskin in her bag, so we stopped to let him take care of his foot.

Around this same time, Archie announced he had low blood sugar and needed to eat. I was doubtful—he'd been snacking the whole time we'd been walking, since breakfast, actually—but I didn't argue. Something about Archie seemed off. His neck was pink, his eyes rimmed red, and he was breathing harder than anyone, like a winded dog. He collapsed his large body in the dirt next to Dunc and pulled out a protein bar.

Since it didn't appear either of them planned on getting up any time soon, I asked the rest of the group if they wanted to go on ahead without us.

"You can even be the navigator," I told Tomás in what I hoped was a patronizing tone.

He failed to take the bait, licking his lips and nodding like he was doing me a favor. "Sure. Where're we going?"

I held the map out. "Hunters Camp. It's not far at all. All you have to do is follow this trail. You'll head west when you reach the junction. There'll be a sign, so you can't miss it. After that, the camp's only a half mile or so farther on your left. You'll pass over the creek to get there, but it should be low this time of year. That's where we're meeting up with Mr. Howe for lunch, but we've got plenty of time. He won't be there for another hour or so, so don't worry if you don't see him. You're still in the right place."

Tomás looked around, pushing his dark hair from his eyes. "All right. So who's coming with me?"

Dunc and Archie both smirked. I noticed this, then watched as a look passed between the two of them. It wasn't a nice look, is what I'm trying to say, and for the first time I felt a twinge of sadness for Tomás. Not sympathy, really, or compassion.

Just sadness.

"Rose, you'll go with your brother," I offered. "Won't you?"

She nodded, dropping my hand at precisely the same time Shelby announced that she'd go with Tomás, too. That didn't make me feel so great, her being with Rose, but then Clay said he'd also go, and that was better. Inwardly, I prayed for Avery to stay behind so that I wouldn't be left alone with dipshit city, and to my surprise, she did.

"Thanks," I told her once the other four had continued on, vanishing around a steep bend in a flash of sunlight and dust.

Avery shrugged as if to say, *I'm not doing this for you,* which, you know, point taken. Then Archie started moaning again about how tired he was, and Dunc rubbed his bare feet like a baby. Avery turned and asked if I wanted to take a walk with her through the nearby woods while we waited for them to get motivated, just to get a feel for the terrain and take in the scenery. Just to do *something.*

I said sure. "Don't go anywhere," I told the other two sternly. "We'll be right back."

"Oh, we're not going anywhere," Dunc said, in a way that was more threat than promise, and as we left, I glanced over my shoulder to see Archie slide a bottle of what looked like Wild Turkey out of his backpack. The expression he wore was one of both guilt and blissful serenity.

We wandered into the trees. It felt nice to walk without purpose. To not be in charge or have my nose stuck in a map.

Avery was quiet as we hiked. I didn't mind. She had a camera in hand, a Canon DSLR that I knew she'd borrowed from school—she couldn't afford something expensive like that any more than I could. I watched as she focused the lens on a large bird that sat way up in the top of a cypress tree.

Shutter click.

"Hawk?" I ventured.

She turned. "Eagle. A golden one."

I nodded. Shoved my hands in my pockets. "Hey, so what're you going to be doing after graduation? You going to school anywhere?"

Avery squatted to take a picture of a glittering toadstool growing at the sappy base of a cedar tree. "Me? No. I'll just be working for my dad next year. I'm not going anywhere."

"Why not? You're smart. You do that theater stuff. You could get a scholarship for sure. Any school'd be lucky to have you."

She stood again and there was that smile of hers. Easy as always. "Smart's not all that matters."

"I know," I said.

"What about you and Rose?"

"Oh, Rose . . . She'll be off at college, for sure. She's in the middle of applications at the moment. She was going to do poli-sci but now she wants to study math."

"I hear it's the only field that's honest."

I glanced at Avery in surprise. "You're right. That's exactly what she says. How'd you know that?"

"She told me."

"She told you?"

Avery caught my eye. "We're lab partners, remember?"

I nodded. "Oh. Right. How's that going?"

"Good. I really like Rose. I like her a lot."

"I'm sure the feeling's mutual," I said, although I actually had no idea.

"What about you?" Avery asked. "Where will you be going?"

I tried out my own smile, one that felt neither easy nor honest. "Same place as you. Which would be nowhere."

"That's too bad."

"Oh, I don't know. I mean, staying at home, working. That's not the worst thing in the world. It's gonna suck, though, when Rose dumps me for some rich frat guy during rush week or whatever."

"You really think Rose is going to dump you?"

It jarred me to hear someone else say those words out loud, but the truth was, I *did* think that. Didn't I? It would explain a lot. It made sense, too, that Rose would be looking ahead, at a life without me, especially given our recent distance and friction. But in response to Avery, I shrugged, noncommittal, as always. "Sometimes it feels like she's destined for better things. But I get it. All I want is for her to be happy."

Avery frowned. "That's sad, Ben. Not that you might break up with your high school girlfriend, but that you think she's better than you."

"I didn't say that."

"You sort of did."

"Yeah, well. I'll live." I cast a sideways glance at Avery. "It's not just about the money, though, you know. My staying here."

"What's it about, then?"

"I can't leave my mom."

Her expression softened. "She's not doing well, is she?"

"She's . . . okay. Still sick a lot, though. In pain."

"Pain?"

"Her back. She hurt it in the accident but it's never healed right. Some nerve thing. Doctors can't figure it out."

Avery paused. "Oh."

"Yeah."

"Well, you do a lot for her. More than you should. It's not fair."

"Life isn't about fair," I said. "She's my mom. She needs me. You'd do the same for yours."

Avery didn't answer.

My cheeks burned. "Shit, Ave. If she were here, I mean! That came out wrong."

"It's fine," she said. "And I get what you're saying about not being able to leave. Even if I got a scholarship, it's not like I could go away to school. My dad's business wouldn't make it without me. Not with all his debt."

I nodded, appreciating for the first time all the similarities in our lives. But a restlessness was building in my bones. It was time to turn around, to get back to the others.

Avery, however, had other ideas. She held her camera up.

"Take your sunglasses off, Ben," she directed.

I took my sunglasses off.

"Now look at me."

I looked at her.

"Smile."

I smiled.

Click.

"How'd it come out?" I asked.

"Blurry," she said, staring down at the screen. "Shutter speed was too slow."

"Oh."

"I'm still learning how to work this thing. Let me take a few more."

I nodded and stood where she instructed me to go, in front of a twisting oak tree, its branches adorned with sharp-edged leaves. Then she told me to move away from the tree, which I did. And then to take a step back, and I did that, too, although Avery squinted and crouched and moved around so much I started to wonder if she weren't trying to figure out a way to take the photograph without actually having me in it. When she held the camera up at last, I didn't bother trying to smile. I stood up tall in an effort to look worthy of a moment remembered.

Click.

Click.

Click.

Finally, I threw my hand over my face. "That should be enough, right?"

"You don't like having your picture taken?"

"The birds have to be more interesting to look at than me."

"I like looking at you," Avery said.

Her words made me stare at the ground very intently. No, I didn't like having my picture taken, but I also didn't want Avery to see my face at the moment. That was a weird reaction, I know, considering she'd just said she liked looking at it.

The thing was, I *liked* that she'd said that.

A lot.

Avery seemed to understand this. Or else she was better with ambiguity than I was. Either way, in the silence that followed, she walked over to me, camera still in hand, and stood by my side, very close. But I didn't dare look up from my staring.

My heart went after my ribs. I felt what Avery felt, of course—that breathless force draped between us, thick and heavy and undeniable. It was a force far greater than desire because it went both ways, that gravitational pull other people called *pheromone heat* or *electricity* or even *magnetism*. But as I stood there, just drip-drip-dripping with it, the whole thing felt more like time travel: a florid heat that had appeared spontaneously where moments ago there'd been none. To me, that said this force could only have come from the future—a cue not of anticipation, but of fate already foretold.

Still, I didn't move or make one. When we were fifteen, Rose had been the one to kiss me first. She did it while I was working one afternoon, after prodding me into taking an unscheduled break when my manager was on a call. I snuck out the back of the store to be with her, and Rose didn't ask my permission or anything. She simply pushed me against the exterior wall and launched herself at my mouth. We were in full view of the street and everything, but I let her do what she wanted and I'd followed her lead, using tongue when she used it and growing hard when she touched me through my jeans. Only Avery wasn't Rose, I realized, which meant I had to make up my own damn mind for once.

Then again, if this was my destiny, I already had.

15.

LOOKING BACK, I CAN SEE NOTHING FOREBODING ABOUT WHAT AVERY
and I did in the forest that day. It was an act of pure instinct. I have to
believe that. I leaned to kiss her and she kissed me back. Then we kissed
some more and groped and slid our clothes off and pulled each other to
the ground. We were both thrillingly naked in the leaves as she opened
her legs and I crawled between them.

Everything after was all that was needed, heat and friction followed
by more of the same—her loose hair sliding like silk against my arm; my
breath quickening into labored panting. The only moment of conscious
thought came when Avery whispered in my ear not to finish inside her.
I nodded vigorously. Rose had always let me, but I did what Avery asked
and it was almost better like that, doing it right out in the open, all over
her sunlit belly, where both of us could see.

I felt bad about it, though, almost immediately. "I'm sorry," I said,
swiping at her with my wadded-up boxers in an attempt to clean her off.

"Don't be." Avery took the boxers from me and did the cleaning herself. "But we should be getting back."

She was right, of course. Scrambling to our feet, we did our best to
straighten our clothes, smooth our hair, and dust ourselves off. Then we
began the short hike back to the others, hustling in forced silence, making sure we weren't touching. There was a bashful look on Avery's face,
and I desperately wanted to do right by her, to tell her I didn't regret
what we'd done.

For a moment that was true. If sex with Rose made me feel like she loved me, then in the brief afterglow of doing it with Avery I felt a little like I loved myself. Okay, I know that sounds bad or cocky or whatever, but I don't mean it that way. I felt *proud*, I guess is what I'm trying to say. A little giddy, too.

But my giddiness was short-lived. Before I knew it, I regretted my actions. I more than regretted them. I hated myself. How stupid could I be? I had no reason to be disloyal to Rose. None. And yet . . .

And yet.

My gut churned with guilt. I didn't understand myself or my choices—how I could be the person who'd done what I just did. How I could want something that made me miserable the instant I got it, when all I'd meant to do in the first place was walk around in the woods and kill time.

But lust is a curious thing, I guess.

It's there,

until it's

not.

My mood grew darker the farther we went. Avery wisely chose to ignore me, continuing to hum and bounce and snap photographs as we walked, both intent on capturing beauty and creating it, as if what we'd done didn't have dire, life-curdling implications. As if it really didn't matter that much to her in the first place.

I sulked more, a brittle sort of pity. However, all my oh-Lord-what-have-I-done sense of self-loathing managed to slip a few rungs down the priority ladder when we reached the clearing where we'd left Dunc and Archie and discovered they weren't there. They weren't anywhere.

So much for staying put.

"Well, shit." I folded my arms and gazed through the trees. We were definitely in the right spot because Archie's protein bar wrapper lay crumpled on the ground by my feet. I couldn't resist pointing this out. "He's such an asshole."

Avery sighed. "They must've gone on ahead. Let's keep going."

We turned up the hillside and resumed our walking. A faint whistle of panic blew through me, a stubborn insistence that *something's not right, Ben, it's just not, you screwed up and this is what you get, this is all your fault.* But I tried not to get ahead of myself. We were only a half mile or so from the junction to Hunters Camp. It would've been hard to get lost. Although this was Dunc and Archie we were talking about. When it came to fucking up, no doubt they were capable of anything.

We left the canopied shade of the forest, stepping once again into the blinding sun. I pulled my weird sunglasses from my pocket and slid them on. The trail grew steep, taking us above the trees, and it wasn't long before we'd reached a wide plateau with views of the valley we'd climbed out of. According to what I knew, there should've been a stream—Hunters Creek—running parallel to the path we were on. But a four-year drought meant no water, and the stream had dwindled to nothing but a boggy seeping, punctuated by a few puddles of mud and brown muck covered with algae and buzzing flies.

"This isn't what the lake's going to look like, is it?" Avery asked.

I shook my head. "Grizzly Lake is spring fed. Plus, there's always, you know, the glacier."

She raised an eyebrow. "Don't think I'm not catching the sarcasm in your voice, Gibson."

I laughed out loud in spite of myself. The look she gave me in return was pure mirth.

Avery pinched her nose while we walked. "Well, I'm glad this isn't what we have to look forward to. Everything smells like farts."

"Oh, wow," I said.

"What?" she asked.

"You're the only girl I know besides Rose who talks about farts."

Avery rolled her eyes. "Maybe you don't know girls very well."

"I won't argue with that."

"About Rose . . . ," she began.

"No," I said quickly. "I don't want to talk about it. It's not something that needs to be talked about."

"Really?"

"Yeah."

She shrugged and nodded, turning to face forward again and walking faster, leaving me to watch her ass sway with each step. That was an activity far preferable to talking about Rose, although pretty soon it got me turned on again. Not in any dramatic, this-is-my-destiny way, like earlier; this was a normal, oversexed, depraved state of horniness. And you might think that would get me to forget my guilt—that lust and disgrace aren't meant to coexist. But for me, in that moment, they did more than exist: They flourished and grew, fusing together into some sickening mass until everything inside of me was mixed up. Until I could no longer tell up from down, good from bad, or my chickens from their eggs.

Ahead of me, Avery stopped walking. Just out of the blue. In my addled state, I slammed into the back of her and tried mumbling a flustered apology—I sure as hell wasn't going to explain *why* I hadn't been paying attention. But she grabbed my arm and dropped to the ground, yanking me down beside her.

The weight of my bag made me tip forward onto my knees, scraping both and leaving me irritable. "What the hell?"

"Shhh!" she said. "I see them."

I righted myself and crouched beside her. "See who?"

"Right there." I followed Avery's gaze. We'd reached the trail junction, which meant the steepest part of the climb was over. A marker clearly indicated that the trail to the left would lead to Hunters Camp and, in another four miles, Grizzly Falls—our final destination. The trail to the right, on the other hand, was lined with sheer granite and led to someplace called Papoose Lake.

There was no way anyone in our group could believe that Papoose Lake was where we were headed, and yet, when I lifted my glasses and squinted, sure enough, about a hundred yards down the granite trail were Archie and Dunc. Their backpacks were off, both propped up against a treacherous-looking rock wall, and the two of them lay flat on their stomachs, peering over the edge of the trail at something I couldn't see.

"What are they doing?" I asked Avery.

"I don't know." She cupped her hands around her mouth. "Hey! What the hell are you two doing?"

Dunc whipped around at the sound of her voice. His dark curls were hidden beneath a grimy baseball cap. He put a finger to his lips, then waved us closer. We slipped our own packs off and crept toward him.

"What's so goddamn interesting?" I sniped as we approached. "You're on the wrong trail, you know."

But this time it was Archie who turned to look at us, and the wicked gleam in his eye told me depravity was a relative thing.

"We found girls," he said. "And they're *naked*."

I sprawled on my belly next to Dunc to gaze down at the view below. Rather than naked girls, however, what I saw first was a stream. It was the China Spring, I supposed. Sparkling like a gift, it dazzled as it ran swiftly through a narrow gorge of granite, a good fifty yards below us, before widening across a pebbly valley shaded by a thick grove of aspen and pine trees.

After a moment, the sun dipped and glinted, the wind whispering through the valley to shake leaves from the branches and ripple the water, and that's when I saw them—the people in the spring. There were two of them. And yes, they were females from what I could tell, and by that I mean they weren't actually swimming, but wading. Waist deep.

That got me scrambling forward, scraping my knees again. My earlier guilt remained, sharp and gutting, but voyeurism suited me. Besides, the women didn't notice us. They were too busy bathing and washing clothes. They soaped their underarms and scrubbed their hair and rinsed their shirts. Bubbles pooled downstream, coming to rest along the shore like pearls that had lost their oysters. In the trail guide, I'd read that China Spring was a drinkable water source, fed straight from the earth, but I can tell you right now I had no intention of drinking anything other people washed their underwear in.

"God, they're, like, *old ladies!*" Avery exclaimed, startling me. I looked up and saw she had her camera out. She was zooming in with that big lens of hers, and her comment pretty much shattered my voyeuristic fantasies. Archie, it seemed, felt the same way.

"Old ladies?" he echoed.

"Well, they're definitely not young," she said. Then she pointed excitedly. "Hey, there's a guy, too!"

We all followed her line of sight, and sure enough, a man—also naked—was walking out of the tall grass and straight toward the pebbly beach. I put my hand over my eyes and squinted. There was a whole campsite back there, set up beneath the tree line. A not-at-all-legal campfire smoldered in a ring of rocks and a ragged beige tent with a large stain on the roof had been pitched downwind. Whoever was sleeping in there was sure to get a lungful of smoke. The man, meanwhile, strolled to the water's edge. We watched with bated breath as he put his feet in, put his hands on his hips.

"Nasty," breathed Dunc. "Think he puts bug spray on his dick?"

I made a face and sat back on my haunches.

"Well, *he's* not old." Avery continued to peer through her lens. "At least he's not all wrinkly."

Dunc snorted. "What's he doing, then? Skinny-dipping with his mom?"

"I don't think that's his mom," she said.

"Hey!" a voice called. "Hey, you! Get down here."

"Oh, shit." Avery scrambled back from the cliff's edge.

"What is it?" I asked.

"It's the naked guy," she said. "He's talking to *us*."

16.

"C'MON NOW, KIDS. COME ON DOWN AND SAY HELLO. THAT'S THE polite thing to do. We won't bite." We all peeked over the edge again, and the naked man, who had very dark hair and very pale skin, stood in the water and waved both arms at us, a gesture that might've seemed friendly enough if he'd had, you know, clothes on, but as it was felt more than a little off-putting.

"Think we should go down there?" Avery whispered before waving back to the dark-haired man.

"No," I said.

"Hell, yes," Archie said at the exact same time.

I shot him a dark look. "The guy's with his naked mom, remember? And what was that crack about not *biting* us?"

Archie crawled to his feet with a grunt. "When'd you get to be such a puss, Gibby? Ain't no one down there going to bite us. Not unless we want them to."

"No way," I said. "We have to catch up with the rest of the group. We're already behind as it is."

"Ah, shit. Now they're putting clothes on." Dunc gestured with a whine of disappointment.

Sure enough, the three bathers had wandered back toward their camp and were pulling on clothing. One of the women, however, remained topless and went to hang her wet clothes in the sun. She had brown skin, glistening and sweaty from the heat, and her breasts were small, supple, reminding me of my Rose, who I missed with sudden urgency.

"We have to go," I said again. "This doesn't feel right. I don't feel right about any of it. We shouldn't be here."

"Come on, Ben," Avery pleaded. "You said we had plenty of time."

"Come on, Ben," Archie taunted, using his best girlish voice.

I ignored him to glare at Avery. "Why do *you* want to go down there anyway? They're just trying to get a look at some tits."

She lifted her camera.

"Seriously?"

She nodded.

"Well, I don't think it's safe," I said.

"Why wouldn't it be safe?" Dunc asked.

"What, haven't you seen *Deliverance*?" I snapped, and no, the irony did not escape me.

Even Avery looked scornful. "Oh, please."

"Ave . . ."

But it was too late. Archie crowed, "Squeal like a pig, Gibby!" and grabbed Avery by the waist, pulling her up to standing. She giggled while he did this, which I hated. I also hated what came after: watching them parade down the hillside trail, arm in arm, with Dunc following right on their heels, as if they were all setting off on some grand adventure.

But I grabbed my backpack and went after them. What else could I do? I tried not to give the appearance of resentment. Or bitterness of any kind. Any more whining on my part would no doubt be used against me once we finally got down to the water and met the trio of naked swimmers. That was the type of humiliating interaction that had happened to me before and was bound to happen again.

I also tried not to get caught up in the weird feeling of doom rattling around inside my chest or the funny tingling in my scalp. Bad omens both, especially together, but in the end, there was no point worrying. My migraines had a way of doing what they wanted. They could come on fast or not at all, but either way, out here in the woods without my medication, there wasn't one damn thing I could do about it.

The path leading us into the canyon was steep. My scalp tingling persisted, eventually giving way to vertigo, and soon I was staring dumbly at my shoes to keep from falling. We'd almost reached the bottom of the trail when Dunc paused in stride, turning all the way around to look at me. His eyes were sleepy, the way they always were.

"You doing okay?" he asked.

"I don't know," I said honestly. "I feel kind of dizzy."

"From hiking?"

"I guess."

"Maybe you're hungry."

"Maybe."

"Or thirsty?"

"Sure."

Dunc reached his hand out and helped me down the rest of the way, a gesture I was more grateful for than embarrassed.

"You still think this is a bad idea?" he asked.

"Yeah, I do."

"Then we'd better not let her get away from us, don't you think?"

Her? I glanced up. Avery, being bolder and faster than the rest of us, was already picking her way across a shallow portion of the stream. A line of boulders had been arranged just for that purpose, and she stepped on each carefully, arms held out for balance, that damn camera still dangling from her neck. Useless as always, Archie had stopped to pour dirt out of his shoe, leaving Avery to approach the strange trio on her own. I hurried forward.

Tried to catch up.

Crossing the boulders was no mean feat. I was loath to get my feet wet, and the sun weighed heavy on my back as I picked my way over, rock by mossy rock. I had no clue what had gotten into Avery in the first place. This wasn't like her—all cocksure impulsiveness and questionable judgment. Although, hell, considering what we'd just done, maybe it was.

I stepped onto the far shore, and that's when my head started to hurt in earnest, a dull throb that circled my left eye socket with cheerless predictability. My stomach weakened, as well, but I continued moving, continued heading toward the unknown—an encounter that hadn't been on any map and one I wasn't prepared for.

The back of my neck began to sweat.

My legs itched from the grass.

The sore call of a bird rang out, echoing down the gorge. It was one I recognized—a killdeer, its tittering song both mournful and sad—and I walked faster, the sun melting my resolve as I struggled to reach the girl ahead of me who couldn't be bothered to look back. Then the bird cooed again—*killdeer, killdeer, killdeer-deer-deer*—and this time I shivered in response, chilled suddenly, even in the heat.

The man we'd seen from the ridge headed straight for Avery. He didn't follow any path but cut his own, arrow true, through the long grass and yellow reeds. His black hair fell almost to his shoulders, and it turned out he'd put on pants, but not a shirt. The man wasn't tall but he was muscular, his chest covered in a pelt of dark hair, and I didn't like the way he smiled at Avery as he closed in on her, a look both long and wolfish.

But the man kept smiling, even as the rest of us rushed to catch up with her. He smiled not only at Avery, but at me and Archie and Dunc. He looked us each in the eye, right in a row, with this strange, glittering type of intensity, and there was something so genuine and disarming about the way he did this that I began to doubt my initial reaction to his presence. Maybe I'd been wrong to judge the guy before meeting him. Maybe my irritation stemmed more from my budding migraine, as well as my own guilt-stained insecurities—of which I had plenty. Maybe this guy was perfectly, absolutely, one hundred percent normal.

When we were all there, standing right in front of him—me wincing and queasy, the other three seemingly far more eager and pleased with themselves—the dark-haired man threw his arms open wide and beamed.

"Jesus saves!" he cried.

17.

AH, SHIT, WAS MY FIRST THOUGHT, AND I DON'T CARE HOW THAT sounds. It wasn't as if I had a problem with Christianity as a whole, or even Jesus, himself—although I'd never counted myself as a believer. But I happened to know full well that people who went around greeting strangers with forceful exultation and references to their Lord and Savior were usually born-agains. I also happened to know that being born twice usually meant you'd fucked up the first time around and were almost certain to fuck up the second. In that way, I guess, history really was good for something. Not for changing the future but for being able to say, *I told you so.*

Out of the corner of my eye, I watched Avery's smile falter at the stranger's words—she seemed to be having the same doubts as me— but in the next instant the man had his arms wrapped around her in this giant bear hug. He wasn't groping her ass or anything, but seeing his hairy chest pressed against her made my skin crawl. I also caught sight of a large tattoo covering his right shoulder: It was a thick black circle inscribed with the same twin Xs I'd seen on the State of Jefferson seal on the drive out here. The infamous Double Cross. Well, you can bet that didn't make me feel any better about the guy, and when he released Avery and turned to me, arms still wide, I stuck my hand out instead.

The man hesitated, then shook it vigorously. "Praise the Lord, son. Praise the Lord."

I said nothing.

He kept holding on to my hand. Eventually, I pulled it back. Let him do the whole greeting thing with Dunc and Archie, who were both grinning and cracking up and looking like fools, which I guess they were.

Avery cleared her throat. "We're on a hike," she said.

The man turned to smile at her again. In addition to his black hair and pale skin, he had very blue eyes, the kind that glowed bright like a warning. "Why, that's a beautiful thing for you young people to be doing. Absolutely beautiful."

"I'm Avery," she told him. "This is Ben and this is Dunc and that's Archie."

The man kept smiling. "Your Benjamin's not too fond of me, I see."

"My name's not Benjamin," I said.

"Maybe Ben doesn't like to see half-naked men." Avery held her camera up and pointed it at the man.

Click.

"Well, I'll try not to take it too personally, then," he said smoothly. "I'm Elvin, by the way, but you can call me Preacher, if that's easier. If that'll help you remember who I am and what it is I stand for."

"Alvin?" Dunc said.

"Elvin. With an *E*."

"Like an elf?" I asked.

The Preacher turned to me, and while he was just as genuine as before, just as intense and glittering and odd, he also appeared determined to see right through me. I stood there, unmoving, under the cool weight of his gaze and the warmth of the day and with my head beginning to erupt, in all its molten pain.

"Yes," the Preacher told me, those blue eyes soaking me in, trying to soak me up. "Like an elf."

"Why don't you have a Christian name?" I asked.

The Preacher's grin grew wider. "Did I say I was a Christian?"

"But you just—"

"Come now," he purred. "I want you all to meet the two lovely ladies

I'm hiking with today. They're just getting decent, you know. They're a little upset, seeing as how you came across us bathing. But that's understandable. It's just you young people, you surprised us coming along that trail like you did."

This made even Archie frown. "But anyone could've come by. It's a public trail."

"Yes, it is." The Preacher's gaze turned skittish, darting up the gorge and back again. "But, you see, we're very private people."

He led us through the grass, all the way to the campsite, where a clothesline had been strung between trees and a pile of camping supplies sat dumped haphazardly beside the fire pit, including a cooler, a few well-worn canvas folding chairs, and a card table with a portable propane stove set on top of it.

It was also where the two women we'd seen earlier—both now fully dressed—sat together on a pair of threadbare tartan blankets spread out in the sun. It turned out they weren't that old, although they weren't young either. Both had leathery skin and lines around their eyes that reminded me of my mother—markers of that type of age not counted in years. They also had dyed black hair, which didn't make either of them appear younger, just ragged and unkempt. A little scary, too. Standing awkwardly beside them, I thought I caught sight of something dark moving among the trees, in my periphery, but when I turned to look, I couldn't make out what it was.

"Hey, is someone over there?" I asked.

One of the women, who had a silver flask in one hand and a black brace on the wrist of the other, shook her head. "Don't think so. Maybe you're seeing things."

"Maybe I am," I mumbled.

"Come sit." The same woman patted the ground beside her. "We were just about to eat lunch."

I sat, because I didn't think I could stand much longer and also because she told me to. Dunc and Archie, however, remained standing. They were disappointed by the company and the women and weren't even trying to hide this.

"You know what," Archie said. "I'll be right back. I need to go do something."

"Me, too," echoed Dunc.

To me it was clear they were going to get high, but the Preacher barely acknowledged their departure, not turning to watch as they jogged off into the woods, vanishing into the shadows and the trees. His attention was fixed solely on Avery, who was fiddling with the buttons on her camera.

"You're a photographer?" he asked.

Avery glanced up, gave a shy smile. "Trying to be."

"Well, the light's perfect down by the water," he said. "I could sit for you, if you'd like."

"Ave . . . ," I said in a low voice.

"Yeah, sure," she told the Preacher. "I would like that. Thanks."

Before I could interject, the two of them headed off toward the riverbank, walking side by side as Avery continued to mess with her settings. I was about to go after her, only the second woman beat me to it. She leapt to her feet, a dark scowl scrawled across her face, and hurried after them. Seeing this calmed my nerves. Somewhat.

Despite telling me to sit, the woman beside me seemed wary of my presence. She was the smaller of the two women, darker-skinned, too— the one who'd made me think of Rose from afar. Up close, however, there was no comparison. Where Rose was a bud, all the promise in the world, this woman was far past her bloom. Her beady eyes latched on to me, watching me closely, and her thin lips twisted into something sour before taking a swig from her flask.

"I'm Ben," I offered.

The woman started to cough, a phlegmy sound that wrinkled my nose. I didn't hold out my hand.

"Maggie," she said finally.

I tipped my head toward the stream. "This is a nice camping spot you found."

"Isn't it?"

"You come out here a lot?"

She paused. "Did Elvin tell you why we're here?"

"Not really. Are you part of his, uh, church . . . group?"

One-half of Maggie's face broke into a ragged smile. "Church group," she said. "Yeah, that's right. We've been doing a little baptizing out here in the mineral water. Supposed to be good for you, you know. Cleansing. In a spiritual sense."

"The water's spiritual?"

"God willing," she said. "So where you kids from?"

"Teyber. We're just here for the weekend."

"Mmm-hmm," she said.

"What about you? Where're you from?"

Maggie nibbled at something out of a can. Tuna or sardines, something fishy and rank. I noticed that the tips of her fingers were smudged with black, like she'd been painting with raw ink or had had a ballpoint pen explode on her. "Arcata," she said when she'd swallowed. "Just drove down yesterday."

"That's a long drive for baptizing."

"What'd you bring to eat?" She leaned forward, pulling my backpack toward her with her grubby fingers, unzipping and rifling through my stuff. I didn't have the strength to stop her, and her probing hands deftly found the mixed nuts and turkey sandwiches I'd packed, along with some Cokes. The only two I had. "Can I have some of this?"

I opened my mouth to protest, but a wave of pain snapped my jaw shut. I reached for one of the Cokes and pressed it to my cheek, while gesturing with my other hand to Maggie that she could have the rest.

"You're not hungry?" she asked.

I shook my head.

She unwrapped one of my sandwiches. "You should eat more, you know. You're too skinny."

"I'm getting a migraine," I said when my jaw decided to work again. "I can't eat."

She paused. "You get those a lot, migraines?"

I nodded.

"Sucks," the woman said. "I get them, too."

"You do?"

"Every month. PMS is a bitch."

"Well, that's not why I get them. I mean, obviously. But I got hurt when I was a kid. Head injury."

"How'd you get hurt?"

"My mom's husband," I said.

"Your dad?"

"Stepdad."

"He hit you?"

"Not exactly."

"What, then?"

I leaned back on the blanket. Closed my eyes and rolled the Coke can up to rest on my forehead. "I shot him."

"No shit?"

"Yeah."

"Did he die?"

"Yup."

"Why'd you do it?"

"I don't remember."

Maggie snorted. "Well, if you did the shooting, how're you the one who got hurt?"

How indeed? "Well, after . . . after I did what I did, my mom drove our car off the road. That's when I got hurt. That's when—"

"Wait, so you were in a *car* when you shot him?"

"No." I couldn't help myself. I rolled over and put my head down, one arm over my face, hunching my body like a pill bug. "I'm sorry. I don't feel good."

"It's okay, kid. You do what you need to do."

It was stupid, but there was something in her words or the way she said them that made my chest tighten, then grow tighter still. "Thank you," I said. "And no, my mom, she put us in the car after I shot him— she was upset about what had happened, I guess, about what I'd done. *She* didn't believe it was an accident, even though that's what she told everyone later. But she was so mad when she found us that she tried to, to . . ." I choked. I couldn't say it.

"Drive you off the side of the road?"

I nodded, then shrugged, but didn't really answer because my stomach was starting to do the thing it usually did in response to the rising tide of pressure in my head, which was to thump around and around, like a clothes dryer filled with shoes. I also didn't answer because what is there to say when everyone believes your mom drove her car off the road in a foolish panic, trying to save her son from the cops in the only way she knew how, but *you* know that they've got it all wrong? That what really happened is *she* tried to kill *you*, to punish you for what you'd done, and in her rage just considered her own life collateral damage?

"Shit, kid," Maggie said, followed by a low whistle, and the funny thing was, she seemed to understand exactly what I meant without my saying anything. I appreciated that more than she knew because it wasn't like I could *tell* anyone in my life about what my mom had done. She had a right to be mad at me, obviously. She still had a right. Guilt was a long game, and I'd ruined her life, after all. That was something we both ended up having to live with. *An accident. It was just an accident,* were words I'd repeated so frequently over the years, there were times I almost believed they were true.

"You want something for it?" Maggie asked. "Your headache? I got Percocet. I'll give you some for the food. How's that sound?"

In truth, it sounded like heaven. I lifted my head, forced open my eyes, and nodded. She reached into a canvas bag that lay at her feet and pulled out a bottle of pills. Handed me two and took one for herself.

Popping the Coke tab, I swallowed the pills gratefully. "Thank you."

"Just don't tell Elvin," Maggie warned.

"I won't."

She gave a nod. "So you the one fucking that girl?"

"What?"

She shrugged. "Well, one of you has to be. I saw the way she was looking at you. You're either boning her or you're her gay best friend. That's a compliment, you know. You got a cute face, kid."

"Thanks?" I forced down more Coke and tried not to blush. "I've got a girlfriend, though. That's not her."

"I didn't ask about girlfriends."

I blushed harder. "So, uh, what kind of church are you with?"

This made Maggie laugh. "What'd Elvin tell you about that?"

"Just that he's a . . . preacher."

She laughed more. "That he is, damn it. Church of goddamn Elvin. Ain't nothing like it."

"Margaret," a voice said sharply, and we both looked up to see the Preacher standing right behind us, his arms folded, his body blocking the sun. "Have some respect."

Maggie ignored him. She winked at me before yawning and stretching her body across the blanket like a cat. "Think we got time for a nap, kid?"

"Uh, we're going to need to get going if we want to get to our campsite before dark. I should probably find my friends." I sat up and looked around. I didn't see Avery anywhere.

"Where's this campsite?" she asked.

"We're trying to get to the lake." I gestured toward the summit. "We'll camp in the meadow by the waterfall, though."

Maggie lifted an eyebrow. "Not worried about the storm, are you?"

"What storm?"

"Some guy in Willits told me there's one coming. Could be snow and everything. I wouldn't go up on that mountain, if I were you."

"It's eighty degrees out," I said, but I was looking right at Maggie and she was looking back at me. She'd said *Willits*. There was no way they would've driven through Willits if they'd come from Arcata. Arcata was north, up on the water, near the Oregon border, and Willits was a hundred miles south of here and inland. It didn't make sense.

"What're you thinking about, Ben?" the Preacher asked.

"Nothing," I said.

"You sure?"

"I'm sure. You know, we really should get going." I cleared my throat and started gathering my things. "We've got a long ways to hike."

"Oh, there's no hurry," Maggie said. "Stay awhile. At least until you feel better."

"I don't think—"

"Stay awhile, Ben." This came from the Preacher, who wasn't smiling anymore. "I insist."

I opened my mouth to argue or, hell, at least do *something*, when I heard my name being called. Startled, I turned to see Archie and Dunc stumbling from the woods, both with huge grins spread across their faces. Clearly drunk off their asses. Or stoned again.

But for once I didn't mind, because the next words out of Archie's mouth were, "Hey, asshole! You deaf or something?"

"Huh?" I asked.

He pointed toward the ridge where we'd sat and spied on the Preacher and the women bathing naked in the water. And there, like the most welcome mirage, was Mr. Howe and the others, all standing in a row, waving frantically, trying to get our attention.

"They're waiting for us, dickhead," Archie said. "So hurry your shit up already."

18.

PERCOCET OR NO PERCOCET, IT WASN'T EASY TO WALK WITH A
migraine, much less hike with one. But I didn't care. Abandoning my
Coke and any questions I might have had about where this group of
people had *actually* come from, I muttered a halfhearted good-bye to
Maggie, leapt to my feet, and grabbed my backpack. Once upright,
however, the ground betrayed me, tilting in this seasick sort of motion.

But I held it together, managing to stagger full tilt toward Dunc and
Archie like a blundering buffalo. My sunglasses offered a slight respite
from the sun's whip-strong glare, and I was relieved to see that Avery
was well ahead of us, as usual, apparently having gotten away from the
Preacher on her own accord—something I hadn't been able to do. In
fact, she'd already made her way back over the China Spring and was
currently climbing out of the gorge.

"Come on," I gasped when I reached the other guys, not bothering
to stop. I lurched right past them. "Let's go."

"What's the hurry?" Dunc asked, loping alongside me.

I glanced over my shoulder, back at the campsite in the woods.
"Nothing. It's just, my head really fucking hurts."

"Your head? Is it one of your migraines?"

"Yeah."

"Shit," breathed Dunc. "How are you even walking?"

I couldn't very well mention being stoned out of my mind on Percocet, so I shrugged. Looked over my shoulder again.

Saw nothing.

My headache grew worse. I turned around and kept walking. I wanted to get the hell out of there. Actually, what I wanted was to go back in time and change the past so that I'd never come down into this gorge in the first place. Regret, it seemed, was becoming a staple of mine.

Archie caught up with us, wheezing from the effort. "Hey, was that Preacher guy trying to convert you or something?"

"No," I said.

"Was he trying to fuck you?"

"No."

Archie shrugged. "Too bad."

"Did either of you happen to see anyone else around?" I asked. "Another person, maybe? In the woods?"

Archie and Dunc both gave me funny looks. Guilty ones, really.

"What?" I asked.

"We didn't see anything," Archie said.

"You sure?"

"Scout's honor."

That was laughable, but whatever. We kept going, crossing the stream and keeping our feet dry. It was heading up the steep trail where I really started to fall apart. My whole body went shaky, and the Percocet made me heave. Archie had to take my pack, which he complained about, but Dunc helped me walk the rest of the way. I kept my sunglasses on. My hand over my eyes. The breeze bruised my skin, and I ached with each step.

When we got to the junction marker, Mr. Howe grabbed my arm and Shelby was the first to ask if I was okay. I thought I gave an emphatic yes, but maybe not, because I got the idea people were really worried about my well-being, which was beyond mortifying. Someone mentioned possibly needing to turn back, taking me to a doctor, but Rose took charge, pushing one of the medicated inhalers up my nose and insisting I'd be fine. Then she held my arm and held me together and guided me the rest of the way to Hunters Camp. I clung to her. If my migraines were punishment—and they always were—then Rose was my salvation.

I met a rebel preacher, I longed to tell her. *Be careful. He'll double-cross you. That's what they all do.* But I couldn't speak, which was for the best. My brain had lost its connection to both my mouth and reason.

Archie, on the other hand, was able to speak just fine, and he recounted our detour into the gorge as loudly as possible, all while walking directly behind me. As if he knew his voice were the last thing I might want to hear.

"Those people were freaks," he crowed gleefully. "They were shady as fuck."

"Could you be any more annoying?" Rose asked him with a glare.

Archie hooted. "Oh, don't get your pretty head ruffled just because your boyfriend was down there trying to bang some old lady."

"You're going to get your pretty head ruffled when I smack you."

Archie ignored her. "Church group, my ass. Those people were hiding something back there. I know they were."

"Enough," Mr. Howe warned. "Whatever they were doing, it's none of your business."

This was true, but it also didn't mean Archie was *wrong*. But at least he shut up about it for the time being.

We reached the camp, at last—a shaded grove. I collapsed in the pine needles beside Rose and put my head in her lap. She draped a T-shirt over my face to block the light, then a hat. She also asked Mr. Howe for a Tylenol 3 and a Zofran. Saying nothing about the Percocet, I swallowed both pills and hoped I wouldn't OD. When I was done, Rose kissed my hand. Stroked my back.

She let me sleep.

19.

I WOKE TO HAZY WARMTH AND AN EVEN HAZIER MIND. I DIDN'T KNOW how long I'd been out, but when I looked around, I was relieved to see I wasn't the only one who'd dozed off. Archie and Dunc were both crashed out. Shelby's eyes were open, but she lay curled in the shade in a tank top with her shoulders bare and pink from the sun. She was staring at the trees, which seemed fairly pointless, although for all I knew, she was counting alpacas in the clouds. Avery wasn't anywhere in sight and I was grateful for that. Rose was the loyal one, the one I needed; she remained sitting beside me, and she was reading a book. I twisted my neck trying to see what it was but couldn't make out the title.

"Any good?" I asked.

Rose peered down at me. "You're awake."

"Yeah."

"Are you okay?"

"I will be."

"You're not going to barf, are you?"

I scowled but shook my head. Rose had a thing about barfing. Only when I did it, though. Not her. I mean, not that I was a fan, but feeling bad about getting sick didn't exactly do a lot to make me feel better. But there was no cause for alarm; both the Zofran and the inhaler had worked, aborting the migraine while I slept, leaving behind only trace amounts of tenderness. My brain remained cottony from the Percocet, but cottony was fine. I reached to pry Rose's book from her hands, realizing that the reason I hadn't been able to read the title was because the cover had been torn off it. In fact, a huge chunk of the entire book was missing.

"What happened here?" I asked.

"You said to pack light."

"So you *tore the pages out*?"

She shrugged. "I read the first half yesterday, while you were talking to Howe, so it made sense to only bring the second. 'Weight matters on the mountain,' you said. Oh, and you were right, by the way. It's a decent book."

I turned to look at the spine. Rose's preference was for old crime novels, books no one else bothered to read, but this was *Into Thin Air.* "Wait a minute. Is this *my* copy?"

Rose nodded.

"That you ripped in half?"

"You already read it."

I bristled. That wasn't the point and she damn well knew it. I also hadn't paid for the book—it was from the FREE shelf at the library—but that didn't mean I could afford to replace it.

But I swallowed my ire. After what I'd done, I owed Rose that. I owed her more.

"So you really like it?" I ventured.

She leaned back on her elbows. "I don't know if I *like* it. Do you like reading about people dying doing something useless?"

"I guess I don't think what they were doing was useless," I said.

"Well, I do."

"Then maybe what we're doing right now is useless. Maybe everything we do is useless, all the time, so none of it matters anyway."

Rose touched her nose, gave a faint smile. "Ding. Ding. Ding."

I felt exhausted. I laid my head in her lap again with a sigh.

She played with my hair, wrapping it around her finger and unwrapping it. "So are you ever going tell me about this old lady? The one Archie says you were trying to bang?"

"There's nothing to tell, Rose."

"You sure about that?"

I rolled on my back. I looked her in the eye.

"Absolutely," I said.

Perhaps it should've followed naturally that if I felt guilty for cheating on Rose with Avery, then the obvious and just thing for me to do would've been to confess. To ask for forgiveness and apologize for my sins.

I thought about doing that. I really did. I thought about a lot of things as I took Rose's hand and we headed off on the second leg of our hike, heading up the mountain and leaving behind the Preacher and Maggie and whoever else they might've been with, as well as the sunlit spot where Avery and I had feverishly torn off our clothes to screw in the dirt like dogs. Truth be told, it made total sense that I should want to clear my conscience and make things right between us.

But I didn't.

Looking back, the only way I can explain it is this: I didn't want to lose Rose. I knew I would someday, but someday wasn't yet. Plus, my guilt was worthless. It always had been. That was the way it was with my mother, whose misery reminded me every minute of every day of what I'd done to her. Not that I didn't deserve my guilt. I mean, when you shoot your mother's born-again asshole of a husband after years of watching him try to beat the devil out of her for her sins, which include your very existence, and then she goes and tries to kill *you* for the trouble—well, there isn't any easy answer for that other than maybe you should've let her continue to suffer.

So, yes, I felt bad for sleeping with Avery. I felt bad for liking it as much as I did and for not being able to control myself and for really not even trying. I also felt bad that Avery had let me do those things to her in the first place, which I know isn't fair and was the exact douchey logic she'd warned me against earlier in the day. But I loved Rose and loving her meant not doing anything that would push her away. So to atone for my cowardice, I resolved to hold her closer, as close as I could. That was the kinder choice, I told myself, because changing the past wasn't in my control.

But Rose not knowing what I'd done to hurt her, well, that was the one thing that was.

20.

THERE WAS SOMEONE, HOWEVER, THAT I DID INTEND TO APOLOGIZE to. I could see no downside to that; he already knew what I'd done.

I waited until we'd hiked for another mile or so, winding higher and higher, as we followed the twisting turns of the Grizzly Creek trail. *Creek*, it turned out, was as big a misnomer as the boggy stream Avery and I had crossed earlier. Fed by the forty-three-acre glacial lake looming above at the mountaintop, this creek was a true force to be reckoned with. Our first face-to-face encounter with it featured the pummeling freight-train roar and sniper-fire spray of a massive twenty-foot cataract shooting down slick rock into a seemingly bottomless fern-lined pool.

For once, it wasn't just me who was overcome by the physical wonders of the world. The whole group of us stopped and stared. Even Tomás was outwardly impressed, which felt a little bit like hell had frozen over.

"Is this Grizzly Falls?" he asked me.

"Check your map," I told him.

He looked down to see what I already knew: that we were still a good mile or so from Grizzly Falls. By comparison, this section of the creek was so small and insignificant it didn't even register on the trail map.

"Shit," he breathed.

I nodded, letting a smile rise to my lips, willing to offer it to him, but he'd already turned away, walking swiftly over to where Shelby and Clay stood. I took that opportunity to slip my hand from Rose's and sought out Mr. Howe, who was resting with his back against a boulder and letting the waterfall wet his face. I sat next to him. Gathered my courage.

"I'm really sorry about what happened earlier," I said. "I screwed up. We shouldn't have gotten separated in the first place. It won't happen again."

"Don't be sorry." He reached to squeeze my shoulder. "I'm the one who shouldn't have left you alone with them. Especially knowing about your health. That was my mistake, you understand? You didn't do anything wrong."

I nodded but only felt worse about things. My health wasn't what had gotten us separated from the rest of the group or made me stick my hand down Avery's pants or led me into the gorge and across the stream to lie in the grass with a strange woman I wasn't sure I should trust. I'd done all those things on my own. Me and my poor judgment.

"Ben?"

"Yeah?"

"You should take it easy for the rest of the day. Rest when we get to the meadow. If the altitude gets to you or anything, you let me know. Okay?"

I nodded again before running my hand through my hair. "Do you hate me?"

Mr. Howe paused. "No, I don't hate you. Not even close."

"Oh, okay. Good."

"I hate that you would think that."

My shoulders twitched. "Sorry."

"Is there something else you're upset about?"

"No. I don't know. Maybe. It's dumb. Forget I said anything."

"Well, you can talk to me," he said. "Anytime. Even about dumb stuff. I'm a good listener. Lucia's taught me well."

I pushed my lips into a smile. "Thanks."

"I mean it."

"Hey, what time is it?" I asked because I needed to change the subject. Disappointing people you cared about always felt worse when they acted so *nice* about it.

Mr. Howe pulled his phone out. "Almost two. Should take us another half hour before we get to the meadow. Then we'll set up camp and do some exploring. But you should really rest."

"I will."

"Good."

I pointed. "Your phone works out here?"

"Not really. There's no reception."

"But you're able to check the weather?"

"What about the weather?"

"It's just, well, I heard there was a storm," I said.

"You heard?"

"Yeah. Those people we ran into earlier told me. One of them said a storm was coming soon. A bad one."

"Who were those people? Archie said something about a church group?"

"They said something like that, but . . ."

"But what?" he pushed.

"But I agree with Archie. I don't think they were who they said they were."

"So who were they?"

"I don't know. They said they were planning on camping for the weekend, but that we should leave before some storm came in."

This got Mr. Howe to lift his eyebrows. "Sounds like they don't want us here."

That was exactly what I'd been thinking, and I was glad he agreed with me, but I still didn't do what I should've done at that moment. I didn't tell Mr. Howe about all the other things that were worrying me. Like Maggie lying about where they'd come from. Or the Preacher's tattoo and how uncomfortable he made me feel. Or that I'd told them both right where we were planning on sleeping that night.

Worst of all, I didn't tell Mr. Howe about the loaded gun in Archie's backpack. I didn't tell him about that or any of those things because I didn't want to disappoint him more than I already had. And besides, right then, Mr. Howe started yelling at Archie, who was pretending he was going to push a clueless Clay into the river. It was a nice sort of yelling—he wasn't mad—and pretty soon everybody was goofing near the water, splashing one another with sticks and throwing rocks in the pool to see how deep it was, and in the next moment Mr. Howe leaned back, turned his face to the sun, and gave this long sigh of contentment, like a dog who'd found his bone after digging for the thing all damn day.

Who was I to ruin that for him?

The afternoon stretched, lingered, and overstayed its welcome, but we finally reached the lush meadow where we were meant to set up camp. Grizzly Lake still wasn't visible, but made its presence known nonetheless in the form of a towering waterfall. From hundreds of feet above, a great whitewater rush shot straight over sheer granite cliffs, arcing in a long, tumbling free fall that came crashing down onto huge piles of boulders. The air foamed with alpine spray as the river thundered through the meadow before continuing down the mountain.

Impressive as the sight was, I have to admit it felt strange knowing we'd be sleeping beneath such a massive—and yet unseen—body of water. That we'd have to trust nature would do just what it'd done for the last ten thousand years, which was to stay put and not kill us all. *Faith*, I guess, is the word I'm looking for. Or maybe *suspense*. Of the ticking-time-bomb variety.

Excused from doing setup work due to my "medical condition," I walked out and sat alone on the far edge of the meadow and took in the view. Something rare and fearsome opened inside of me as I did this.

Whether it was exhaustion from the day, my weakness, my migraine, I didn't know. But rather than gaze up at the waterfall, at what lay ahead, I stared down at the valley we'd come from, at the road we'd driven in on and the snaking river we'd camped beside.

All of it, I realized from where I sat, was a reminder of perspective, of futility, of the fact that every system we thought we knew was in reality so much bigger than ourselves. Big enough that our insignificance—in time, in space—was all but guaranteed. This even got me thinking about God a little, which wasn't like me. Pondering questions about creation or the afterlife or how I might be punished for my sins was rarely worth the effort. Or so I'd found.

But introspection can only last so long. By the time I returned to the campsite, Rose had already gotten the tent all set up, which made me feel shitty. A dumb reaction, seeing as it was her tent in the first place and she knew what to do with it. I'd practiced setting it up on the lawn of the inn on numerous occasions but had yet to put it together on my own.

I crawled inside while she was changing clothes so that I could unroll my sleeping bag—well, that was Rose's, too, since I'd borrowed most of my gear from her. The rest was on loan from Mr. Howe. In fact, the only piece of backpacking equipment that was actually mine was my compass, which had been my grandfather's. My mother had hated him with a passion, so when I'd found it in the garage in a box along with some of his other stuff, including his ashes, most of which had spilled everywhere, I didn't bother asking if I could have it. I just took it.

"Want to lie down with me?" I asked Rose with as much optimism as I could muster. I thought it would be nice to close my eyes and put my hand between her legs.

"Can't," she said as she double-knotted the laces of her Nikes. "I told Shelby I'd walk with her."

"Walk where?"

"I don't know. Up by the waterfall I guess. Avery's got a camera. She wants to take pictures of us."

"Since when are you friends with Shelby and Avery?"

"Since when am I not?"

I didn't have an answer to that question. Not one I wanted to tell her about, anyway, so I tried a different approach. "Well, aren't you tired?"

"What's there to be tired of?"

"Not being with me."

"I'm sure we'll have time for that later." Rose squeezed out of the tent and started to walk away.

"Time for what?" I called out.

She didn't look back. "For me to get tired of you."

When the girls were gone, I wandered over to where Dunc and Tomás were arguing over how to build a fire. They'd even made this giant ring of rocks and piled a bunch of sorry-looking twigs in the middle of it.

"You know you can't do that," I told them.

"Why not?" Dunc swiped at his forehead with the back of his hand. He'd gotten an awful sunburn on his face, despite repeated sunscreen warnings from both me and Mr. Howe, and currently looked like a cross between the lady who worked at our local tanning salon and fucking Donald Trump.

"You're going to burn the mountain down," I said. "Also, it's illegal. Or did you not see the ABSOLUTELY NO FIRES ALLOWED signs when we drove into the park?"

Tomás pointed one of the twigs at me. "You know, you can be kind of a dick."

"Thanks."

Dunc sniffed. "Those people we met had a fire."

"Those people we met probably had a lot of things they weren't supposed to," I muttered. "Doesn't mean we're having a fire."

"Who were those people anyway?" Tomás asked.

Dunc kicked at the rock circle, sending stones rolling. "Dude said he was some sort of preacher, but he was full of shit."

"A preacher? Like, a religious person?"

"Yeah. A preacher. That's what I said."

I nodded at Dunc. "Why'd you think he was full of shit? I mean, I thought that, too, but I want to know why you did."

Dunc kicked a few more rocks, then shoved a pile of Skoal in his lip before answering. "Don't tell anyone, but Archie went through some of their stuff while you were lying down in the grass with that lady. Let's just say some of the things he found in that tent of theirs sure didn't make it seem like the guy was a preacher."

I gaped. "He seriously did that?"

"What lady?" Tomás asked.

Dunc sighed. "Yeah, he seriously did that."

"What'd he find?"

"Just some booze and stuff. Arch might've taken some."

"Taken some what?"

"Booze."

"Jesus," I said.

"What lady?" Tomás asked again.

A line of brown drool ran down Dunc's chin. "One of the Preacher's acolytes. He had two of them. Apparently their God-given job is to walk around naked while he prays for more ass or something. Arch and I got an eyeful before Gibby and Avery showed up and ruined the whole thing. It was a pretty nice scene to come across. But you wouldn't know about that, would you, Tomás?"

"Know about what?"

"The pleasures of naked girls."

Tomás looked at me. "What were you doing with Avery?"

"We were just, uh . . . taking some pictures." I fumbled for the lie, and even I could hear how awkward my words sounded.

"Yeah, I bet you were," Dunc said. "But hey, Arch thinks he knows who those people really are."

I blinked. "How's that?"

"He told me he heard about two convicts escaping from that state mental hospital down in Napa yesterday, then robbing a bank. Guess they were last seen heading north with two female accomplices."

"Oh, come on," I said. "I heard that, too. It was on the news at the gas station. That's not them. No way."

"How would you know?"

"Well, first of all, we only met one guy down there. Not two."

Dunc shrugged. "Arch says there were four sleeping bags in that tent."

"Why would they come here?"

"Why *wouldn't* they? I'd hide out somewhere remote if I were them. Apparently they're carrying half a million dollars in cash."

Half a million dollars. I'd missed that part of the news story. And I shivered a little, picturing all that money and what I could do with it. But I also recalled that eerie movement I'd seen in the woods behind the campsite. Maybe that hadn't been some migraine-induced trick of the eye. Maybe I really had seen something.

Or *someone.*

"Listen," I said. "I don't know who those people were, but there *was* something off about them. That woman I was talking to? Maggie? She told me they'd driven here from Arcata."

"Arcata sucks ass," Dunc said.

True, but not relevant. "Yeah, but *later* she told me about a weather report she heard all the way down in Willits. That doesn't make sense. That's almost three hours in the other direction."

Tomás looked at me. "What do you make of that?"

"I don't know what to make of it. It just makes me wonder, you know?"

"See, that's what I'm talking about." Dunc wagged a grubby finger at me. "It *is* them. It has to be. Coming from Napa, they would've gone straight through Willits. I bet they have that cash on them. That's why they were so sketchy earlier, following us around everywhere."

"Maybe," I acknowledged. "But then why'd the Preacher call us down there in the first place?"

"To find out who we were. What we're doing here."

"I guess." It still didn't make sense to me, though. He'd let Avery *photograph* him. In fact, he'd invited her to do so.

"Think we should tell someone?" Tomás asked me.

I looked at him. "Who?"

"I don't know."

Dunc tipped his head as he spit again. "Yeah, I don't know, either, but you better be careful telling Archie any of this. Give him proof he's right about who those people are, he's going to go after a whole hell of lot more than a bottle of Jim Beam."

Tomás gave an exasperated sigh. "We're talking about fugitives who broke out of a *state mental hospital*. That means they were waiting to be assessed to see if they're criminally insane."

"Yeah, well, I don't need to wait for someone else's assessment. This is Archie DuPraw we're talking about. I know insanity when I see it. Hell, Gibby, *you* ought to know better than the rest of us. Takes one to know one."

"I guess." I didn't have the energy to get sucked into the taunting nature of his words. No one had ever said I was *criminally insane*; I just had to see a court-ordered therapist for a year or so after what happened with my stepfather. I was also assigned a social worker, who made sure my mother got on disability on account of her back injury and did his best to keep her sober. Trust me, even though I'd killed someone, to everyone outside of our house, I was seen as a victim. I was treated like one, too.

This time, though, I doubt I'll be so lucky.

21.

AVERY FOUND ME AFTER DINNER WHEN I WENT TO GET WATER FROM
the river so that Clay and I could wash the dishes. The sun was setting
and the sky was bursting with color—bright pops of it, here and there
and there—and even though I didn't plan it like that, my whole body
kind of felt the same way when I saw her walking toward me.

That long black hair.

Those soft, soft thighs.

She sat on a rock by the water's edge, at a spot where the river ran
wide, taking pictures of the sky and the dragonflies and maybe of me.
For my part, I pretended not to see her while I crouched to fill the
dromedary sack, which was just a fancy name for a nylon bag that held
water. We were hidden from the others by a thicket of weeping spruce
and feather grass, and I don't know how it happened, but pretty soon
we were sitting together and letting our knees touch and talking about
things that felt urgent and deep, like how much we liked each other but
didn't want to hurt Rose. Pretty shitty stuff, I realize now, looking back
on it, because if I were getting played, the last thing I'd want my signifi-
cant other talking about was how bad she felt for cheating on me. But
in that moment I was stupid and eager and maybe there was a certain
chaos I craved.

The sky dimmed and after the talking, Avery and I fooled around
for a bit. I want to say I couldn't help it, but I could and I did it anyway.
The colors popping in the sky and popping inside of me grew brighter,

more brilliant, the more I ran my hands along her skin; soon I was panting again, all heat and original sin.

Avery, for her part, was earnest in her lust—eager, too, which I liked, and submissive, which I didn't. But she touched me back and things were good for a while until it ended up kind of fizzling out. Embarrassing, but I was honest and told her how that happened to me sometimes, that my head and my body didn't always work well together and that it was probably due to brain damage, although that was impossible to prove because it wasn't like I had a sex life *before* I'd been hurt. I also told her that some people with traumatic brain injuries wanted to do it all the time and could also be really emotional, but that I was the opposite and that it was frustrating and irrational, because how could I *want* something but not really have the desire to do it?

Avery looked confused with my explanation. But then she shrugged and patted my shoulder, like I was a good little donkey who'd just carried her up a steep hill. "Makes sense to me," she said. "Want and desire aren't the same thing, you know."

"What do you mean?"

"Well, want is for when there's something missing. Desire is for going after what makes you feel good."

I'd never heard that before but thought she might be right, so then I told Avery that maybe the reason desire was hard for me was because going after what made me feel good was a choice and that I didn't like making choices. She sort of frowned when I said this, her eyes filling with more compassion than I could bear, and she told me she hoped that someday I might see things differently. Then she said she had to go.

By that point the sun was almost gone from the sky and it was true, we both needed to get back to the campsite. We couldn't go together, so Avery left first. She didn't really say good-bye or act like she'd miss me as she slipped back through the grass, and I felt sick with abandonment.

Guilt, too, for failing Rose again for no other reason than lust. Also shame, for being so damn bad at it.

Kicking off my shoes, I went and sat on the boulder Avery had been perched on and dropped my feet into the black pool beneath. Then gasped. The cold nearly stopped my heart, pure polar melt, but I didn't pull back. I let the depths of the water chew at my bones with its unrelenting force.

I thrust my legs in deeper still, to my knees, watching as bubbles frothed at the surface. Eager to indulge the greedy pull of the current, I was of half a mind to let it take me. To let it pull me under. Just to be wanted, if only in death.

I closed my eyes.

I let my hips slide forward, to the boulder's very edge.

"Hey!" a voice said.

My eyes flew open, and I whipped around to see Clay Bernard holding a flashlight, which he was shining right in my face.

"What is it?" I yanked my feet from the current.

"What are you doing?"

"Nothing."

Clay gave me a pointed you're-full-of-shit look. "Well, you got that water or what? I've been waiting for you for, like, forever."

"Yeah, I got it." I scrambled off the rock before gathering up the dromedary sack along with my shoes and socks. "Let's go."

When the dishes were done, Mr. Howe announced that he would be leading a stargazing hike to a spot about a mile away up on the western ridge, where the entire sky would be visible. He'd brought a portable telescope and the view would be stunning, he said. No light pollution to dim the stars or crush our dreams. Plus, a meteor shower was happening. Long-lost pieces of ice and comet dust bursting and shimmering in their final fall to our ground.

I didn't end up going on the hike. Someone had to stay back and keep an eye on the campsite. Not to mention I hadn't been doing very well at the whole resting thing.

Archie, Rose, and Shelby also ended up staying behind, which worked for me. I planned on staying close to Rose and far from Avery, since I clearly couldn't be trusted around her. I was starting to feel pretty lousy about that, especially given the fact that Avery wouldn't look at me, not even out of the corner of her eye.

So I focused my attention on Rose. On all that I loved about her and all I could do to show her that. She'd cut her hand on a serrated knife while drying dishes and although she tried gamely to be brave, I could tell it hurt—Rose hated nothing more than physical pain. So when I got her alone, I sat her down outside our tent in the grass and insisted on tending to the wound with a first aid kit.

Her eyes brimmed with tears while I poured antiseptic on it.

"It stings, doesn't it?" I asked.

She nodded.

After washing off the blood and cleaning the cut, I spread antibacterial ointment on her finger, making sure to cover the whole thing, before stretching an oversize Band-Aid across the area.

Rose smiled when I was done, although tears lingered to stripe her cheeks. "You're always gentle when I hurt myself."

"I try."

"But you do more than that. You do more than just try."

I looked up at her. "I hope that's a good thing."

"For me it is," she said. "I don't know what it's like for you."

While the others were off stargazing, the four of us spread a tarp on the grass and played cards by the light of a glowing lantern—first Asshole, then Blackjack, and finally a game Shelby taught us called Spite and Malice. I hadn't heard of it, but Archie pulled a bottle of Jim Beam out of his bag—I knew full well where it had come from—and we all did shots while she explained the rules.

The game itself was simple enough: an exercise in the zero-sum conundrum. Or the tragedy of the commons. The goal was to get rid of a stack of facedown cards before anyone else got rid of theirs, but that task required the cooperation of others. I played dutifully, only I drank too much, too fast, and soon my mind got stuck on all the things I could think of that required the cooperation of others: from conception to love to betrayal. Did that list include death? Suicide seemed to say otherwise, but I kept trying to make it work. After all, someone had to sell the gun or sharpen the blade. But it was the forces of nature I couldn't reconcile. Leaps from high cliffs. Or into fast-moving currents.

Anyway, as these things go, when only one can win, cooperation goes out the window, meaning Spite and Malice is really a game of trying to screw one another over.

"Jesus, Archie. Play an ace already," I growled, because the game had stalled over his stubbornness. Archie was a mean drunk, it turned out. A spiteful one, too. I got the distinct feeling he was hoarding cards, not for his own advantage, but just to piss everyone else off.

Without his ace, I couldn't do anything. I picked a card up from the center pile. It was a nine, which did me no good. Only I couldn't figure out what I was supposed to do next, so rather than ask, I dropped my cards and reached for the Jim Beam. Took a longer swig than usual.

"Careful," Rose warned.

"Careful," mimicked Archie, which made Shelby giggle. I'd never heard Shelby giggle before.

"You sound like a bird," I told her.

"What kind of bird?"

"A loon."

"That's rude," she said.

"Calling you a loon?"

"Not finishing your turn."

I swiveled back to Rose. "Wait. What do I need to be careful about?"

"Huh?"

"You just told me to be careful."

"About the drinking. You don't want to get sloppy, Ben. Not tonight."

"I won't get sloppy," I said.

"But you already have."

"What does that mean?"

Rose dropped her gaze to the ground, to a spot right in front of me. I looked and saw that in setting my cards down, I'd somehow placed them all faceup, for everyone to see.

I swore and grabbed for them. Shelby giggled more, like we were all goddamn loons, and I guess I really was sloppy because I started to laugh, too. Rose shook her head but in a way that looked playful. I leaned to kiss her cheek, to feel her breath against my skin, but I caught Archie leering at us in an odd sort of way.

"So, Rose . . . ," he started.

"So, Archie," she finished.

"About that brother of yours."

"What about him?" Rose said. "And no, I won't tell you who he's fucking."

"So he is fucking someone?"

"So you care who he fucks?"

Archie gulped more whiskey. Didn't bother wiping his mouth. "I don't care about anything, sweetheart. That's just it."

"And yet here we are, the way we always are. With you asking questions and me still not answering them. You have a funny way of not caring."

"Yours is even funnier," Archie said, nodding at the way Rose's elbow was resting on my thigh, and I frowned—I wasn't laughing anymore—because what did Rose mean by *the way we always are*?

And what did Archie mean?

Dread spooled through my gut, a live wire of unease, but I didn't ask. I didn't say anything. What I didn't know couldn't hurt me, right? Instead I stayed very still and swallowed the shard of blackness rising in my throat. After a moment, I glanced at Shelby, who gave me a sweet smile in return, one of her prettiest.

It's okay, she mouthed to me. *It's going to be okay.* I wasn't sure what she meant by that or if she really meant anything at all. What I did know was that I didn't deserve to feel jealous or upset or angry. I deserved nothing because *I* was the worst of all. A cheater. A liar. And terrible at both. But maybe Shelby understood some of what I was feeling—that it was possible to hate the person you were but also feel deeply sorry for yourself, both at the same time—because she reached to hand me the liquor bottle, and honestly, it was about the nicest thing she could've done.

Thank you, I mouthed back.

22.

ARCHIE.

Rose.

Rose.

Archie.

After swigging more Jim Beam than was prudent, I set myself to sulking. Abandoning my cards for good, I promptly turned my back on the others—I was too drunk to storm off on my own. Instead I squeezed my eyes shut and proceeded to mine my brain for every instance I'd seen the two of them together. There wasn't much. How could there be? Rose wasn't merely too good for Archie; her worth was measured on a different scale than his, if his was even worth measuring in the first place, which I highly doubted.

A few encounters did spring to mind: the two of them getting paired together for driver's ed sophomore year, much to Rose's distaste—she said he drove with his dick, not his balls, whatever the hell that meant; that time we'd given Archie a ride home from our class cleanup day by the Eel River. He'd spilled Mountain Dew all over the backseat of the Pathfinder and left without saying anything. The most notable instance, however, was something that had happened last spring during a party out at the Richards' miniature-horse ranch that was located on the eastern side of Teyber.

I hadn't meant to go to the party that night. I really hadn't. My mom's back pain had been flaring that week. Worse than ever, and it scared me to see her like that—writhing helplessly, unable to get out of bed even to use the bathroom. I fretted and tried dragging her to the ER; hell, there was only so much *I* could do, no matter what she said about those doctors, how they looked down on her and made her feel like crap for needing help. For needing *anything*.

She wasn't having it, though, and after going a few rounds with me, she ordered me to leave the house. To go be with Rose and not come home until morning. I tried to protest—she'd never kicked me out before—but I wasn't dumb. My mom was forever warning me off sex, despite my swearing up and down I wasn't doing it. But that never stopped her from lecturing me on the subject, always at times when I was least interested in hearing about it.

"You can ruin a girl," she'd hiss at me, "without even knowing it. That's what boys don't understand. They don't understand anything. They think nothing of their few seconds of thrusting, and then they're gone. Onto the next one. The girl forgotten. But she'll remember, Ben. It's in her nature to be changed by that, to let someone else inside of her." It always made me shudder to hear how gross I was for ruining Rose's body or whatever—although when had I ever *forgotten* her?— but when my mom went off like that, the best thing I could do was smile and nod and pray she didn't bring Jesus into it, like she would've if Marcus had still been around.

The point is, my mother's pushing me to spend the night with a girl she hated let me know very clearly who she'd be inviting over to the house once I was gone and why. And, look, you can spare me the sanctimonious lectures on enabling and addiction. I'm neither stupid nor willfully ignorant, but I don't make it a habit to police my mother's choices. Pain is always personal. I should know that better than anyone.

So I left, and by the time I got over to the Richards' farm, the place was packed. I had to park the Ford in the far pasture, way past the barn where the horses slept, and close to the waterline in a low spot slick with mud. Then I made my way back toward the main house. Everyone was crowded outside on the back patio because Connie Richard wisely didn't want her parents returning to a trashed home. Walking up the drive, I witnessed my classmates doing the things they always did when they found themselves out of reach of adult awareness: laughing, shouting, drinking, fucking, whatever.

Bad music blared from a blown speaker, the air reeked of alfalfa dust, and that night there was a weight on my chest so heavy it almost got me to turn around and sink myself in the river. No one would miss me; I hadn't told Rose I'd changed my mind about coming—or really, had it changed for me—because autonomy equaled pride and getting kicked out of my own house so that my mom's dealer could drop by was wholehearted shame.

I made a beeline for the keg instead. I must've looked desperate, because Walt Nunez, who lived two doors down from me, shoved a beer in my hand even before pouring his own. Then he peeled away from the crowd to stand with me in the dark beneath a giant willow tree.

"Cheers," I said, before gulping half the beer and ignoring the foam spilling down my arm.

"Cheers." Walt watched me drink before taking his own sip. "Rose is here, you know."

"Yeah, I know."

"I don't see you much without her these days."

"I don't see you much at all."

Walt's eyes widened, like I was being an asshole or something. That wasn't my intent, and my first impulse was to apologize—it always was—but I resisted. Drank more instead.

"You having a good time?" I asked after a moment.

He shrugged. "Not really. It's been kind of a shit year. Guess that makes tonight kind of a shit night."

I nodded. Once Teyber Union's prized defensive back, Walt had torn his MCL during a losing game that fall, tearing more than one heart in the process, along with his Division I dreams. Multiple surgeries later and no more football meant he'd gained a good twenty pounds since. Walt and I had never been close, despite our proximity, but even I knew there was nothing about his current situation that wasn't depressing as hell. I caught sight of him every now and then, limping around school, around the neighborhood, with his eyes dull and his head hung low. More than anything, he'd come to resemble a shelter dog nearing the end of its days, and it was hard sometimes, not to look away.

"Want to smoke?" he asked brightly, tapping the breast pocket of his shirt.

"Sure," I said, because that was the easiest answer. It was Humboldt, after all, and smoking meant weed not tobacco. Walt's eyes lit up at my agreement, making me wonder if the cause of his newfound moroseness wasn't so much that he could no longer play a game he loved, but that no one had a reason to hang out with him anymore.

We walked back down the hill toward the rows of cars. I sat in the front seat of his truck while Walt rolled a joint on the knee of his jeans—his good knee, although I couldn't tell you why he bothered. Then we got high together. It was a soft, lazy high that didn't take me anywhere I hadn't already gone but which made the stars loom large and my heart ache less.

The air inside the truck remained crisp, our breath mingling with the weed. Walt put music on—he didn't seem to want to talk—and after a moment, I closed my eyes, rested my head against the seat back. The weight on my chest didn't ease, but I'd stopped caring. Not caring was easier, a languid release, and there was a word, I realized, for my preferred mode of travel along the path of least resistance; it was called surrender.

Someone tapped on my window, making me jump. My eyes flew open and I turned my head. Saw nothing.

"What the fuck?" Walt growled.

I shoved the truck's door open, letting in the night breeze and the crappy thud of the bass from the music playing up the hill. I'd placed one foot down on solid ground when Rose sprang from the darkness with a roar. She bounced against me hard, a feral girl, then fell into my arms, bubbling over with laughter.

"Ben!" she exclaimed. Her eyes were brighter than I'd ever seen, her pupils like saucers. "Come on!"

"Shhh," I told her.

"Don't shush me."

"I'm not shushing you."

"You just did."

"It's just . . . your voice, it's kind of loud right now."

"My *voice* is loud?"

"Not in a bad way," I said quickly.

"Uh-huh." She took a step back from me. Put her hands on her narrow hips. "Well, you need to tell me where you've been. Tomás said he saw you pull in over half an hour ago, but I haven't seen you anywhere. You didn't even text me."

"I'm sorry."

"I didn't ask if you were sorry."

"Walt and I were just hanging out."

"Walt?"

"Nunez."

"Oh." Rose made a sound of impatience. She clearly didn't care what I'd been doing. "Well, come on. They're *waiting*."

"Who's waiting?"

"Just come on!"

She laughed and pulled my arm, harder than I liked, and I didn't have time to do more than shout a harried "Bye!" to Walt before turning and racing with Rose back up the drive. Despite the inside of the house being off-limits, she pushed through the crowd and dragged me up the porch steps and marched straight into the kitchen. The lights were on and the place was a mess, food was everywhere, bottles, too, but the room was empty.

Rose stormed around the kitchen. "Goddamn it."

"What?"

"They're all gone!"

"*Who's* gone?"

"Everyone!"

"Hey, assholes, I'm still here." I glanced over the bar into the adjoining family room and spied Archie DuPraw slouched in an oversize recliner. He was a mess. It looked like he'd been up for days: Solo cup in hand, stubbled chin to chest. His hooded eyes were bleary, and his greasy hair fell past his shoulders. Not to mention, there were unflattering food stains—or worse—dotting the front of his T-shirt. He was also looking right at Rose. At her tits, really, from what I could tell—she had on this little tank-top thing—giving me the urge to strangle him.

Rose made a face. "Forget it, let's go."

"Who were you looking for?" I asked.

"Doesn't matter. Let's get a drink."

"All right," I said, eager to be alone with her or at least out of that brightly lit room. We turned to leave.

"So it's going to be like that?" Archie called after us.

Neither of us answered.

"You're a bitch, Rose Augustine," he called out louder. "You know that? Una puta. A stuck-up Spanish bitch."

I tensed. Froze mid-step at his words. "You want me to say something to him?"

Rose rolled her eyes before kicking open the door and pushing me through it, back into the night. "God, no. That's the last thing I want."

Then we were outside on the porch, and despite her bravado, she looked small suddenly, fragile, just standing there, with her bony shoulders shivering, while duskywing moths dove and danced against the carriage light above us.

I reached to touch her, protect her. "You sure you don't want me to talk to Archie? He shouldn't have said that to you."

Rose shoved my hand away. Smacked it really. "What did I *just* fucking tell you?"

I recoiled. "I'm sorry."

"Why?"

"Why what?"

Her eyes flashed. "Why the hell are you sorry?"

"I don't know." I stared at my feet and wondered what was wrong with me. My head felt fuzzy. Miserably so.

But then Rose was in my arms again, returning to me with her own winged dance, cooing and stroking and kissing me everywhere. "Shit. *Shit.* I'm the one who's sorry, Ben. All right? Forget it. I was just being a bitch. I love you. Okay? I love you and I don't deserve you and I hope you know how goddamn good you are."

Rose never told me what she'd been doing in the kitchen that night or who she'd been doing it with, but I also never thought to ask. My takeaway was that Archie thought Rose was a stuck-up bitch, and that was fine by me. I wouldn't have wanted it any other way.

But now, being up on that mountain with both of them, drunk and jealous, my ego wounded, my heart brimming with guilt, the events of that night began to jitter around inside my mind. Over and over.

Because *something* had happened between them. It also seemed more had happened since. And I, who was indeed never without my Rose, had no idea what it was.

23.

NOTHING GOOD CAME OF MY MOPING. NOTHING GOOD EVER DID. BUT I was saved from saying anything stupid or drinking myself into a coma when Shelby shook my shoulder and told me to get up.

"Leave me alone," I mumbled.

"You really don't want me to do that."

"Why would I say it if I didn't want you to do it?"

"Are you joking right now? Rose, is he joking?"

"Move your shit, Ben," Rose said lightly. "You can thank us later."

Thank who? I opened my eyes and saw what the rest of them had already seen: the bobbing lights in the distance indicating stargazing had ended and that Mr. Howe and the rest of the group were minutes away from returning to camp.

Shit. I scrambled to my feet. The four of us flew into action. Shelby sprayed everyone's mouth with Binaca while Archie jammed the Jim Beam into his backpack so fast he managed to kick over the camping lantern we'd been using. It rolled away from us, straight down a small incline before coming to rest in a patch of yellow grass.

"Glad that runs on batteries," Rose noted wryly as I scrambled after it. Shelby gave a sharp bleat of laughter, and that's how that song about the Chicago fire started running through my head. The line about the cow kicking the lantern over seriously gave me the urge to hoof Archie DuPraw in the face.

And then they were back, the whole group, flooding over us in a discordant wave of laughter and warmth and stargazing camaraderie—they'd all just glimpsed the heavens. Avery flopped down in the spot where I'd been sitting and picked up my cards. Dunc followed right behind, while Tomás and Clay went to sit side by side on the edge of the meadow, both leaning back on their elbows to continue their gazing and leaving me with little doubt as to who Rose's brother was fucking. Mr. Howe called to me from where he was standing near the tents. I jogged over to him and hoped to God the Binaca didn't fail me.

"How was the hike?" I asked, because that seemed like a totally normal not-underage-and-trashed-out-of-my-mind type of inquiry.

"Fine. It was fine." Mr. Howe rubbed at his forehead the way I sometimes did when I felt unwell. "We saw Venus out there. Jupiter, too."

"With the telescope?" I nodded at the case he'd set by his feet.

"Yes. But they're visible without. You can see them, too, if you want. Just head around that bluff far enough so the peak's not in the way." He yawned, covering his mouth with his hand. I made myself stare at the sky, to act like I was interested in what was out there, but tilting my head back set the universe spinning. A sickening loop of stars and galaxies and the vast unknown. I straightened up and focused on Mr. Howe's bearded face instead.

"You look tired," I said.

He smiled. "It's been a long day."

"Yeah, it has."

"How's your head?"

"It's okay."

Mr. Howe pulled his phone from his side pack and turned it on. "By the way, I wanted to show you this."

I stared at the glow in confusion. "I thought that didn't work out here."

"The phone doesn't. But there's a barometric sensor built in that does. I used it to check the weather after what you said about a storm."

That got me to lean closer. All I saw on the screen was something that looked like a car speedometer, with a needle swaying between an illustration of the sun and a gloomy rain cloud. "What's it say?"

"Looks like the atmospheric pressure's dropping."

"Does that mean a storm's coming?"

"It means we'll probably get some cloud cover tomorrow. Maybe a touch of moisture. We can check again in the morning. It's a pattern over time that really tells you something."

I nodded. We were both silent for a moment. Until anxiety wrestled away my better judgment.

"Can I ask you a question, Mr. Howe?"

"Sure."

"How'd you meet Lucy?"

He slid his phone away before answering. "We met in college. At Berkeley. We ended up in the same co-op our sophomore year. Although we didn't start dating until after we'd graduated."

"Why not?"

"Well, we were both with other people at the time, and we were really good as friends. I guess we didn't want to change that."

"But you had to know at some point, right? That you wanted to be together? And that you made each other happy?"

He beamed. "Absolutely. I still know it. Every day I have with her is a joy."

"That's cool," I said, although I wanted to ask if their life together was such a joy, why'd they spend so much of it apart? Her in DC, trying to change the world. Him on top of mountains, trying to conquer it.

Mr. Howe glanced over at me. "Where are these questions coming from? Is something going on with you and Rose?"

"Sort of. Maybe. I don't know."

"What don't you know?"

"I guess I don't always know if she likes me."

"You don't know if she *likes* you?"

"No."

"How many years have you been dating?"

"Two."

"And that's not long enough for you to figure that out?"

I rolled my shoulders and shuffled my feet, but liquor inspires honesty if nothing else. "Not really."

"I see." Mr. Howe did his beard-tugging thing. "Then can I give you a piece of advice? Something you might not want to hear?"

"Yeah. Sure."

"Well, look, first of all, I know your mom. I've known Jana a long time, okay? We grew up together."

"Okay."

"I also know her life hasn't been easy. With her mom dying the way she did, and her dad—well, none of that changes the fact that she probably doesn't make your life too easy, either." He paused. "But now you're with Rose, Ben, and she's different from your mom. That's a good thing. It's really good. But different can be tough to figure out sometimes. Just like it's tough to grow up being told that when someone doesn't want you it means they need you. Or that if something hurts it means you're meant to do it again. It's also tough to find out that with other people the opposite can be true."

I was confused. "But Rose doesn't hurt me."

"Maybe that's because you won't let her."

I frowned. I didn't know what to say.

Mr. Howe put a hand on my shoulder. "Do you want me to explain what I mean?"

"No," I said, more abruptly than I intended.

"Are you sure?" He drooped at my response, making me feel like an asshole and also embarrassed for him, because he seemed pretty eager to share whatever advice he had in mind. But I wasn't in the mood for a father-son pep talk, despite knowing how deeply he longed to be someone's father. More proof, I suppose, at how terrible I was at being a son.

"I'm sure." The world beneath me was spinning again. I wanted the conversation to be over.

"All right, then," Mr. Howe said. "I think it's time for me to turn in. Make sure you get some sleep soon. Tomorrow'll be another long day."

"I will."

"Those guys, too." He nodded at the card game, which was growing rowdier by the minute.

"I'll do my best."

"I know you will." Mr. Howe stretched and stifled another yawn with the back of his hand. "You're a good kid, Ben. You really are. We make a good team, you and I. I hope you know that." Then he smiled and gave me a quick wave good night, and I nodded and waved back and watched as he shuffled off with his telescope toward his small one-person tent.

Those were the last words he ever spoke to me.

DAY THREE

24.

I WOKE TO THE SOUND OF VOICES. WHISPERING. LAUGHTER.

Followed by furtive shushing.

My eyes opened. I let them stay that way, despite a pounding headache. I was reluctant to slip back into dreaming. There was too much darkness sloshing around inside of me. Booze, too. Struggling to sit up, I realized I was still extremely drunk. And none the better for it.

The light inside the tent was grainy. We'd left the fly off, which meant I could see to the sky, those dappled bursts of the Milky Way, a swirling mix of stardust and memories. I turned my head to the side and looked for Rose. She wasn't in her sleeping bag. In fact, she wasn't in the tent at all. That was strange. She'd been in there earlier. I remembered that clearly. She'd put me to bed—giving me water and patting my back, imploring me not to puke in my sleep and die. I'd promised I wouldn't. After that, I'd assumed she'd stayed with me.

Clearly not.

More whispering. It sounded farther away now and I was intrigued. I also had to piss, so I slipped on a pair of track pants and my hiking shoes with no socks and squeezed my way into the night.

"Shit!" I inhaled with a hiss as soon as I was on my feet, darting across the meadow like a rodent. I had no clue what time it was—it had to be after midnight—but the temperature had dropped significantly. My teeth chattered and bumps rose on my arms. I hurried to find a tree and a shadow, which was all the cover I needed. Pissing by moonlight wasn't meant to be complicated, and that, I thought, was a wonderful thing.

When I was done with all that wondering, I searched for the voices I'd heard. The campsite itself was dark and still, but not far beyond the line of tents, at a point where the ground sloped toward the water, I spied a light. Or what I thought was a light. I stared at it for a few moments, my brain working slowly, unsure if I could trust what I was seeing. Finally, I staggered forward. Slowly at first, then faster.

There was nothing stealth in my approach. But the roar of the waterfall hid my footsteps and my chattering teeth until I came upon the source of the light and the whispers. Lights, plural, to be more precise. Because every single one of the six figures huddled together by the waterfall was holding a flashlight.

They didn't notice me, just kept up with their talking or whatever it was they were doing. The sight of them out here in the middle of the night more than confused me. I was *mystified*. Because I recognized them all, even in my drunken haze: Archie, Dunc, Shelby, Tomás, Clay, and yes, Rose. *My* Rose.

I stood gaping at them. They were dressed in dark clothes, their voices low, urgent. And despite the moonlit cloud of pot smoke hovering in the air, it was clear this was not a party or a raucous game of cards or even a late-night round of drunken shit talking. No, this was a conversation.

A serious-sounding one.

My immediate inclination was to turn and leave. Because, like whatever it was Archie and Rose got up to when I wasn't around, this clearly wasn't meant to be my business.

But my cowardice became a moot point when Dunc turned and saw me. That goofy smile broke across his face.

"Hey, Ben," he said easily. "Whatcha doing?"

"Who the fuck are you talking to?" That had to be Archie. He swung his flashlight into my eyes so that I couldn't see.

"*Ben?*" someone else said.

Now there were more flashlights pointed at me. All of them. Hand over my eyes, I stumbled back, my foot landing in a hole and turning my ankle.

Someone grabbed my arm from behind. Steadied me. "Are you okay?"

Shelby. It was Shelby gripping me. I stared at her. Those wide blue eyes. That alluring mane of white-blond hair.

"Am I dreaming?" I asked.

She laughed, a high, tinkling sound. "I've heard that when you can't sleep it means you're awake in someone else's dream. So maybe you are dreaming, just somewhere else."

"Huh?"

"What's he want?" Archie called. "What the hell's he doing here?"

"I don't know," Shelby called back, but then she leaned close, her soft lips grazing my ear. "Maybe you should go back to bed. I don't think you want to be here. Not for this."

"Bring him over," Archie shouted. "It's okay. We need him."

"What's he saying?" I asked Shelby. I didn't understand what was happening.

She shrugged, then motioned for me to follow her, which I did. Shelby loped ahead of my drunken stumbling with all the grace of a prancing horse before gesturing in a dramatic flourish as she delivered me to Archie. I stood before him as he lowered his flashlight, allowing me to see the wide Cheshire grin stretched across his face.

"What'd you need me for?" I asked.

"What else?" he said smoothly. "Your navigational skills."

———

"Wait." I stared at the others and felt lost. The constant rush of the waterfall was sucking sound and reason from the air. An aquatic event horizon. "What are you talking about? What are you guys doing?"

"Ben, Ben, Ben." Shelby continued her bouncing, skipping around the circle like something out of a fairy tale, wild hair flowing behind her. The rest of them just stood like statues, watching me, the expressions on their faces unreadable.

I went to Rose.

"Hi," she said.

"You left me."

"You were passed out."

"I was asleep."

She shrugged. "I couldn't wake you."

Had she tried? Archie swooped in before I could ask, slinging his arm over my shoulder like we were the very best of friends. I felt ready to vomit. He reeked of whiskey and worse.

"Gibby," he boomed. "You sure you don't want to go back to bed? You look like shit, you know."

"You're supposed to be asleep," I said. "All of you."

Archie held me closer, practically choking me. "You're no fun, you know that?"

"Let go!" I squirmed.

"But we're having a debate."

"A *what*?"

"A debate. An ethical one. Maybe you can help us figure out what we should do."

I wanted him off me. "Okay, fine. What is it?"

Archie grinned and released me, taking a step back. "Now we're talking."

"Hurry up. It's cold."

But he didn't hurry up. Archie being Archie, he took his sweet time.

"Here's a hypothetical situation. Say someone commits a crime. A self-serving crime. They take something of value simply because they want it. That's wrong, isn't it?"

I nodded. "Sure."

"So if someone else were to take what they'd stolen and use it for something good, would that be a moral action?"

"You mean give it back?"

He waved a hand. "Say that's not possible. But the second person can do something good with that item. They can make the world a better place."

"Well, no," I said. "That's stupid. That's not even debatable. Two wrongs and all that."

"Not even if they're going to give it to the poor? To people who really need it?"

I snorted. "Who is this? Robin Hood? It's still not moral. And besides, altruism isn't about morality in the first place. It's about looking good and social status. In other words: self-serving."

"Cynic," scolded Archie. "Wrong answer."

"Right answer," I muttered, although it was starting to dawn on me what he was talking about. "Wait, Archie. This isn't about the Preacher, is it? Dunc, you didn't tell him about Willits, did you?"

Dunc, who was draining the last of the Jim Beam, shot me a rueful look, shame rimming his hooded eyes, which told me all I needed to know.

"Archie," I said. "You're not this fucking stupid. I know you're not."

"Maybe not," he agreed. "Maybe this is all hypothetical. That's what I said, right? So maybe you'll go back to your tent and fall asleep, and when you wake up in the morning, your life will be exactly the same as it is right now. Unlike ours."

A chill went through me. "So you're planning on stealing that money? How?"

Archie smirked as he tugged on the sleeves of his black hoodie. "Don't you worry about how. We might just use my cloak of invisibility here. Those guys'll never know what hit them. They won't even know we're there."

One by one, I glanced at the others. "This is . . . You're all fucking with me, right? This is a joke?"

Dunc pointed at me with the empty whiskey bottle. "I don't think money that would let me leave Teyber once and for all is a joke. Do you?"

"Why the hell do you want to leave so damn badly?"

He huffed. "Have you met my dad?"

"What's wrong with your dad?"

"He's a shit-kicking asshole is what's wrong. And unless you're willing to come over and shoot him in the head for me, I'd kind of like to get away from him. For good."

I whirled around. "What about the rest of you? Are you serious about this? Or are you just drunk?"

Clay looked at me with solemn eyes. "I don't talk about it a lot, but my little sister's sick. Really sick. My mom can't work anymore, and we can't pay for all her hospital bills."

I knew Clay's sister. She was seven years old and had a gap-toothed smile and braids and wore ladybug rain boots every time she came into the grocery store. Even in summer. "What's wrong with her?"

"Cardiomyopathy. Her heart's failing. She's probably going to need a transplant."

"Well, I don't think your family would be happy knowing that this is how you tried to help them."

"I think my family just wants her not to die, Ben."

I turned to Tomás. "What about you? *You* know this is crazy. You told me. What do you need money for? Your parents not funding enough trips to Europe these days?"

144

"I want to help Clay," he said flatly.

"Shelby . . . ," I said.

She stopped skipping long enough to fold her arms and set her jaw. The indignant fairy. "You know what? My life's not any of your fucking business."

Archie cut in. "I'm getting the feeling you don't want to be our navigator. That's disappointing."

"No," I breathed. "I really don't want to do that."

He shrugged. "Tomás'll do it, then. Shame, though. I trust you a hell of a lot more than I trust him."

It was a moment of surreality that followed. I stood and watched, disbelieving, as Archie—who'd shed his sullenness to become something animated, enthralling even—hoisted his backpack onto his shoulders. With a toss of his head, he beckoned for the others to follow, before turning and walking into the woods, heading toward the trail leading back down the mountain.

And then they did it. One by one the rest of the group went after him, their lights bobbing before them, like beacons in the darkness.

"I'm getting Mr. Howe!" I called after them.

"No, you're not," Archie called back.

Shelby waved at me as she took off, hair still floating as she moved. Clay and Tomás went next. Followed by Dunc.

"Rose . . . ," I pleaded as she turned to go. I couldn't believe she would leave me. "This isn't what you want, is it? You, out of everyone, you have no reason to do something like this. You don't need money. Who could you possibly be trying to help?"

The smile she gave me nearly broke me with its tenderness. "You really don't know?"

"No!"

She whispered in my ear, "*You.*"

———

I know now that what I should've done was go and wake Mr. Howe right off the bat, tell him what was happening, how I'd lost control of everything. But I didn't. And I don't know, sometimes when you're in the middle of seriously fucking something up, it can feel as if what's been done can still be contained. That it's not *so* bad yet that anyone needs to know how stupid you've been.

That was the feeling that kept me from doing anything smart or right, after I'd watched the six of them march down the mountain, straight into a hell of their own making, and maybe it's what makes faith so damn dangerous in the first place. Because I believed things would get better. That I could fix what was already so very broken without having to answer for my failures.

I went and found Avery instead. Back at the campsite, she lay curled in her sleeping bag on a tarp beneath the stars. A pang of guilt went through me to see that, to know Rose was the only reason I had shelter. I fell to my knees and shook Avery. Her head tossed and her long hair was strewn all around her, as if she were rooted to the ground. I shook her again. Harder.

"Ave!" I whispered. "Ave, wake up!"

Her eyes fluttered and opened.

"Ben?" she mumbled, her voice throaty and thick.

"You have to wake up," I told her, tugging on her arm with pit bull persistence. "Please!"

She let me pull her up to sitting, but remained bleary. "What is it?"

"It's the rest of them. All of them! They've gone and done something stupid."

"Rest of who?"

"Everyone! Except Mr. Howe. They're going to—"

She rubbed a fist on her eye. "They're going to what?"

"They're going to go steal money from the Preacher!"

"Huh?"

"I'm serious!"

Her nose wrinkled. "What money? Who has money? That doesn't make any sense."

"No, it doesn't. But they're doing it anyway. They're drunk. They're fucking trashed. We've got to stop them."

Avery still hesitated, so I explained it all to her. How it was that Dunc and Archie had come to believe the Preacher and his friends were the fugitives who had robbed a bank down in Napa, and that if they were, they were more than likely carrying over half a million dollars in cash. Honestly, it sounded stupider than ever once I said the whole thing out loud, and Avery, for her part, remained skeptical.

"I think they're just playing with you, Ben," she said with a yawn. "Archie's a dick. You know that."

"You really think Clay and Tomás are teaming up to play practical jokes with *Archie*?"

"No," she admitted. "But still—"

"But still *what*?"

"Well, where's Rose? Didn't you tell her about this? She'll know what's going on."

"She's with them," I said. "She went with them!"

Avery blinked. "Without you?"

I was glad for the dark, to hide my burning cheeks. "Yeah. She went without me."

"Oh."

"Archie's got that gun, Ave. You know that. Even if they're just fucking around, something bad could still happen."

This got her moving, got her scrambling out of her sleeping bag and reaching for her shoes. "Shit. *Shit.* You're right. You're absolutely right. We have to do something."

"But what?"

"Do you know where they went?"

"Back down the mountain!"

"Then go stop them!"

"How?"

Avery was on her feet. She tossed a headlamp at me. "You go. Find them. I'll get Mr. Howe. You can tell them that he's coming. That'll stop them."

I nodded. I turned and ran.

25.

I FLEW DOWN THE MOUNTAIN, AS FAST AS THE NIGHT WOULD LET ME,
cursing Archie and wishing I'd had the nerve to swing at him. Or do
anything to break his hold over the others, who were apparently mind-
less enough to follow him wherever he might go.

I also puked pretty much the whole way, something that was
both unfortunate and seriously unpleasant to do while running. But I
couldn't help it, all that sloshing and booze and fear and adrenaline. Although my getting sick was only partly due to being woefully drunk on
cheap bourbon. I also understood, somewhere deep inside of me, that
if anyone were to get hurt on my watch—seriously hurt—I wouldn't
be able to live with myself. There wasn't a single part of me, not one,
that could bear the thought of once again having someone else's blood
on my hands.

It was a seemingly endless scramble down the dirt trail that twisted
back and around to the other side of the mountain. My legs pounded
and pounded and pounded, but finally I reached the ridge where we'd
spied on the naked swimmers. Switching my headlamp off, I crouched
low and peered into the black gorge, that remote spring-fed canyon that
lingered against the thicketed woods, on the edge of utter desolation.

Other than the burbling stream and the occasional owl hoot, there
was nothing but silence. Fog hovered over the water, curling wisps of it,
and the air was rich with the scent of wet granite and pine. I could see

nothing of interest. The Preacher's campsite was too far away, set back from the shore, closer to the trees.

I had no choice but to descend into the gorge. Stealth seemed wise, but without the headlamp, I slipped a few times, sending dust and rocks flying down ahead of me. I swore under my breath and tried crab-crawling the last stretch, finally giving up and sliding on my ass the rest of the way and breathing a sigh of relief when I touched solid ground.

Walking upstream, I kept my back to the cliff wall so that my body was in shadow. This felt safer, to have cover behind me, and I was glad for the burbling of the creek that masked my halting steps.

Still I heard and saw nothing. I reached the boulder crossing that would take me to the far side of the stream and stepped from the shadows amid a flutter of nerves. Moving from rock to rock over the dark water, my legs quavered and I held my arms straight out. Balancing in the moonlight like that made me feel obvious. Laid bare.

But I reached the other side. From there it happened swiftly, a clattering downfall, like the clipping of an angel's wings. First, I heard a noise. It sounded like a grunt. Only I couldn't tell where it had come from. Or how far away it was.

I stumbled forward, tripping on rocks—that pebbly shore. The tent and the campfire were straight ahead, I knew that, and I followed the scent of burning wood, the pungent smoke. Reaching the edge of the shoreline and stepping into meadow grass I was able to walk faster. Dew gathered on my ankles. The glow of flashlights came into view. Or what I thought must be flashlights: shining orbs in the night, all moving erratically.

I started to run.

That's when I heard the first gunshot. Followed quickly by a second.

"Fuck!" A third gunshot rang out, a sharp bang, echoing off the canyon walls so loudly it was as if the earth were being split in two. My flight response took over and I ran on instinct, desperately, veering sharply from the campsite and heading back down the gorge, before turning into the shadowed woods to seek shelter.

I pulled up as I swept beneath the trees, into darkness. Gripping the needled branches of a crooked sapling with one hand, I bent over, clawing my lungs and gasping for air. My legs shook and my chest heaved.

"Ben!" a voice hissed. "Ben! Over here!"

I yelped in terror, shying sharply to my left before whirling like a top and straining to see who was talking to me. Relief flooded my veins. It was Shelby and Clay. They were crouched in the underbrush not five yards from where I stood and both were waving frantically at me.

More flight. I bolted toward them, diving into the brush and crawling as close as I could. I huddled against their warmth. "What the hell is *happening*?"

Shelby squeezed my arm. Clay opened his mouth to answer.

That was when the screaming began.

It was a woman's voice. Or a girl's. That was all I could tell. The screaming went on and on, piercing the night and scraping my soul. A whole symphony of anguish. Was it Rose? My Rose? I lunged forward, driven to do something.

Shelby grabbed for my ankle, holding me back. "You can't go down there!"

"Someone has to! Don't you hear that?"

"They have guns! They're *shooting*!"

"I know that!"

"Then stop! You're being stupid! You'll get killed."

There was another gunshot right then, making us jump. This was followed by more shouting.

And then silence.

Shelby whimpered. Clay looked like he was going to cry.

"Oh, shit," I breathed. "*Shit.* Who's down there?"

151

Clay wiped his nose. Then wiped it again. "It's Dunc, Archie, and Rose. They were going to . . . they weren't supposed to actually run into anybody. This wasn't supposed to happen. Arch said their plan was foolproof. They were going to make sure those people were all sleeping before they took anything. No one was supposed to get hurt. Not like this!"

I was dumbfounded. "He thought he could just walk up and take half a million dollars? That they wouldn't notice? Did he actually believe he was fucking invisible?"

"I don't *know*! Don't yell at me!"

"What are you two doing out here?"

Clay looked at Shelby. "We couldn't do it. I didn't really think we'd make it down here in the first place. Then when . . ."

"When what?"

"Archie had a gun, Ben," Shelby whispered. "A real one!"

My throat tightened. "Yeah. I know."

"You *knew*?"

"I saw it earlier today. That's why I came down here. To keep him from doing anything stupid with it. It's why Avery's getting Mr. Howe."

"She is? Are they here?"

"They're coming behind me. That's all I know."

"We need them now," Clay whined.

"What about Tomás?" I asked. "Where's he?"

Shelby shook her head. "I don't know."

"What?"

"He's not here," Clay said. "He turned back before we even got down here."

No, he didn't, I thought. I would've passed him.

"Let's see if we can get closer," Shelby whispered. "Maybe they're fine. Maybe they're doing what they said they would and something else is going on."

That seemed doubtful, but inaction was impossible. We crept toward the campsite, as quietly as we could. Someone was wheezing, a rattling sound that pricked my nerves and set my heart racing. I assumed it was Clay who was breathing like that, but soon realized *I* was the one making the noise—my lungs betraying my fear. Shelby, on the other hand, was absolutely silent as she snaked forward, her jaw tense, lips tight, as if she were holding her breath. As if she planned to hold it forever if she had to.

We kept going. There was no fog in the woods, just gloom on all sides and above. It didn't take long before lights flickered ahead and we heard voices. We inched toward the campsite, following smoke scent like moths to their maker. The fire came into view first, the flames crackling and hot.

Then horror.

26.

TWO MEN STOOD IN THE CLEARING. ONE I RECOGNIZED: ELVIN THE
Preacher, dressed in all black, a leather jacket and jeans, his thin face
sweaty and tense. He paced restlessly while another man, one I hadn't
seen before, aimed a military-style rifle at a group of people who sat on
the ground with their hands on their heads.

Hunkered in the shadows, I had to lean forward, stretching my neck
to confirm who they were: Archie, Dunc, and Rose. My first reaction
was a shaky sort of rapture; Rose wasn't dead. She wasn't the one who'd
been screaming.

The Preacher swore, throwing something against the rocks circling the campfire. Whatever it was shattered, making him swear again
and kick at the dirt. The rage on his face was in sharp contrast to the
cool, collected mannerisms I'd found so distasteful when we'd met
earlier.

My stomach burned; I wanted my Rose. Shelby pinched my arm
and grabbed for Clay's. She pointed at something that was on the other
side of the fire, away from the armed men, but not more than ten feet
from where we were.

Clay clasped his hands over his mouth. It was a body, right there in
front of us. A woman's body. Not Maggie—it was the woman I hadn't
spoken to, the one who'd followed Avery and the Preacher down to the
water. She lay sprawled on her back in a dark pool of what could only
be blood.

Archie yelled something. I couldn't make out what it was, but I saw his mouth open and his face go red. Beside him, Rose lifted her chin, beautifully defiant in the firelight, while the Preacher stalked over and shouted back, spit flying from his mouth, his body rippling with violence.

"Did Archie shoot that woman?" hissed Clay.

"I don't *know*," Shelby whispered.

"That's what it looks like," I said.

Clay fretted. "We need Howe. We need him now."

I looked at Shelby. She looked back at me.

"What're we going to do?" she asked.

"Clay," I said. "Do you think you can make it back across the stream and up to the ridge?"

"Yeah." His shoulders twitched. "Definitely. I definitely can."

"Then go, okay? Avery and Mr. Howe can't be that far behind. Go find them. Tell him what's happening. He'll know what to do."

He faltered. "You want me to go alone?"

"I'm not leaving Rose."

"I'll go with you," Shelby offered.

"Thank you," I said. "But be careful. Both of you."

Impatience danced in Clay's eyes. He tugged at Shelby's sleeve. "Let's go. I want to get out of here."

"Don't die," she said to me.

"I won't," I told her. "I promise."

They left, and I couldn't just sit there. I turned and slithered back into the woods on my stomach. With my arms shivering and teeth chattering, I slowly made my way around to the other side of the campsite and approached again from a different angle.

To stay in the shadows and out of view, I stopped maybe twenty yards away from where Archie, Dunc, and Rose were being held at gunpoint. Everything was clearer from this angle. More desperate, too. The fire burned bright, launching firework sparks high into the air, aiming for stars and brittle trees.

Rose was closest to where I was. She sat with her back against the stack of firewood and her knees curled close to her chest. Everything she wore was filthy, her sweatshirt torn, her shorts smeared with dirt and blood. A welt swelled beneath her left eye, raw and shiny, and her short hair was a matted mess.

I couldn't take it, to see her like that. Stupidly, I inched forward, all while praying the Preacher wouldn't see me. I didn't have to worry, though; his attention was focused on the other man with the gun and, more than anything, Archie. Imperious, insolent Archie. With his eyes sharp and his jaw tensed, he looked more alive in that moment than I'd ever seen him, facing down his own death.

"You know you're not going to kill us all," he was saying. "You're not that fucking stupid. So just let us go."

"You need to keep your mouth shut, son," said the second man, and I finally got a look at his face. He was older than the Preacher, it seemed, shorter and heavier, too, but there was enough in his sharp chin and black hair and glittering blue eyes to convince me they were brothers. And maybe the more rational of the two. The Preacher paced around the dead woman, before rearing back and kicking Archie in the face.

Archie rose up to lunge at him, but the Preacher's brother was there in a second with his rifle. He held it to Archie's head.

Rose closed her eyes.

"Fuck!" Dunc yelped. "Fucking just sit still already, Arch. Come on."

A baleful look simmered in Archie's eyes, but he settled back down. Wiped blood from his nose.

The Preacher picked up his own gun from the card table that was propped up close to the fire and stared into the woods, not far from where I hid. "Where's that other kid you were with? The tall, skinny one with all those moles on his neck."

Well, that wasn't a very flattering description, but I knew he meant me.

"I don't know where he is," Dunc said. "That guy's not my problem."

"You sure? You just happened to figure out who we were all on your own? That kid knew something about us. I know he did." He turned to his brother. "That bitch of yours told him."

"Maggie's no bitch."

"We don't know who any of you are," Dunc said. "I told you that. We were just screwing around."

The Preacher stood right in front of him, rage barely controlled. "You shot my Fleur because you were *screwing around*?"

"It was an accident! You scared the shit out of us coming at us like that. What were we supposed to do?"

Shut up, Dunc, I thought. *Just shut your fucking mouth.*

The Preacher was incredulous. "So you thought you'd show up here armed in the middle of the goddamn night and we'd sit you down for a drink?"

"*No.*" Dunc's voice twisted into a whine. "That's not how it was."

"Then why don't you tell me how it was."

I crept a few feet closer to Rose, hoping she'd notice me. Her eyes remained half closed and glazed over. Like she was willing herself out of the situation she'd found herself in.

I took a chance. I whispered her name. "Rose."

There was no response.

"Rose," I said again, and this time she heard me. Sweat glistened on her forehead, and I caught the moment of recognition. An intangible thing—she threw something back at me without moving a muscle, a spark of hope, or a flare of danger. Whatever it was, it was clear as day.

I pressed my finger to my lips and racked my brain for what to do. The only action that came to me was the one I'd seen in movies: jumping in front of the guns, absorbing a hail of bullets while the others scattered and ran for freedom. In truth, there was a draw to martyrdom—if I were to die, I'd be remembered fondly. That was worth something, wasn't it?

I pushed onto my hands and knees and tensed my shoulders. Then I said a brief prayer, and I don't care if that sounds hypocritical or cowardly or whatever. I'm only telling you the truth.

That's when I went for it. I jumped to my feet. I opened my mouth to shout.

27.

THE PAIN CAME DOWN SWIFT AND IMMEDIATE. THE SECOND I MOVED, something cracked against the back of my skull, snarling the nerves at the base of my neck. My whole brain stem, probably. I crumpled in an instant, hitting the ground hard before flopping over onto my back. With a groan I looked up, only to see a scowling face staring back at me, along with the barrel end of a carbine.

Maggie.

I said nothing and neither did she. Instead she gave a jerk of her head. She wanted me to get up and I tried. I really did. But my legs wouldn't work. I lay there gasping, but Maggie indulged me with her patience, waiting until the numbness in my legs faded enough, and I was able to crawl to my feet and limp to where the others sat.

Archie snorted when he saw me, making me want to reach out and kill him myself. Instead I collapsed on the ground between the other two. I snuck a glance at Dunc, who stared straight ahead, his cheeks pale and his jaw trembling. But Rose, I couldn't look at. I'd failed her.

The Preacher sidled over to loom above me. He looked me up and down just as deliberately as he had that afternoon. Only there was no hostility in his gaze at the moment. Just curiosity.

Maybe a touch of amusement.

"Hello, Benjamin," he said.

I glared up at him. "I already told you. My name's not Benjamin."

"Then what is it?"

"Bennett."

"Well, Bennett, you came to save your friends, didn't you?"

"Yes."

"Even though they attacked us?"

"Yes."

"You know, and I hope you don't mind me saying this, but you don't seem very well equipped to handle that job. Perhaps you should've brought your photographer friend. She seemed smart."

I didn't answer, but from where she stood by the fire, Maggie called out, "Don't underestimate that one, Elvin. He's a killer, you know."

He looked at her. "What do you mean?"

"Kid killed his stepfather when he was little. Shot him right in the head."

The Preacher turned back to me. "Really?"

"It was an accident," Rose said stiffly. "He didn't do it on purpose."

Maggie shrugged. "That's not what he told me, sweetheart."

"I'm not your sweetheart."

"So which was it?" the Preacher asked me. "Murder or an accident?"

"I don't remember," I said.

"Bullshit."

"It's true. I was ten. My mom found me with the gun and him dead. She told the cops it was an accident. But . . ."

"But then *she* tried to kill him," Maggie finished proudly. "Because she knew what he was really capable of."

Now I felt the weight of everyone staring at me. Not just Maggie and the Preacher and the Preacher's brother. But also Rose and Archie and Dunc. They all stared in what I assumed was some sort of repulsed silence, since even Archie didn't manage to crack a joke or insult my intelligence.

"Well, that's all very interesting," the Preacher said. "But seeing as

Bennett is unarmed at the moment, I'm more concerned about why his friends came down here in the first place."

I shook my head. "Don't ask me. I wasn't part of it."

"But I know you know. I know you know why we're here."

I licked my lips. I did know, didn't I? That was just it. And so maybe, just maybe, that meant this was all *my* fault. Because I hadn't kept my dumb mouth shut.

"Yes," I said, after a moment. "I know why you're here."

The Preacher gave a long sigh, real resigned-like, like maybe it was simply a string of bad luck that was responsible for this situation. My ultimate hope was that if we kept playing this blame-game thing, maybe he'd figure out that *he* was responsible for his own actions.

"Thank you, Bennett," he said, tipping his head at me like a gentleman. "That's all I needed to know."

He turned then, in the most casual of ways, lifted his arm, and shot Dunc in the head.

Rose screamed. I closed my eyes and cringed. The air reeked of heat and gunpowder, and Rose reached for me or I reached for her, but we found each other before diving for the ground, scrambling to get away from the woodpile, from the Preacher. From everything.

There was a huge crash behind us. I wrenched my neck to look over my shoulder just in time to see Archie and the Preacher locked together, grappling for the gun, with the overturned card table between them. Half the camping supplies had slipped into the fire, including the camping stove and propane. The Preacher's brother had his rifle lifted, waiting for his shot, and I couldn't breathe, knowing what was going to happen. That Archie was going to die. That I couldn't do a damn thing to save him.

Only it didn't happen like that.

Instead Mr. Howe stepped out of the woods, from the other side of the fire ring, near the clothesline and Fleur's dead body. I recognized the flare gun he held tight in his hand like he was trying to give the impression it was more than what it was.

Oh, thank God, I thought. *Thank you for saving us.*

"Just step back and put that down," Mr. Howe said sharply. His gaze was fixed on the Preacher's brother, who froze at the sound of his voice, at the sight of the flare gun.

"Who the hell are you?" he demanded.

"You heard what I said. Put your gun down."

"Yeah, yeah. Okay. I heard you." The Preacher's brother leaned forward to set his rifle down, and it was right at that moment that the propane from the camping stove exploded.

There was a loud *whoosh* as the flames leapt upward, a streaming arc, followed by a massive fireball that burst in every direction—an eruption of heat and debris that shook the earth. My ears rang but I could still hear shouting coming from all around me. Smoke was everywhere, and it was through the haze that I saw the Preacher's brother lying on the ground. The blast had knocked him down—his face was charred and bleeding—but he'd never set down his gun. In a single twisting move, he rolled onto his stomach, lifted the rifle to his shoulder, and squeezed off two shots, striking Mr. Howe in the chest and neck.

Mr. Howe fell back with a grunt. The Preacher's brother took aim again, this time at Avery, who'd been standing farther back, and I ran at him, charging full speed with my head down. Only Archie got to him first, tackling him from behind and sending the rifle spinning. I fell to my knees and grabbed for it, snatching it off the ground and nearly sliding into fire for my effort.

Another gunshot went off somewhere behind me. Then another. My breath came in short bursts as my hands fumbled to slide the rifle's safety into the locked position. Finger on the trigger, I scrambled to my feet and stalked the campsite, whirling around and around, searching everywhere for the Preacher. The smoke and the night made it too hard to see.

Archie remained on top of the Preacher's brother, hands wrapped around his neck, shouting expletives. I was fine with that. What had been Dunc lay slumped by the firewood, but I didn't let my gaze go there. I couldn't. A flurry of footsteps came from the woods, and I lifted my head in time to catch sight of Maggie fleeing into the darkness.

My lungs burned. I coughed, then couldn't stop coughing. I pounded my chest and lurched forward, my feet catching on something. I glanced to see what it was and my mind swayed into madness— it was the Preacher. Dead. He lay on the ground with his blue eyes open and his gun still clutched tight in his hands, only now there was a hole in his head. And worse. I staggered back, sick at the sight. All that gore.

"You asshole!" Archie was screaming and kicking the Preacher's brother in the chest. Over and over. His eyes were wild, rolling. Tears stained his cheeks, and I wanted to tell him to stop, that his dead brother was the one who'd killed Dunc. But then I froze. Because I saw what he must've already seen: Shelby and Clay huddled on the ground with Mr. Howe in their arms.

Time slowed down then. Halted, really. Denial, they say, is one of the five stages of grief, and my brain did all it could to fight back, to reverse time, to turn what was all wrong all right.

"Shelby!" I called out, and she looked at me, her lovely eyes melting. She knew what I was asking but didn't answer. I walked toward her in my slow-motion steps, but no matter how surreal the world felt, with my burning lungs and smoke-filled eyes, time refused to swing backward. It inched forward, defiant.

"Shelby," I said again.

She shook her head. Clay wouldn't look at me.

"No," I said. "Shel, no."

"Yes."

"No, he can't—"

"He's gone." Her voice choked. "He is."

My mouth hung open, and I stared at Shelby, watching her lips continue to move but unable to take in what she was telling me, unable to take in anything other than her stricken expression. The strident ringing in my ears.

"Ben," Shelby was saying. "*Ben.*"

I forced myself to respond. "What?"

"You need to check on Rose," she told me.

I cocked my head. Rose? That didn't make sense, what she was saying, but I turned to take a halting step toward the woods, back where I'd left her, where we'd cowered together in the shadows.

The first thing I noticed was Avery, which was also wrong. How had she gotten here? Last I'd seen her, she'd been standing behind Mr. Howe. Yet there she was, sprawled on the ground with her long legs splayed and twisting in the dirt. Mad thoughts ran through my head, like not letting Rose catch me looking at Avery's legs, which was the stupidest thing because she wasn't going to care about that *now*.

The gun fell from my hand to clatter on the ground. That was when I saw her, my Rose. She was a wounded bird, a fallen flower, a crumpled form, lying beside Avery. Avery tried desperately to help her, her face grim and focused. Only Rose wasn't grim. She smiled at the sight of me, despite having been shot, and I watched in horror as the bright blossom of red seeping from her midsection, staining her shirt, grew. And grew.

A whimper escaped me.

"Oh, Ben," she said, still smiling as I approached, dropping to my knees to be at her side. "Don't faint."

28.

GRACE UNDER FIRE WASN'T A PHRASE I WOULD'VE EVER USED TO describe Rose. Not until that night, that moment, when she lay in my arms, all gossamer softness and fragile courage. When she murmured soothing words to me, despite the blood and the bullet hole, and kept me from losing my shit and losing consciousness.

This was in stark contrast to the roles we'd played over the prior two years, when she'd been the unsettled one—flashes of brilliance among the storm clouds. But there could be no shine without the drab, the dependable, and that was where I'd always come in. Although I never saw our relationship in the crass way Avery had put it; I never once bemoaned that Rose was better than me.

In fact, I needed her to be.

Looking back, it is true that in the first few months we were together, I had a hard time conceiving of myself as being joined with Rose. Being joined with anyone, I guess. It wasn't that I didn't have friends or people in my life to make small talk with, but after the accident, that only went so far. In the ways that mattered and perhaps only I understood, I was separate, isolated: pitied for my injuries and loathed for my sins. Studying was the only thing within my power, and to that end, I set myself to staying up at night, memorizing facts, rewriting essays, and solving equations. I yearned to be measured and validated, to be deemed acceptable, in matters of grades and rubrics and honors. If nothing else.

But sophomore year, that all changed. That was the year Rose found me studying in the theater lobby. When she made me hers, which wasn't freedom but felt far less lonely. And if freedom wasn't free, at least Rose was. She was more than that, in the ways she pushed me to be better than whoever I was born to be. When I blurted out that I loved her after only knowing her for five short weeks, she didn't say she loved me back. Instead she sat me down and made me watch some old movie she liked in which a couple argues over the definition of love. Unsurprisingly, in the end, it's the girl who gets the final say on what love is: trust, admiration, and respect.

"Do you trust me?" Rose whispered in my ear when the movie was over.

I was ashamed—mortified, really—about what I'd told her, so I answered honestly, "I don't trust myself."

"You should."

"Well, I don't."

"Why not?"

"Because I'm always wrong."

Rose wrinkled her nose. "You're not always wrong. You're scared to be right. What did you tell Johnny Rheem when he asked if I was your girlfriend?"

I blushed. "I don't remember."

"You told him you didn't know *what* I was."

"Yeah."

"Not knowing what I am to you doesn't sound like trust."

But I admire and respect you, I longed to say. *That's more than what I feel for anyone. To me, that's love. It's everything. It's all I have to give you.* But that wasn't what she wanted to hear.

"You're right," I said. "I'm sorry."

In return for my acquiescence, Rose offered one of her most winning smiles. The kind that set my body ablaze and reminded me that keeping her happy was the most important thing I could do. It also reminded me that, like studying, I could apply myself and learn what to do and what not to do until I excelled at her happiness. Until I was the very best at Rose tending.

"Don't be sorry, Ben," she told me, her eyes twinkling with victory. "Be *better*."

Shock is a powerful tool, I guess. Like Rose's grace, it ended up being the thing that kept us from breaking down as a group. That let us set our emotions aside momentarily and do the things we needed to. Like taking care of Rose's wound—the Preacher's bullet had gone in and out of her left side, seemingly missing any major organs—and while it looked awful, she wasn't in immediate danger. She was awake and talking, and we were able to stop the bleeding with towels plucked from the clothesline that stretched between the trees. The exit wound was the nastier one, her flesh ripped apart by the force of an object it couldn't contain.

Infection was probably the biggest concern, Clay said in a hushed voice, while he and I were crouched beside her, trying to figure out what we should do. I argued for leaving right then, for racing down to the staging area where the cars were parked and driving for help, but Clay convinced me that getting lost or injured in the dark wouldn't do Rose any good. The steep access road, with its fallen trees and washed-out sections of trail, was sketchy enough in good light, and we had no maps or compasses. Nothing.

"Besides, Tomás could already be getting help," Clay whispered. "Maybe he saw what was going on and knew what to do. That's possible, don't you think?"

"I don't know," I said because I had no clue where Tomás had gone in the first place. He hadn't turned up and that didn't feel like a hopeful thing. But I didn't tell Clay that. I couldn't.

We agreed to leave the instant the sun came up, a choice that left me sick and edgy. But it was late already. It wouldn't be long before Rose would be in a hospital and under a doctor's care. She nodded and smiled when we told her this. Then Clay and I lifted her, as gently as we could, to move her into a camping chair we'd set by the fire. We put blankets on her.

We did our best to keep her warm.

Then came the things we did that I prefer to keep hidden, buried in the depths of my memory, far from reach and consciousness. That's understandable, I think. The way I see it, survival's often a shameful act, maybe necessarily so, but I guess the point is that at least you're around to feel bad about it.

It turned out Archie had beaten the Preacher's brother senseless, but he was alive and we didn't take any chances. Avery worked to unthread the belt from the man's pants and the laces from his shoes, and we tied his hands together, his feet, too, before using the clothesline to hog-tie his limp body to a nearby tree, securing him as tight as we could.

Then we set about the terrible job of wrapping Mr. Howe and Dunc in one of those blankets Maggie had sat on by the stream the day prior. No one wanted to linger on this, on the tragedy that had been made of their bodies, but we didn't want to forget them, either, and we couldn't just leave them on the ground. They were a part of us, and there were people who loved them. It was up to us to remember that. To contain what was left in any way possible. Shelby started to cry at this point. Archie did, as well—these big drunk-heaving-sniveling-type sobs that got me worried he might really be lost to us. But he held it together. Enough.

Next we had to deal with the Preacher's body. My assumption was that Archie would be foaming at the mouth to impale his head on a stake, but to my surprise, he said nothing, just nodded grimly and waved me off when I suggested dragging both the Preacher and his dead girlfriend into the woods and leaving them in a spot where others could find them.

When I bent to pick up the Preacher by his shoulders, however, I noticed something strange. My understanding was he'd been shot with his own rifle while fighting with Archie. Only from what I could tell, the bullet had entered through the *back* of the Preacher's skull. I showed this to Clay, tried to explain why that didn't make sense, but his face went white and he ended up walking away. After a moment, I saw him puking in the bushes and Shelby rubbing his back, so I called Archie over and showed him.

"Well, who the hell shot him?" he asked.

"I thought you shot him."

"Nope. He was alive when I left him to beat the shit out of that other guy."

"You mean his brother."

"Whatever." Archie leaned closer, inspecting the bullet hole. "So then who did it?"

"I don't know." I whirled around, remembering the moment when I'd seen Maggie bolting for the woods. It was possible she'd done it: shot the Preacher in cold blood.

Then fled.

Together we dragged the Preacher's and Fleur's bodies deep into the forest, far from the campsite. Archie retrieved his own handgun from the waistband of the Preacher's jeans, which I hadn't known was in there. Then, without ceremony, we rolled them down a gully in a dry pile of leaves and tree litter and left them there. And maybe I should've felt a twinge of sadness at more lives lost or the knowledge that they'd been lovers and he'd grieved her death. But no, there was no sentiment in me for those two. Only anger. A red, red rage.

By the time we returned, it was close to sunrise and the pain set in. Not just Rose's suffering—her grace was quickly eroding—but all of ours. Everyone except Archie gathered around the fire and we all held hands. Avery recited the Lord's Prayer—for Dunc, for Mr. Howe, for all of us. There were tears on her face as she whispered the words in Spanish first. Then she said them a second time in English, and Clay lost it when she got to "deliver us from evil." Soon everyone was crying, except me, of course, and even though I held their hands and stood by their sides, I longed for them to know how deeply I cared and how wounded I felt, too, even if I couldn't show it.

Avery's soft words stirred up such crushing sorrow, laying bare both the truth of loss and the inevitable pain of living, that even the wind responded in kind, gusting through the trees with a brutal snap and roar. I tipped back my head to gaze at the night sky, to search for a sign, or at least the two planets Mr. Howe had said would be visible. Venus and Jupiter, in all their late-summer glow. I searched and searched. I had to see them, to know the world he'd loved was still out there. To know that everything hadn't changed and that ultimately we weren't alone in this.

But I couldn't find them, those planets among the stars.

At least, not that I could tell.

29.

NIGHT INCHED TOWARD DAWN. ARCHIE BROODED FAR FROM THE REST
of us with the Preacher's rifle laid across his lap. His own gun, he'd returned to his backpack, which sat at his feet. Driven to know where
all weapons were at all times, I went and found the second rifle, the
Preacher's brother's, which lay in the dirt where I'd left it by the woodpile. Dropping to one knee, I held the barrel skyward while I ejected
the magazine and emptied the loaded round from the chamber. Then I
secured the whole thing high off the ground, in the branches of a tree,
and that was the only thing I'd ever been grateful to Marcus for: teaching me my way around a gun.

Clay and Avery set about righting the card table and the camping chairs, then worked to stoke the fire, sending flames leaping, while
Shelby boiled water. The heat was welcome; her earlier adrenaline gone,
Rose's face had turned pale and shiny, her eyes glassy, and she shivered
when I stroked her cheek. Then shivered when I didn't.

Our roles were slipping back to what they usually were—me, the
backdrop to her tender light—and it killed me to know she was in pain,
real pain, that I'd failed in taking her bullet. She began to whimper, an
anguished keening, and I prayed she wouldn't ask for her brother, since
for all I knew, he was lying at the bottom of a cliff or had gotten himself
mauled by a bear. I tried calculating how long it would take me to get
up the mountain and back so that I could retrieve the first aid kit that
held my painkillers. Then I remembered Maggie's Percocet. She'd had a
whole bottle of it.

"I'll be right back," I whispered to Rose, sliding my arms out from under her. I found my headlamp and switched it on, heading for the threadbare tent that sat downwind from the smoke.

The inside of the tent was as much a mess as the outside. Amid their filthy clothes and sleeping bags, everything smelled like mildew and body odor. I found beer cans, food wrappers, condoms, a stack of water-stained papers, a dead cell phone, and most ironically, a small dog-eared copy of the Bible. I also pawed through what looked like the contents of a wallet—credit cards, driver's license, some cash, all held together with a rubber band. I slid the license out and peered at it beneath the light. The man in the photo was the Preacher's brother, and if the license wasn't a fake, that meant his name was Abel Trent Faulkner and he was thirty-eight years old, five feet eight inches tall, hailing from Susanville, California, which was on the eastern side of the state, near the Nevada border.

Maggie's bag was buried under a bedroll. I dug through it, hastily finding the Percocet rolling around loose in the bottom among crumpled cigarette packs, boxes of black hair dye, spare change, lottery scratchers, her silver flask, and bottle of personal lubricant. I shoved the medication into the front pocket of my pants.

"What do you think you're doing?" a voice asked.

I jumped, then relaxed. It was just Archie. He towered in the tent entrance, his large face staring right at me. He looked sweaty and flushed, like he had when we'd first started out on the trail that morning after I'd told him to put his gun away.

"Nothing," I said.

"Doesn't look like nothing."

"I was looking for medicine for Rose."

"Not the money?"

"No."

"You sure about that, Gibby?"

"Very sure. You know, funny thing, money's really not all that important to me at the moment. In fact, it never was." I went to push past him, but he grabbed my arm.

"It should be important." He spat the words in my face.

"Four people are dead, Arch."

His eyes blazed, a wild look, as if fueled by some inner furnace of will. "*That's* why it matters. Dunc, Mr. Howe, they didn't die for nothing. I'm going to make damn sure of that. You hear me? This, everything's that happened, it's going to mean something. I swear to God."

"Fine." I wrenched free and pushed past him, dragging one of the sleeping bags with me. "Do what the hell you want. You will anyway."

Back with Rose, I laid the sleeping bag over her, and when no one was looking, I slipped two Percocets out and put them in her mouth. I whispered for her to swallow them dry. She did, rewarding me with a grateful smile. It wasn't long before she drifted into a heavy sleep.

I watched her for a bit, the rise and fall of her chest, the brown-gold glow of her cheeks, and did my best to focus on all the ways I loved her and not that she'd been stupid enough to follow Archie into harm's way. She didn't deserve to be hurt for that. After all, she wasn't the one who'd shot Fleur. That was Archie. Although if Maggie had intentionally shot Rose before fleeing—and I was beginning to think she had—it was possible there was more to the situation that I didn't know.

After a few minutes, I got up and walked over to where Clay, Shelby, and Avery stood on the other side of the fire, their hands held to the flames for warmth. I glanced back to look for Archie, but he must've still been in the tent. Or somewhere else I couldn't see.

"We need to get out of here," I told them, keeping my voice low.

Clay looked up. "Daybreak, right? That's what we said."

"What time is it?"

"I don't know."

"Well, maybe we should go now."

"You think?"

I nodded. "Someone has to come with me, though. It's probably an hour hike back to the staging area where we parked. Maybe less. The trail's sketchy, but we've got the headlamps, and it'll be light by the time we get there either way. We'll be able to drive right out."

Avery bit her lip at my words.

"What is it?" I asked her.

"I don't have the car keys," she said. "Do you?"

Fuck. We spent the next five minutes searching Rose and Mr. Howe, combing through their pockets. No keys on either of them.

Finally, I gave up. "This is pointless. They're not here. They're back up at Grizzly Falls."

"Maybe we could just flag someone down on the road," Shelby suggested.

"No one's going to come down that road," I said. "It's a dead end. Access for this trail only. We need the keys."

She sighed. "Then we'll have to get them in the morning. I can't climb up there again, Ben. Not now."

Archie, who'd returned from wherever the hell he'd been, sauntered over to the fire, looking more flushed than ever. "Keys aren't going to do you any good."

"Why's that?" Avery snapped. "And can you put the fucking gun down?"

"No, I cannot put the *fucking gun down*. That bitch is out there. You know that, don't you? You want to get yourselves killed?"

"Who're you talking about? Maggie? I saw her leave," I said.

"Doesn't mean she's not out there. Waiting for us. So she can get that money. I know she wants it. She probably wants this asshole, too." He jerked his head toward where the Preacher's brother—Abel Faulkner, I supposed—lay.

"She shot his brother, Arch. I don't think she's coming back for him."

"Yeah, well, maybe these two planned it that way all along. Only now they don't have any way out of here. You go down to that parking lot and I bet she's waiting for you. Waiting to take that car. She'll kill us for it."

"You sound paranoid," I said.

He sneered. "Do I?"

Shelby looked at me, alarmed. "Did that woman really have a gun?"

I paused. "Yes."

"Well, are there other ways out of here?"

"Only through the original trail, the one heading south. It leads all the way down to Junction City. But that's over ten miles away—it's not an easy trail, either."

"So what are we going to do?"

"We're going to get the keys like we planned."

Clay shook his head. "I don't want to get shot. We should just walk out the long way. The ten miles or whatever. I don't want to fuck around with any of this."

My chest went tight. "Rose can't wait that long."

"Then find the money," Avery said.

"What did you say?"

She shrugged. "If that woman's really out there, it's your one bargaining chip."

Was she serious? "We don't know where it is! We don't even know that it's here! You guys just assumed it was!"

"Calm down," Shelby told me. "Stop yelling."

"I'm not yelling!"

"Yes, you are," Clay said.

"Jesus," I said. "Forget it. This is stupid. Let's just wait until morning. Get some sleep. We'll figure it out then."

"You know, you're not in charge anymore," Shelby said peevishly. "You don't get to tell us what to do."

"Yeah. That's becoming pretty goddamn clear."

"I'm not sleeping," Archie growled. "I'm going to find that bitch."

I threw my hands in the air. "Everyone do whatever the hell you want. I'm not in charge. I'm not anything. Just don't get yourselves killed, okay?"

30.

I HELD ROSE IN MY ARMS FOR THE REST OF THE NIGHT. THERE WASN'T much left of it, but it was the best and only thing I could think to do.

"Ben," she whispered at one point, her voice foggy with codeine.

I pressed my ear to her lips. "What is it?"

"Thank you for taking care of me."

"I'll always take care of you. You know that, don't you?"

She gave a faint smile. "Can I ask you something?"

"Anything."

"Does she make you happy?"

"Does who make me happy?"

"Avery," she said.

"Avery?"

"It's okay, Ben. I'm not mad. I told you that this summer. I want you to be happy. I want that more than anything."

"I don't know what you're talking about," I said. "I am happy. With you."

"But you shouldn't be. I ask a lot of you. More than I should."

"Shhh." I held her tighter. "You need to rest."

Rose didn't answer. She leaned her head against my chest and gazed up at me. She reached to stroke my cheek the way she always did when my head was hurting, and for some reason, that made me feel terrible, like a terrible person. Well, I suppose the reason I felt terrible was because I'd lied and cheated on her. Because I was still lying. But I couldn't understand why she was asking me these questions in the first place. It wasn't like I was going to confess to anything *then*.

"Is this about Archie?" I whispered.

"In a way," she admitted. "But not like how you're thinking."

"Then how?"

"He's the one who told me about you and Avery. How you two went off into the woods today. Alone."

I tensed. "Come on, Rose. You know he's full of shit. He's a total dick."

"But I already told you. I'm fine with it."

I didn't *want* her to be fine with it. "Can we stop talking about this? Please?"

"Archie says you two hung out over the summer. Maybe that's when this all started. While I was in Peru."

"We did not hang out! We talked *once*. About my car. Hardly enough to make her like me."

Rose shrugged. "I liked you before we even talked."

"That's your problem!"

"You're right," she said. "It is."

I rubbed my temples, pushing in small circles at the pressure points. "I spent my whole summer alone, Rose. I swear. While you were gone, I didn't go out or see anybody. I didn't do anything fun. Not once."

"Why not?" she asked.

"Because you weren't there!"

"So your happiness depends on me? On my telling you to do the things you enjoy?"

"What I enjoy is being with *you*."

"The way you enjoy being with your mother so much it makes you physically ill?"

My mouth went dry. "What?"

"You spend more time with her than you do me, that's for sure."

"I don't have a *choice*. And are you talking about my migraines? Those aren't her fault."

"But stress makes them worse. Your doctor told you that. And I know he thinks you're depressed. You don't deserve to feel bad all the time like you do, Ben. I promise. It's the being depressed that makes you believe that."

"He just wants me to take more drugs. They all do. And I got a migraine *today*. What was I stressed about then?"

"You tell me."

I took a deep breath. Forced myself to calm down. Rose was hurt and sad and scared. Like a wounded dog biting its owner's hand, she didn't mean what she was saying. So I kissed her forehead. Then her hair. And I told her I loved her.

Rose melted at my touch.

"Ben," she said softly. "Your mother. What she does to you. It's not right. And what she said you did to your stepfather, that's—"

"Don't." I was starting to tremble. I felt like I might get sick. "Don't do this now. We'll talk later."

She nodded, her eyes heavy with pain. "You're right. I'm sorry. I don't want to upset you. Let's sleep. Okay? We both need sleep."

I woke to a hint of daybreak. The air was wet and drippy. More fog had settled, but the sun was just barely rising, pushing back gloom and setting the world aglow with a pinkish char. Beside me, Rose breathed deeply, her eyes shut tight. After checking her wound, I slipped from beneath her and got to my feet. I walked around the fire, poking the flames with a stick as I eyeballed the remaining wood. It would last the morning but not much longer. That was enough, though. Soon we'd be gone. Off this mountain.

For good.

Beyond our clearing, the world was still and silent. Deathly so. I spied Archie sitting beneath a tree not far from the tent, with a blanket slung across his knees. He was snoring loudly. The Preacher's rifle still lay in his lap, and I fought the urge to swipe it from him. My teeth chattered. It felt as if the temperature had dropped twenty degrees during the time that I'd been sleeping, and more than anything, I needed more clothes. So I shoved my hands into my pockets and marched out toward the spot where we'd dragged the bodies of the Preacher and the dead woman.

It wasn't hard to find. I followed the trail of flattened leaves and mud. What had seemed like an endless slog during the night turned out to only be a short walk through the trees and down a fern-lined gully. I stopped once to piss against a tree and lamented the sight of heat leaving my body, in any form. When I was done, I jogged the rest of the way despite aching muscles and the nagging bite of queasiness.

We'd rolled the Preacher into the gully first. Meaning he lay beneath the woman and only the bottom half of him was visible. Cupping my hand over my mouth and avoiding looking directly at either of their faces, I crouched and strained to pull her off him. Her limbs had gone stiff and cold, and I tried not to get blood or whatever else there was on my hands.

Dropping her unkindly into the leaves, I went for what I'd come for, wriggling the Preacher's jacket off his body. The coat was leather and lined and it felt good to slide it on—a pleasing heft. I flirted with grave-robbing guilt as I pried off his shoes to take his socks, but the payoff wasn't worth it. Anything I did to the Preacher now wouldn't hurt him. Plus, I figured he kind of owed me.

Sidestepping away from the bodies and not bothering to slide the shoes back on his bony feet, I rummaged through the jacket's pockets and found a few items of interest: a roll of cash—there had to be at least a thousand dollars, just rolled up and loose in there—a receipt from a Denny's down in Santa Cruz, and a scrap of paper with the letters EUR AMTK followed by a bunch of numbers written on it and the words *For Jules* scrawled at the bottom. I had no idea what that meant, but maybe it had to do with euros. After all, the stolen bank money would have to eventually be laundered overseas, as far as I knew about things like that—which was really nothing but phrases and concepts I'd picked up from television and heist thrillers. "Overseas" was about as tangible a place in my world as Jurassic Park.

I shoved everything I'd found into a pocket on the jacket's interior before turning back toward the campsite. The money offered a certain amount of relief; if Maggie were truly prowling around, waiting to ambush us, she would've already found these bodies and searched them for anything valuable. It was no half million dollars, but no one would let that much cash sit around and rot.

Trudging back up the gully, I went over the details of what needed to be done in the hours ahead. Someone had to first hike up to Grizzly Falls to retrieve the car keys and medical supplies and some food. When that person returned, another group would have to walk down the mountain to the car and drive for help. All told it would probably be another six hours before we got off this mountain and before Rose could see a doctor. During that time, I vowed not to fight with her or get drawn into any of her moods or arguments. She was hurt and deserved compassion. And she could say whatever she wanted about Avery, but I planned to deny it forever.

I also didn't intend to let anything Rose said about my mother get to me. It was a frequent topic she liked to rail on about to make me feel bad. She'd tell me I was codependent. Or enabling. Worse, she'd act like I was some pathetic slob being manipulated in all sorts of awful ways without even realizing it. A Stockholm son held captive by my own weakness.

None of that was true, by the way. My mother was sick and had issues, yes, but she couldn't help who she was or what she'd been through, and even if she could, it would still be up to me to care for her. It's what any child would do, because it's not like there's a choice. Not to mention, it was especially important for me to step up, seeing as *I* was the one who'd hurt her. And don't get me wrong: I knew full well that she was the adult in that situation. That she was the one who'd brought the young, hot-blooded Pentecostal minister Marcus Salvatore swaggering into our lives—he might as well have had LOVE and HATE tattooed across his knuckles—and it was a little like a hen opening the door to her house and letting the fox just march on in. Or more accurately, the way I remember it, it was like the hen carrying the fox's bags inside, taking his coat off, and setting the table for him.

But in the end, I was the one who shot him and whether it was an accident or otherwise didn't much matter. What mattered was making sure the door to our home stayed boarded shut from there on out. And if that meant me buying groceries and working to pay our bills and staying home with my mom when she didn't hate me and letting her push me around when she did, then I did all of that. Willingly. And maybe I did other things, too, things I didn't dare tell Rose about because I knew she'd never understand, like lifting bottles of vodka from the storeroom at work when we couldn't afford to buy them. Or pouring myself a glass of said vodka before going upstairs, turning off the light, and crawling into my mother's bed to be with her on those nights when she was lonely and drunk and needed to feel needed. And no, I didn't do what it is you're thinking. But maybe I let my mother believe otherwise.

Maybe that was easier.

Walking with heavy shoulders and an even heavier heart, I finally made it back to the campsite. Only when I got there, something was different. It took a moment to figure out what it was because Archie still snored beneath the tree and Rose still lay sleeping, her cheeks pale, but her breathing steady and even, and the other three were still in the tent from what I could tell.

It wasn't until I glanced across the fire through a haze of white wood smoke that I saw what it was—the Preacher's brother. He was awake.

And standing right beside him was Tomás.

31.

I DIDN'T SAY ANYTHING AT FIRST. I JUST STARED AT THE TWO OF THEM
staring back at me in that grainy pinkish light. I couldn't believe what I
was seeing.

"Hey, Ben," Tomás said after a moment. And he didn't say it in a
nice way. It was his same old sneery Tomás way.

My jaw tightened. But I still didn't say anything.

"Do you know where Clay is? I kinda need to talk to him."

"What do you need to talk to him about?"

"That's not any of your business."

"Excuse me?" Something dark simmered inside me. I stalked over
to where Tomás was standing—he was smoking a *cigarette*, for fuck's
sake—and there was nothing I wanted to do more in that moment than
rip the cigarette from his mouth and punch him in his stupid, pouting
face.

"Do you know what happened last night?" I snarled. "Do you have
any idea? Where the hell have you been? And why exactly are you talking to this asshole?" I jabbed a finger at Abel, who was watching us from
where he lay on the ground.

"We're not *talking*. I just got here and I saw him and he was awake,
so I asked him who he was and what was going on."

"Yeah, right."

Tomás narrowed his eyes as he took another drag from his cigarette.
"You know, you're the asshole in this situation. No one else is walking
around screaming at anybody."

"*What* did you say?"

"I said you're being a real prick."

I balled my hands into fists. "Don't you even care about *Rose*?"

"Rose? What does this have to do with Rose? I saw her over there. She's sleeping, right?"

"She was shot! By your new fucking friend!" Abel made a cackling sound as I said this.

"Wait, what?" Tomás's jaw dropped, his cigarette falling to the ground. "What do you mean shot?"

"I mean he shot her in the stomach! Or someone did. And they killed Dunc and Mr. Howe!"

He shoved past me. I shoved him back, but then let him go. He raced around the fire to Rose, his face ashen. He fell to his knees by her side.

"Is she—?" he gasped.

"She's sleeping," I said. "She's hurt, but I don't think she's in any immediate danger. She's been talking, drinking water. The bleeding's slowed. I gave her pain medication. She needs a doctor, though."

I don't know if he heard me. Tomás gently gathered Rose in his arms, pressing his cheek to hers. Even from a distance I saw tears welling up on his lashes; he'd always been able to cry when I couldn't. Rose's eyes opened and she murmured something to him, something I couldn't hear. He murmured back, then kissed her hand, her nose, and soon the two of them were lost in their strange twin place that I'd never understood or been invited to enter.

"Nice fucking jacket you got there, Bennett," a voice said.

I looked down.

Abel lay on his back in the dirt, his four limbs still tied together, and where the left sleeve of his T-shirt was pushed up, a black ink tattoo identical to the one on his brother's arm was visible. XX. I leaned to inspect it while he glared at me through bloodshot eyes. As helpless as his situation was, he still had the arrogance of his brother, which meant he acted like he was better than me.

I straightened up. The smug look on the man's face was ugly and cruel, and for a flash, I felt good. I was glad he'd noticed the jacket. Wearing it felt like hard-won victory, an antlered trophy mounted on the wall.

"Your brother's dead," I told him. Just to make sure he knew.

The man didn't answer.

"And Maggie left you," I added. "Guess she's the real rebel, huh?"

Abel still didn't answer, refusing to give me the satisfaction of a response. Instead his eyes fluttered shut, and it was impossible to tell whether he was ignoring me on purpose or whether he'd drifted out of consciousness again.

I sat and I watched him, my nerves strung tight, waiting for his next move. But he never stirred again. The campsite fell quiet, and Tomás and Rose both appeared to be dozing. I didn't know what else to do, so I ended up sitting there, not doing anything, until the light changed, going from pink to gold to bronze, a lazy roll past daybreak into dawn. And as the sun came up at last, rising high to meet the day, the wind blew harder. Colder. It nipped my cheeks.

I was startled by a noise behind me. Peering over my shoulder, I spotted Avery, Clay, and Shelby crawling from the torn-up tent. Haggard and filthy, the expressions they wore were more shell-shocked than the night before, as they took in the reality they'd woken to. Chilled sunlight and blood spatter. A wounded Rose. Abel tied to a tree. The two blanketed figures wrapped and reverently covered near the pile of firewood.

Clay and Shelby made their way over to me, their shoulders hunched and shivering, their skin sallow. There were fresh tears and I understood that, even if I didn't particularly want to deal with it. But at some point, Shelby began to sob helplessly, and finally I put my arms around her. She kept sobbing, wetting my neck with her tears, and I noticed scratches on her hands, bloody ones, only I didn't know how or when that had happened.

I glanced at Avery but she didn't look at me. She walked over to where Archie sat and shook his shoulder until his eyes opened. He held tight to the rifle resting across his legs but pushed her away with a groan. She shook harder.

Clay went to stand by the fire, but something about him seemed off. It took a moment to realize what it was—his legs were trembling. His whole body was.

"Hey, Clay," I called out. And when he didn't answer: "Clay!"

He turned toward me, his expression flat.

"You need to sit down or something. Seriously. You don't want to pass out in the flames."

"He was sick all night," Shelby whispered. "It's his anxiety. It's really bad. He even got—"

"Hey, is that *Tomás*?" Clay asked suddenly.

"Where?" Shelby squinted.

"Right there."

"Yeah, that's him," I said. "He got back a little while ago."

Clay set off around the fire on those wobbly legs of his. I held my breath watching as he stumbled first over the burned-out propane tank, then again on the ruined stove, both feet catching in a charred metal clatter. Archie laughed loudly to see this, while Avery advised him to shut the hell up; and the whole commotion ended with waking Tomás, who sat up and stared at us with haunted eyes.

"Clay," he said thickly. "You okay?"

Clay wiped dust from his pants in obvious disgust. "Yeah, I'm fine. What're you doing here? What happened to you?"

Tomás gave a quick shake of his head. "I'll explain later."

I didn't want him to explain later, and from the look on Clay's face, the feeling was mutual; but I also didn't want to get sidetracked. We had a plan. We needed to stick to it.

"I'm going to go get the keys," I announced. "I'll bring back food and anything warm I can find. Then a couple of us can walk out to the parking area. Drive for help."

"Will you get my bag while you're up there?" Shelby asked. "Please?"

"Mine, too," echoed Clay.

I scowled. "Well, someone has to come with me."

No one answered.

"Are you kidding?"

Still no answer, which was just fucking great. Out of the corner of my eye, I caught Avery whispering something in Archie's ear again. Cheeks flushed, he shook his head vigorously and shoved her back. Avery said something else—I couldn't hear what—before turning and marching away from him. Her eyes burned with frustration.

"Hey." I tried catching her attention, but she brushed past me, arms crossed tight, dark hair falling in her face, to storm off into the trees.

I made a move to go after her.

"Leave that girl alone, Gibby," Archie warned.

"But I need someone to go with me to get the keys."

"Well, it's not gonna be her."

"Is it going to be you, then?" I asked. "Because I'd kind of like to get out of here."

Archie snorted. "Fuck getting out of here. I'm not helping you do shit."

"So you want Rose to die?"

"I don't care if we all die."

"Jesus," I breathed. "You're an asshole."

He flipped me off, and this was the Archie I knew. Callous. Uncaring.

Bitter as hell.

"Whatever. I'll just go by myself," I said.

"Wait!"

I turned. It was Rose who'd called out to me. She'd managed to sit up in the camping chair, separating herself from her brother. Her face was pale, drawn, but her jaw was firmly set.

"I'll hurry," I told her. "I promise."

"No. That's . . . that's not what I want."

"What do you want?"

"It's the money." Her gaze darted from me to Archie to me again. "I know where it is. You have to get it while you're up there, Ben. It's our one chance to have this mean something."

"Huh?"

"That guy." She took a deep breath, then pointed to Abel, still lying motionless on the ground. "He—he told me where it was."

"He did?"

She nodded. "When you were gone. Getting that jacket."

"Why would he tell you that?"

"Because I promised we'd let him go if we found it."

"Oh, Rose." My heart foundered. "You didn't."

"I did."

"So then, where the hell is it?" Archie demanded. "Tell us, already."

Rose lifted her chin. "I'm not telling you anything, dickhead. I'll tell Ben. You go with him and help him and maybe he'll show you."

"Don't fuck around like this, Rose," he said. "I'm serious."

"Don't talk to me like that."

"Then tell me where it is!"

"No."

Archie rose from the tree stump and stomped his way over to where Abel lay curled in his own blood and piss and who knew what else. He didn't hesitate. Gripping the Preacher's rifle by the barrel, Archie brought the stock of it down on the back of the man's head, the blow landing so hard there was an audible *crack*. Blood sprayed onto Archie's pants. Abel moaned and writhed against the ropes.

"What the fuck?" Tomás shouted, leaping up from his chair. "You're going to kill him!"

"I want him to wake the fuck up!"

"He's not going to if you keep doing that!"

Archie looked at Rose.

"Go with Ben," she ordered. "Put the gun down. Leave it here. Then go with him up the mountain, and if you don't piss him off and you don't act like an ass, maybe he'll take you to where it is."

"What?" I squeaked. "I'm not doing that. No way. I'd rather go alone."

"No, you wouldn't."

"I absolutely would."

"Come here." Rose beckoned me with her finger, wincing as she did it. Sweat beaded her upper lip. Her brow.

I walked over and knelt in the dirt beside her. "I don't care about any money. I don't want to look for anything. I just want to help you. I want to get out of here."

"Then listen to me. Come closer."

I nodded. Dropped my head. Cupping my chin in her hand, Rose leaned forward to whisper the location in my ear.

I stared at her. "Really?"

"Yeah."

"Why do you want me to do this?"

Her eyes puddled. "Because this—everything that's happening, everything that's gone wrong—it's *my* fault. It's all my fault. I have to fix it. As much as I can."

"I don't understand."

"You don't have to. Just go up there with him. For me. Please?"

I relented. "Okay."

Rose leaned back. Gave a sigh of relief. "Thank you, Ben. I can always count on you."

"That's a good thing, isn't it?"

"I hope so," she said.

32.

ARCHIE AND I SET OFF ALMOST IMMEDIATELY. I WAS GRIPPED WITH panic leaving Rose behind, but in leaving I also found purpose. This was how I would save her. This was a chance for me to make the right decisions, and I wouldn't screw up. Not again.

The trees rattled overhead, the wind racing the branches, and I glanced back only once as we left the clearing, my gaze falling on Abel's motionless form. He'd done nothing but spit blood after Archie struck him, but his eyes never opened. And while I was glad Rose had made Archie leave the rifle behind, it wasn't like I didn't know about the hand-gun resting in his backpack. There was nothing safe or honest about him. I had to remember that.

"You shouldn't have hit him," I told Archie when we were out of earshot of the others. "It wasn't cool."

"Oh, shut up," he said. "You think people like him deserve mercy?"

"He could be lying about the money, you know. He's probably full of shit."

Archie snorted. "Why the hell would he lie?"

"Why the hell *wouldn't* he?"

"Because he has to know I'll kill him if we don't find it."

I had no answer for that. We made our way across the stream and began the steep hike up out of the gorge. My legs protested the effort, but I pushed myself to go faster. Soon I was coated with sweat.

Archie was silent as we climbed, but I watched him drink from a silver flask that I recognized as Maggie's. He didn't bother trying to hide it, the drinking, and I didn't bother caring. Together we wound our way past Hunters Camp—the shady spot where we'd eaten lunch and I'd slept curled in Rose's lap.

The trees thinned as we hiked higher, and the exposure threw sun in my eyes, a mid-morning assault, but one I needed. Rather than retreat, I tipped my face into the day's glow and tried soaking it in, all that light, the clarity. Something broke inside me as I did this, tight cobblestones of grief dislodging to remind me of all we'd lost—not just now, but from the future, too. There were mountains that would never be climbed; shitty homes never escaped.

Another half mile and we stopped to splash water on our faces from the frigid depths of Grizzly Creek. That felt good. My head spun from lack of food, lack of drinking water. But when I stood again, after kneeling by the creek, a swarm of colored dots filled my field of vision. I instinctively sat back down and shoved my head between my knees, waiting for the light-headedness to pass.

When I felt better, I looked up, only to catch sight of Archie staring at the sun rising over the mountains, just as I'd been doing earlier. I don't know what expression I expected to see on his face. Arrogance, I suppose. Or maybe resentment at forces beyond his control. After all, weren't those the reasons we were in this situation in the first place? Wasn't *that* how we'd gotten here?

What I saw instead was pain. Of the wet-cheeks-and-heaving-chest variety. I turned away, embarrassed for Archie the same way I'd been embarrassed for Mr. Howe when he'd tried giving me relationship advice I hadn't wanted to hear. Whether sorrow or need, some emotions were best left unexpressed.

"Let's go," I said gruffly and started walking again before Archie had a chance to answer. For all I knew, his weepy mood wasn't because of Mr. Howe or Dunc or the grim finality of death, but because he was grieving for himself. For the realization he just might have to answer for his own stupidity.

We made it to the meadow at last, our small campsite coming into view with a burst of bright color amid a sea of green. I made a beeline for the tent I'd shared with Rose. Crawling inside, I made a mess as my shoes tracked dirt everywhere while I tore through our belongings, searching for the keys to the Pathfinder.

Only I couldn't find them. They weren't in her backpack or mine. Or anywhere I could see. I searched more, going through all the tent compartments. Then going through them again.

Still nothing.

"Shit." I sat back on my haunches, and there was that weight of uselessness again, a familiar beast settling in to rest heavy on my chest.

The answer came to me then, a swift gut-kick of insight. I lifted Rose's sleeping bag and pulled it to me. Reaching inside, my fingers roamed before landing on a zippered pocket stitched into the lining, opposite the hood. Tugging hard, I worked the pocket open. Sure enough, the keys were in there. I slipped them into my own breast pocket with a grunt of satisfaction—well, technically, it was the Preacher's pocket, but it wasn't like I planned on giving the jacket back.

Crawling from the tent, I felt more purposeful than ever. Capable, too. Not only had I found what I'd been looking for, but it was my studied knowledge of Rose that had led me to the keys. She was different from me in a lot of ways—most, actually—but there were two things central to her nature that I was absolutely certain about: First, she liked to use things for their intended purpose; she wasn't one to carelessly leave her keys in shoes or hats or on the ground, the way I might. And, second, if something was truly important to her, I knew that Rose would always, always keep it close to her heart.

———

Archie had vanished by the time I got back outside. I jogged the perimeter of the campsite but couldn't find him anywhere. The wind blew harder, pushing the lush meadow grass around so that it swirled and bent. I didn't bother calling out for Archie. Doing that would've felt like I wanted him to return and that wasn't a desire I wanted to put out into the universe. Besides, I was starving.

Our food hung in a bear-proof canister twenty feet off the ground, tethered to a white pine near where we'd been playing cards. I walked over and undid the anchor at the base to pull it down, hastily flipping off the lid when it reached me. I grabbed for the first things I saw: a package of Pop-Tarts and a bottle of Gatorade. Not my favorite, but I forced them down, followed by a handful of almonds and some beef jerky.

Still no Archie. I began gathering supplies I wanted to take back to the others. Spreading a tarp out on the ground and placing items on it, I didn't even try to grab people's personal belongings. Those would have to wait, although I made an exception for Avery's camera. I knew she'd want it, not because it was hers but because it wasn't. I also picked out a small selection of food that didn't need to be cooked and wasn't too heavy, plus salt, matches, and water-purification pills.

Ducking back into my own tent, I grabbed my compass and trail map, before moving on to Mr. Howe's, which was this fancy blue-and-white four-season North Face deal. He'd boasted that he'd slept in it up on Denali when the temps dipped below zero. Personally, I didn't see how that was a feat worth bragging about since it meant admitting you'd been foolish enough to go camping in weather like that in the first place.

But kneeling in that narrow tent, knowing he was gone, I could scarcely breathe. Everything inside was arranged so neatly, his belongings waiting for his return. It wasn't hard to imagine Mr. Howe was just outside in the meadow, finishing breakfast, getting ready to hit the trail. I reached to touch his shirt, his hat, then flipped my way through the trail journal that lay by the head of his sleeping bag.

A few photographs slid from the pages. I picked them up and held them to my face. Some were of mountains, places he'd been, but most were of Lucy, an account not of distance or place, but of time—here she was glowing in her youth, sitting cross-legged in a college dorm, her hair short, beer in hand, wearing a faded Jane's Addiction T-shirt; in another she stood atop a rocky cliff overlooking the pounding ocean, pointing to a ring on her finger, her cheeks wet with joy; the most recent shot showed her walking through a California vineyard at sunset, arms outstretched, her smile wide, her long hair blowing in the wind.

I searched the photos for what I knew of Lucy—that moment when her hope for a family had vanished. I thought I would see it in her eyes, in the way she looked at her husband, who'd failed to give her what she wanted. It wasn't there, though. In every photo Lucy gazed back at the man behind the camera with absolute adoration. Her love, it seemed, didn't come with conditions.

After tucking the photos back where I'd found them, I gathered the items I'd come for: the truck keys and his phone, which I briefly turned on to check the barometric pressure. It had dropped again, only I didn't know what that meant because Mr. Howe wasn't around to tell me. I also grabbed the larger of the two first aid kits, which contained not only my medication, but also gauze and antiseptic and other tools that could be used for cleaning Rose's wound. Maybe more. I unlocked the lid to peer inside.

What I saw confused me. My prescriptions were there; I quickly stuffed them all in my side pack. But there were other medications, too. Ones that didn't belong to me, which was strange. *I* was the sick one. I always had been. But rolling around with my own meds, I found a bottle of Zoloft with Tomás's name on it. That wasn't such a huge surprise—it wasn't pregnant-lady porn—but it turned out Clay had a prescription for Xanax, and Shelby, one for a medication I'd never heard of called Sulfazine, which had a lot of dire warning labels and got me worrying

that something might really be wrong with her. Most surprising, however, was a bottle of Risperdal, which was a drug I happened to recognize because it had been prescribed to my mother in the past. It was
meant to stabilize her moods and keep her from hurting herself. She
hated it taking it, which probably tells you a lot about either the medication or her. I held the bottle up and squinted to read the patient's name
on the label: DUNCAN STRAUSS.

I put the pills back.

I finally found Archie when I went down to the river to fill my water
bottle. Well, *found* is the wrong word, since I wasn't exactly looking. But
there he was. And just as I had the night before, he was sitting on the
very edge of a rock with his shoes off and his legs dunked in the current, deeper than they should've been. Unlike me, though, he had his
open backpack beside him and that damn flask in his hand again and
was clearly dead set on getting wasted.

A few images flitted through my mind: a drunken Archie tumbling
into the water, yelling out for help before being dragged under. My honest, heartfelt testimony about being unable to save him. There was also
the darker scenario where I shoved him into the river on my own, making my testimony less honest but all the more heartfelt.

But murder, like decisiveness, wasn't in me. Not anymore. So I
stood, watching him, until he turned and saw me. There was a different
expression on his face, an almost wistful look, but it vanished fast.

"You ready?" he asked.

I gave diplomacy my best shot. "How about we take the food and
stuff back down to the others? Someone else can walk out. Get help
for Rose. Then you and I, we can come back up here and look for the
money. If it's really that important to you."

Archie's eyes gleamed as he pulled his dripping feet from the
water. "So it's somewhere up here, then? Is that what you're saying?
It's close by?"

"Yeah. Supposedly."

He rubbed his hands together. "Then we're not going anywhere, Gibby. Let's get it now before that bitch finds it. Or"—he looked me up and down—"you can tell me where it is. I don't need your help."

I sighed. Because the thing was, he *did* need my help.

He just didn't know it.

"Fine," I said, all resigned-like, because the path of least resistance did *not* involve arguing with Archie DuPraw. "Let's go."

"Where're we going?"

"There." I pointed up, high, to the very top of the waterfall, that majestic rise of granite cliffs and craggy peaks, a whole fortress of rock doing what it could to control the massive lake sitting hundreds of feet above, relentless in its effort to break free of its hold and come tumbling down upon us.

33.

CLIMBING THE WATERFALL BY WAY OF THE FORMIDABLE GRIZZLY
Scramble was a challenge I'd planned for meticulously over the past six
weeks—both physically and mentally. I'd taken to working out as best
I could in my bedroom, trying to increase my upper body strength, as
well as my endurance. I'd also scoured the internet for photos and personal accounts of the climb from other hikers, reading and rereading
their words over and over, until I could lie back on my own bed, close
my eyes, and actually visualize myself in their bodies, reenacting their
every movement, every step, every decision.

What I knew about the Scramble was this: It began as a steep ascent
by way of stone steps, risers set into the earth that would take us a good
third of the way up the cliff, hugging close to the waterfall and the spray
of the river. After that, the steps faded, trailing off into a narrow, almost
impossibly steep path that cut back and forth, winding upward in a precarious serpentine.

A break in the trail came roughly fifty feet from the top in the form
of a stone plateau, one that was wide and flat, overlooking the falls and
valley below. Technically it was possible to pitch a tent on this ledge
and sleep among the clouds, though from what I'd read, dueling wind
streams made this a risky choice. But ahead lay the roughest part—
a slick pile of shifting rock and crumbling granite that could only be
climbed using all four limbs. At the very top, we'd have to pull ourselves
up onto the cliff before leaping the waterfall outlet to land on the far
side. This leap was the section I'd studied the most and I knew full well

how harrowing that last crossing would be. Not a long jump, by any stretch. Just one you'd never get a second chance to screw up.

I explained this all to Archie as we stood at the base of the Scramble. He stared up at the rocks and the waterfall and nodded like it was no big deal.

"So you're okay with heights?" I asked him.

"Why wouldn't I be?"

"Oh, I don't know. There's always the possibility that you could fall to your death."

"You're an idiot," he said. "That's, like, the least of my concerns."

Well, there were a lot of things I could've said in response to that. None of them nice. But I let it go, and we started off on the trail with me leading the way. The path was narrow from the start and Archie had to fall in line behind me, requiring him to walk with his face in my ass, which felt like a certain brand of justice. *Spite*, maybe, was the proper word.

Archie had problems right off the bat. His face did that red thing and his breathing grew labored. If I hadn't seen him like that the day before, I would've guessed he was on the verge of altitude sickness—we were above 5,000 feet. Although he'd been fine on the earlier hike, he now struggled with each step. Pretty soon he was swearing.

"What's wrong with you?" I finally asked.

"Asthma," he gasped. "But I'm fine."

"You have *asthma*? Don't you have an inhaler or something for that?"

"No," he said, wheezing more. Then a minute later: "Tell me where we're going."

I hesitated. There didn't seem to be any reason *not* to tell him. I didn't care about the money. I was only going to make sure he got up and back down the waterfall safely. "Okay, there's a cave," I said. "About a half mile past the lake. We're going to walk around the perimeter of the lake, then follow a sign pointing toward the summit. When we turn north, there should be a tall cairn on our right. We'll enter the woods there, and the cave'll be a few hundred yards back and covered with rocks. I don't know. It be might be hard to find, but that's where Rose said to go."

Archie nodded, seeming to take this all in. We soon came to the end of the switchback, reaching the part where we had to climb—scramble, really. Staring up at the talus slope and piles of loose rock, I took time to point out the easiest routes.

"You don't want to choose the shortest way up," I warned, echoing the words I'd read on countless climbing blogs and websites. "You want to pick the smartest. There aren't any ropes and I sure as hell can't help you if you get in trouble. You got it?"

"Yeah, sure. I got it."

"Rest if you need to, Arch. I'm serious. You don't look good. This isn't a race."

He sneered. "Jesus. Don't be such a pussy. Let's go already."

We started climbing. It wasn't long before I was gasping, too. Progress was slow, the sun rising to lick our backs as the wind whipped harder. I'd selected the most direct route toward the top, which meant crawling along the spine of a steep ridge, clambering up boulders and over fallen trees—those brittle victims of drought. Archie, on the other hand, veered east, his choices more deliberate and cautious than I would've predicted.

A narrow ledge jutted up from the ridge peak, and I pulled myself up and over to land on solid ground. I still had a ways to go, but I took a moment to breathe; the view from the ledge was vast and yawning, and Archie was nowhere close to reaching me. I peered over to watch him toil below, picking his way from marker to marker and having to rest every couple minutes in a way that felt more lazy than necessary.

I stayed there like that, leaning over the side on my hands and knees, until a rush of dizziness closed in on me—a sudden bout of vertigo that seemed to come from nowhere. Alarmed, I straightened up and crawled back, then tried pushing myself to standing, only to have my arms crumple under my weight. I collapsed forward onto my face. With a groan, I rolled to one side, scissoring my hips, and struggled to rise again. And again. But something was wrong. My limbs had gone all pins and needles, as if my body had fallen asleep without me. I lay there, like a dying horse, my right foot churning uselessly in the air.

I had no clue how long I was on the ground like that. Time spiraled into something bleak and unreliable, and I was vaguely aware I was experiencing the precursor to a migraine—aura, it's called and mine takes many forms. I also knew the pain would consume me soon, battering me with suffering, bright and flashy. If I couldn't get to my meds, my only hope for relief would be to die of a stroke or else find a way to roll myself over the edge of the cliff.

Heavy breathing signaled the arrival of Archie onto the ledge, which was followed by the sound of him gulping water from the bottle I'd brought with me. He hadn't bothered bringing his own.

"What the hell are you doing, Gibby?" he asked when he was done.

Migraine, I wanted to say. *With parasthesia.* That was the word for the numbness and lack of coordination winding through my limbs. It was also the reason I couldn't form words to tell him what it was I needed and why opening my eyes felt like trying to grasp objects that had fallen to the bottom of the deepest well. These were the worst of my migraines; the ones that came on fast, without warning, only to leave me ruined.

Archie stood over me. "You having a seizure or something?"

I still didn't answer. I gaped like a fish.

He made his wheezing sound again. "Well, now, crap, Gibby. You don't look too good. But like you told me, if you can't climb, I sure as hell can't do anything to help you. I'm real sorry about that. But I'm gonna keep going. Catch up with me if you can."

I groaned again as he reached down to unzip the side pack I wore around my waist. A spark of hope flared within me as he rummaged around in there. Maybe he was getting my pills. But instead, he plucked out both sets of car keys, my compass, and the trail map, jamming all the items into his own backpack.

"You really can't blame me," he said before he left. "You'd do the same thing if you were me. I know damn well you would."

34.

TECHNICALLY SPEAKING, THE TYPES OF MIGRAINES I GET ARE DUE TO
a condition called persistent post-traumatic headache. It sounds simple
enough and, in a lot of ways, it is. All the name really means is that my
brain still hasn't gotten over what happened when I was ten, when my
mother drove her gold Kia off the highway, hitting a light pole as she
went before rolling twice and ending up at the bottom of a hill in front
of a defunct gum factory. I was thrown from the vehicle—I wasn't wearing a seat belt—and it's always seemed ironic that despite not being
anything close to athletic, I'd somehow succeeded in hurling my body
through the front windshield.

I don't remember anything after that. I've been told I landed facedown in a drainage ditch that was filled with maybe four inches of rainwater and algae. Shallow, but still deep enough to drown. I don't know
how long I was underwater but apparently I had to be resuscitated. That
sounds overly dramatic, if you ask me, and I'd like to think that if I'd really died and come back to life, I'd *know*. Even if my mind couldn't hold
on to the memory, I want to believe there's some part of me that would.

When I woke up in the hospital two days later, no one told me anything other than I'd had an accident and hit my head. Well, maybe they
told me other things, too, and I just forgot. I did a lot of that in those
first few days. Forgetting. Sleeping, too. I was instructed not to move
without help, a directive I didn't understand until I tried making it to
the bathroom on my own, too bashful for a nurse's help. I was upright

for mere seconds, the world seemingly unmoving, while inside my own body, I spun and spun, circling the drain of consciousness before sinking to the waxed linoleum floor.

My head hurt all the time in those early months. I don't think that's surprising given what happened. A lot of people wanted to know the details of what I'd done to Marcus, forcing me to repeat over and over that it was a moment my damaged mind had stolen from me. That I didn't remember a thing.

What was known was that he and I were alone in the house together with a loaded gun that he'd foolishly left on the coffee table. Apparently, I'd picked it up, it went off, and he'd died from a bullet to the brain while sleeping on the couch. Accidental, it was deemed. How could it be anything but? I was a timid kid, not an angry one, and in the end, Marcus was lamented as both a good man and a bad gun owner. But I refused to give him that, even in death, and so I'll tell you this: Timid or not, I *hated* him for hurting my mother. For hiding behind Scripture and righteousness and making her feel as if she deserved to suffer at his hand, by making her hate herself.

By making her hate *me*.

No one worried too much about my headaches at first. They were the least of my problems, compared with cops and social services and my mother's black, black moods. They were also ordinary, given my injury, and I was told I would heal. However, healing, like God's mercy, failed to appear. The headaches grew worse. More frequent, too. And when the numbness and vision loss kicked in, that was when I had to go see a specialist.

The doctor I went to was a neurologist, who ran a bunch of tests and made me wear a stupid medical alert bracelet. He also let me know that while my most severe symptoms closely resembled a rare condition known as hemiplegic migraine, which carried the risk of coma and possible death, it was usually due to genetics, not injury. In the end, I was diagnosed with plain old regular migraine of the persistent, post-traumatic variety. But the more I learned about the hemiplegic thing, the greater my doubt. Perhaps the truth was that my injury had only set off what was already there, lying in wait.

Perhaps pain had always been a part of who I was.

And look, there's no point not to anymore, so I'll tell you this, too: I remember *everything* that happened that day with Marcus, and here's what the coroner got wrong—my stepfather definitely wasn't asleep when I shot him. It also wasn't an accident. He woke up that afternoon to find me standing beside him, holding the gun he'd taught me to fire to his temple, and he knew what I was going to do. He also knew why, which was how I wanted it. *I* was the one who squeezed my eyes shut before pulling the trigger, and I don't think I opened them again until hours later, when my mother came home and found us. And no, she never once asked what I'd done or how it had happened.

She never had to.

After Archie abandoned me on that ledge, there wasn't much I could do about the situation. With great effort, I managed to reach into my unzipped side pack for my medication. My fingers fumbled with the blister packs, but I finally popped a Zomig out only to have it roll out of reach, somewhere near the edge. I whimpered at the loss—I wasn't about to go searching for it—then fumbled for another pill. I held on to that one, shoving it under my tongue and letting it melt, before chasing it with two codeine-laced Tylenol. Then I prayed for sleep, the way I always did. I didn't care if it was the easy way out.

A rumbling came from above. Followed by the sound of crumbling earth. Twisting my head, I glanced up just in time for a rush of falling rocks and dirt clods to hit me square in the face. I spat mud from my lips in disgust. Archie had done that on purpose. I was sure of it.

Laying my head on granite, I closed my eyes. Soon I was conscious of nothing but the wind prickling my skin, the rising pain in my head, and the yawning free-fall distance from the ledge to the ground below. My mind grasped for reason, an analytical solution to my current problem. Geometric even, because like points to a triangle, it seemed my strange trio of perceptions must have something to tell me—if only I could figure out what it was. But my awareness was far from equilateral, the pain most acute, and if I knew anything right about relationships, then that meant the Pythagorean theorem should hold.

I labored with the calculations. Rose was better at math than I was, but I determined that the distance to the ground was farthest, meaning it had to be the hypotenuse. Would its square be measured in yards or meters? Yards were easier, and I estimated the ledge I was stuck on hovered maybe two hundred yards in the air. Only I had no clue how to convert pain into any equivalent value, much less wind velocity.

Solutions drifted from reach. Hope, too, and I gave in to the glove grip of failure, having come to the very end of my reason. My brain was broken, addled by pain. By drugs. By more. Twisting onto my back, I forced my eyes open only to have them roll into my head. The blue sky above sparkled, dreamlike, but its beauty was wasted; I could stand neither the weight of the sun nor the cruel shove of the breeze.

Flailing my arms to the side, I propped my legs against the cliff wall and stayed that way, lying backward, half suspended in the air. My mind shimmered toward madness; I was sinking but I was also hanging, a pig on a meat hook, and I craved my gutting. I could picture the act in vivid detail—the first thrust of the knife; the deep carving of flesh; the ragged wound running all the way from breastbone to rectum. Everything after would be easy. That's what I told myself, as the blackness rushed in.

Release.

Death.

Nothingness.

———————

I awoke cold. Freezing, really.

My lungs contracted, gripped with chill, making me cough. I had no clue how much time had passed, as I lay curled on that ledge in a state of codeine-induced half consciousness, half death. I did know that when I opened my eyes, it was because I was shivering. But this awareness filtered in slowly as I untangled myself from sleep and pain, only to realize the sun had ceased to warm my skin.

I sat up. Tested my limbs. I was relieved to find everything working in all the right ways. That relief was trampled, however, as I remembered Archie's betrayal. That he'd stolen the *keys*. That he'd left me here. Alone.

I felt it again—the frigid blast of air that had woken me in the first place. It washed over the cliff top and hurtled straight down the mountain to lap my bones, a greedy slurp of winter. I shuddered, bleary-eyed, and looked up. Shadows fell across my face as I stared at the darkening sky. What had been blue was now steel-gray and churning, but it wasn't night. I knew that. I couldn't have slept that long.

That left only one other explanation.

I braced myself. The storm's door slammed open with a bang. Wind whistled in with primal force, slapping my face as the rain began to fall, those first drops runny and large. They landed, one after the other, like a leaking faucet, but soon fell faster.

And faster.

The hail came next, mixing with the sheets of rain to pelt me with ice and welt my skin. Thunder boomed in the distance and the wind tore at my clothes, screaming as it blew through every opening and weakness in my body it could find.

I was soaked in an instant. Shelter was imperative. I had to move. I had to do something. Or I was going to die out there.

35.

ATTEMPTING TO MAKE MY WAY UP THE REST OF THE SCRAMBLE TO THE top of the waterfall appeared at best Sisyphean, at worst suicidal. The earth turned to mud, melting before my eyes, and each time I lifted my head torrents of water barraged my face, rushing to fill my nostrils and throat.

Gasping, sputtering, I stayed crouched on the narrow ledge with my hands over my head and pondered my dwindling options. The water pooling at my feet had found its own current, sloshing, splashing toward the edges before spilling into the abyss. I couldn't stay there much longer, but I couldn't go down, either, which meant I had no choice; hell, I was only twenty feet from the top. Slipping my ugly sunglasses on and hoping for the best, I began the climb.

The rain fell harder as I ascended, matting my hair to my face. I focused on moving one limb at a time, straining with each shift of weight and balance. The frigid wind grabbed me, shaking my body the higher I climbed, causing me to cling desperately to keep from being blown away. As I held on, raw fingers digging into dirt, I dipped my head and peeked below. The view was horrifying, a sheer drop straight down into the massive waterfall's thundering maelstrom, a foaming pool ringed by boulders and sharp edges—a gaping mouth, its teeth slick with rain. I whipped my head up, then shouted as one of my hands slipped, sending me sliding back toward the ledge.

I managed to throw one leg out, kicking it into the dirt as hard as I could. My hip wrenched at the action, torqueing sharply but stopping my fall nonetheless. I squeezed my eyes shut with shuddering gratitude, then pressed my face against the mud. I was a fool for coming out on this mountain in the first place. For ever believing I could take on nature and be more than who I was. All those nights doing push-ups on the floor of my room or running up and down our single flight of stairs when I knew my mom wasn't going to wake up—those had been acts of willful ignorance. No different from believing in pots of gold at the ends of rainbows or in the hands of criminals willing to hand them over. Everyone crafted their own brand of dreams, I supposed, but from where I crouched that made hope the most Sisyphean act of all.

Eventually the wind and rain eased slightly, allowing me to breathe, and I dug deep for a sliver of resolve. Not in myself, but in the girl I longed to save.

I resumed climbing. Slowly. At last I reached the very top of the waterfall, the cresting edge of the massive Grizzly Lake—visible for the very first time. My heart rocketed at the sight. The icy water was a living creature, a body organic and wild, its waves choppy, smacking against its own shores with obvious ire. I stood balanced on the ridge that spindled out over the waterfall, the rock below hollowed from the current's force, a powerful testament to both gravity and the whims of fate.

On the other side of the ridge was the trail to the peak, the one I'd told Archie about. I saw where it wound upward through the trees before vanishing in a mass of black clouds. To get there all I had to do was make the leap from where I stood to an equally precarious ledge on the opposite side of the waterfall. The gap was maybe two feet at most, but would have been terrifying even in good weather. One slip would send you tumbling into white water, down to the rocks below. And while I wanted—needed—the car keys, for all I knew, Archie already lay smashed at the bottom, his possessions—and mine—all lost for good.

I stood frozen in the gusting wind and driving rain and stared at where I needed to go. I couldn't possibly do this and yet I had no choice.

I held my breath.

And leapt.

Landing on the other side, my feet skidded and slipped, throwing me forward onto my knees. I splayed my hands out with a yelp, managing to catch myself before spinning sideways off the rock face. I lay, trembling, before realizing that I'd made it. Alive. Pushing up with filthy, bleeding palms, I somehow got to my feet and started to run, slipping, limping steps that carried me up through the trees and toward the trail Rose had said to follow.

The rain came down harder the faster I tried to move, turning the earth to slurry beneath my feet. I flailed and slid. It was like running on ice, and I stumbled with each stride, falling over and over until I was covered with mud. It was in my nose, my ears, oozing from my shoes.

But I kept going, step by futile step, until the hairs rose on the back of my neck and the air crackled with ozone. My skin went taut, and the sky lit up with shattering brilliance while sending two simultaneous bolts of lightning to strike the ground right in front of me.

My shouting was drowned out by the earth-splitting crack of thunder that followed immediately after. I bolted straight into a forested thicket located just off the trail, diving beneath a canopy of dripping aspen trees and army-crawling through the mud, as low as I could, before wriggling on my belly into a makeshift shelter formed by a set of crisscrossing tree trunks that had collapsed against the hillside.

The pelting of rain echoed off the branches high above where I'd buried myself, but the dark spot I'd found was relatively dry, a decent waiting space. I wiped water from my eyes as they adjusted to the darkness. Only when I could see again, I found I wasn't alone. Hunched mere inches from where I was, soaked and miserable—his eyes wide with fear, his back pressed into the soft dirt of the carved-out hollow— was Archie.

36.

"GIBBY," HE SAID, AND IT WAS IMPOSSIBLE FOR ME TO READ HIS VOICE. Was he relieved to see me? Angry? Fearful? It didn't matter. I hated him even as my teeth chattered and I trembled horribly with cold and wetness. My migraine, which had waned in the face of adrenaline and certain death, now swelled and pulsed its way toward a sickening crescendo unlike anything I had ever experienced.

More thunder crashed down on us. Shaking the ground and rattling the trees. It was as if hell itself had set up shop on that mountain, a deafening force capable of sparking images I never wanted to see again, shooting them straight into my field of vision—Marcus bellowing with his hands wrapped around my mother's neck, his face bulging with fury; the righteous gleam in his eyes as he tore at her clothes, pinning her body with his, seeking to punish her with what was meant to be love; and me, cowering and helpless, forced to bear witness to it all.

Archie repeated my name and reached out to push my shoulder with his foot, pushing harder when I didn't respond. I leaned forward with a groan to vomit between my legs. Then I did it again. And again after that. And then I couldn't move. I just sat there, frozen, hands bleeding, knees bleeding, covered in mud and puke and drool and rage, and every nerve in my body was on fire.

"Shit," breathed Archie. He didn't touch me again. He just sat and watched me, something I begrudgingly appreciated since the worst thing people did when I fell ill was to try and shove food or water in my mouth or ask me a ton of questions about what they could do to help, when what I actually needed was absolute silence or, more precisely, the absence of all sensory input.

The migraine seemed to peak after I got sick, the way they often did, flaring then fading until I was able to collapse backward onto the ground and open my eyes without feeling like death.

"You okay?" Archie asked with a frown.

I didn't answer. I had nothing to say to him.

"Those headaches of yours are pretty shitty."

I still didn't answer.

He lay back on his elbows. "So that's how it's going to be? Well, why the hell'd you come all the way up here if you weren't gonna talk to me?"

I flipped him off.

Archie laughed. "You're pissed, aren't you? You're pissed, but you're not going to say it. That's not how shit gets fixed, you know. That's how you let life just keep pissing you off, day by goddamn day."

"What do you know about fixing shit?" I snapped, turning to glare at him. "All you've done over the past few days is get people killed."

"Maybe that's all I need to know," he said.

"You're sick."

"And you aren't?"

"Rose is suffering because of you. She's in pain."

"Because of *me*?" Archie huffed. "You came up here on your own. You *chose* to climb that waterfall and dick around with me when you could have been saving that precious girl of yours."

"Bullshit! You made me come up here! You stole the keys!"

"I didn't make you do anything. You had the keys before we even started climbing. You could've left the campsite any time you wanted and been off this mountain by now."

"But I promised Rose. I promised her I'd go with you."

Archie wiped dirt from his hands. "You can't seriously be that stupid. What'd you think would happen if you didn't?"

"I'm not stupid," I told him.

"Oh, yeah? What do you call it when you're so desperate to make someone happy you end up becoming the thing that hurts them the most?"

"I'm not stupid," I repeated.

"No," he agreed. "You're something worse."

"What's that?"

"Pathetic."

I wish I could say Archie's baiting and name-calling didn't get to me. That I was able to be the bigger person and set my mind to doing what it was I needed to do so that we could both get back down the waterfall and the mountain safely and with the keys needed to lead us to help.

But his words stung and the storm raged and I stewed soppy in guilt. Hurting Rose was my deepest fear and hadn't I already done that? Maybe she didn't need to know of my infidelity in order for it to matter. Maybe betrayal bore its consequences with or without confession. After all, if Rose was right and math was the only thing in this world that could be counted on to be honest, then trust was an illusion. And without trust there could be no love. And without love, *her* love, I was nothing.

Nothing at all.

"You know," Archie said after a moment, his voice lower, more solemn. "Maybe I'm being too hard on you. Taking the keys was a dick move. I admit that."

I glanced over at him. "Yeah, it was."

"But that girl, Rose, she's not making any of this easy on you. You know that, right?"

"Not making what easy?"

Archie's eyes widened. "Oh, come on."

"I have no idea what you're talking about."

"You really don't?"

"No."

"Shit." He dipped his head. Looked away from me before looking back. "Okay. I'm going to tell you something. I'm going to tell you about Rose. You remember that party we were at last year? It was in the spring. Out at that baby horse farm?"

"Miniature horses," I corrected.

"Whatever. I was really fucked up that night. Just in a bad fucking place."

"I know. I saw you."

"Yeah, well, the thing is, before you got there, I was drinking with some of the guys inside the house. Manny fucking Grossman broke into the Richards' liquor cabinet, so we were drinking all the clear stuff, replacing it with water."

"Classy."

"At some point your girl waltzes in, all by herself, just out of nowhere. But she's smiling and giggling and the whole thing, wanting to sit with us. I'd never seen her like that, but I say, sure, you're cute, come have a drink. Next thing I know she's on my lap, touching my face, my hair—"

"I don't want hear this," I said.

"You should."

"Well, I don't."

"Well, I'm going to tell you anyway. But first of all, I didn't fuck your girl, so you can get over that, all right? That's not what this is about."

I didn't answer.

"Look, she kept touching me, had her hands everywhere and at some point I asked her what she was doing. She missed you, she said, she needed you, and I told her she had a funny way of showing it. Then she whispered in my ear that she was rolling, which made sense because the bitch was high as fuck."

"What?" I was confused. That didn't sound like Rose. She didn't do drugs. Not that kind, at least. Or so I thought. Then again, she hadn't known I was coming and I recalled her energy from that night, electric and charged, so different from how she usually was. The way she'd laughed and lit the air as she bounced against and away from me, a glittering ball of mirth and movement.

Archie shrugged. "I told her to give me some, but she just sat and drank with us. Then someone said they'd seen you drive up. Girl was out of my lap in an instant and dancing away. 'That's it?' I asked her, and she nodded and said something like, 'I have to find him now.' I told her, 'You seem perfectly happy right here.' Well, she gave me this dopey smile and that's when she said it."

"Said what?"

"She goes, 'I *am* happy, Archie. That's why I have to find him. I can't hurt him when I'm feeling this good.'"

"Hurt me how?"

"You tell me."

"I have no idea."

Archie scratched his chin. "Rose told me you'd say that. She says you insist on pretending everything's fine, even when you're miserable. That you've trained yourself not to see the hammer hitting you in the head, and that you'd rather just complain all the time about having a headache."

I went cold. "She did *not* say that."

"Not that night," he admitted. "But she did say it."

"When?"

"Doesn't matter."

"Then I don't believe you."

He laughed. "Believe whatever the hell you want. You think I care?"

"Why'd you call her a bitch that night, then?" I demanded. "If you two are so fucking close?"

"I called her a bitch because she treated me like trash. She left me to be with *you*, some useless white boy, which made me feel worse than trash, actually. More like a pile of shit."

I was aghast. "You hate me, don't you? That's what this is about. You've always hated me. The only time you even acknowledge my existence is when you're drunk. Or stoned. Or you want something."

Archie pulled his flask out as if on cue and took a swig.

"Nice," I said. "Thanks a lot."

He swallowed whatever was in there with a smack. "I don't hate you, Ben. If I did, you'd know. Trust me."

That was all I could take. I hunched forward and twisted my head to look the other way, out into the dark woods, where the sound of rain echoed off the sheltering trees and mist pooled on the ground as if the earth was struggling to stay warm the same way we were. Whatever thoughts were in my head at that moment were not ones I wanted to be having. At all.

"Hey," Archie said after a minute.

I didn't respond. He reached out and pushed me with his shoe again, like he had when I'd gotten sick. He did it lightly at first but then he kicked me, sending fresh waves of pain sloshing through my head.

"What?" I snapped.

"*Look.*" He pointed. I turned and looked, facing away from the woods and out onto the mountain and the lake and the distant valley below.

"Oh, shit," I said.

It was snowing.

37.

"WHAT THE HELL IS HAPPENING?" ARCHIE HISSED. I DIDN'T ANSWER, just stared in disbelief as the cacophony of hail-thunder-rain gave way to the peaceful silence of white puffs tumbling down from the sky. Gathering on the ground in swirling drifts.

"I don't know," I said. "I really don't."

He pushed his wet hair back. Gave a barking laugh. "Christ almighty. Which one of us do you think pissed God off? It's *October.*"

"We need to get back down," I said. "This is bad. We're going to get stuck up here if the storm gets any worse."

Archie grabbed his backpack and crawled forward in the mud, carefully skirting around my puke as he prepared to leave the shelter of the thicket. "Yeah, about that. I'm not going back down."

"Wait, what? What does that mean?"

"It means I'm doing what I came up here to do. I'm not quitting now. I'm going to get that money. No one else is going to get it. That's for damn sure."

"You're serious?" I asked.

"Very."

"That's *insane.*"

"Yeah, you're right." He squeezed his way into the storm, leaving me behind. "It probably is."

I crawled after him. I had no fight left. "Okay, you win, Arch. Let's just go. Let's get this over with so we can get off this fucking mountain."

He turned to gawk at me, still on his hands and knees. "You're *staying*?"

"I don't really have a choice, do I?"

Archie gave me the strangest look. "You tell me."

"Let's just go," I said again. I felt itchy. Anxious. I wanted to get moving.

"Hell, all right, then," he said. "Let's do this."

It was easier to hike in the snow than the rain. The trail smoothed out and we trudged side by side. Archie kept drinking from that flask of his, until his words were slurring and his gait was wobbly, and finally I drank some, too, against my better judgment. I needed the warmth, I guess. Or the courage. I also made him give me back the map and the compass. He didn't know the first thing about using them.

Another quarter mile on, with the icy summit looming above, we rounded a steep bend in the trail only to have a second alpine lake come into view, a smaller one, with snow dusting its shore, its water black and deep.

"Hey, what's this one called?" Archie asked.

I pulled the map out, clutched it in my freezing hands. My teeth wouldn't stop chattering. "Granite Lake."

He shuffled right to the lake's edge. Stared down its depths. "Looks like a good place to drown."

"You think?"

"It's like a quarry," he explained. "You jump in, there's no way out. Rocks are too high from the waterline."

He was right. Unlike Grizzly Lake, Granite Lake was snow fed, which meant the low water was due to the drought. A paradox of sorts: What little water there was meant it was more likely to kill you.

We stood there, unmoving. The snow kept falling, the clumps growing heavier, thicker. It melted on the lake. It gathered on our skin.

"My aunt drowned," Archie said softly.

I looked at him. "Avery's mom?"

"Nah, I'm not talking about her." He took another swig from his flask. "That was shitty, though. How that happened."

"Yeah."

"It's still shitty. My uncle, he's never gotten over that. Probably never will. Same with Avery. She's always been the Girl Whose Mom Died. She fucking hates it, you know. It's like people always put their own sadness on her because they figure she'll know how to deal with it."

Well, that was a more astute observation than I would've expected from Archie DuPraw. And, much to my chagrin, I realized it was also a pretty apt description of the way I'd always seen Avery. Maybe the way I still saw her.

"You're close with her, huh?" I asked. "Avery."

He wiped his red nose, then wiped it again. "You'd better not fuck her over, Gibby. She's a nice girl. Smart, too. She's been through a lot."

"I don't plan on doing anything to Avery."

"No . . . don't say it like that." He shook a wet, boozy finger at me. "That girl's too good for you. I've told her. I don't know what the hell she sees in you."

I rubbed my hands together. "Maybe you should tell her I'm with Rose."

He snorted. "Maybe you shouldn't have screwed her yesterday."

"Tell me about your aunt," I said quickly. "The one who drowned."

Archie's head bobbed. "Yeah, that was my dad's little sister. Laney. She was eight when it happened. Long fucking time ago."

"It happened in a lake?"

"Nope. Ocean. The Pacific. Down near Bonny Doon, north of Santa Cruz. You been there?"

"I've never been anywhere."

He stared at me. "You serious?"

"Absolutely. This trip is my first time out of Humboldt."

"No way," he said. "That's kind of crazy, you know. It's sad."

I folded my arms. "It's true. And I don't need you telling me how sad you think my life is."

"Yeah, yeah, okay, I got it. Don't shit yourself. Anyway, they were on the beach, playing by the water, building goddamn sandcastles or something, when my aunt and my dad got caught by a sneaker wave. He was twelve. Pulled them almost a mile offshore. She couldn't swim. He kept trying to hold on to her."

"But he survived?"

"Clearly."

"Who rescued him?"

"No one rescued him," Archie said. "That's just it. He saved himself."

"How?"

He gave a sick grin. "By letting her go."

"Jesus."

"Yeah. Growing up with him, with someone who could do something like that. It's been . . ." His voice trailed off.

"It's been what?"

"Fuck it. Never mind. Let's keep moving." He turned and started walking again.

I dragged after him. My pants grew stiff with ice, making them even heavier than before. The temperature was plummeting, and if I was cold, Archie had to be miserable. Stuck in a freak snowstorm, he didn't even have a jacket, just a dumpy hooded sweatshirt and some ugly beanie cap he'd pulled from his backpack. It had a walrus stitched on the front. "Archie, come on. This is stupid. We're gonna die out here."

"Maybe. Maybe not."

"Is it worth it if we do?"

"Is it *worth it*?" Archie stumbled at that point and nearly went down. The flask in his hand went flying into a snowbank. I scrambled to retrieve it. "Look around us, Gibby. I already *have* nothing! My life, everything about it, is nothing!"

"What's that supposed to mean?" I asked.

"It means, at this point, *anything* would be worth it."

The desperation in his voice was painful to hear, but before I could respond, Archie regained his footing. His sense of purpose, too. Shoulders square, his head held high, he marched forward, leaving bold depressions in the snow. The prints were his, large and unmistakable.

I did my best to keep up.

My best was far from enough. The snow fell faster, thicker, and I was continually smacked back by the storm sweeping over the mountain's peak. It barreled straight for us, and I was no match for its building force, the pelting rush of ice and more. If climbing the Scramble in the rain had been Sisyphean, this struggle made me feel more like Icarus— a journey flawed more by delusion than difficulty, and not only was it clear we were destined to fail, failure was quickly becoming a matter of life and death.

It wasn't anything I'd planned for, obviously, but I knew a lot about hypothermia—all the survival guides I'd read covered it, complete with gruesome examples throughout history: the Donner Party, who'd been stuck not far from where we were; the Antarctic *Terra Nova* expedition, in which the heroic Captain Lawrence Oates had sacrificed himself to the elements, only to have everyone else freeze to death anyway; and Oregon's horrific Mount Hood disaster, which was almost too awful to contemplate. I'd also learned how in the throes of dying, people often tore off their clothes or sought to bury themselves in snow. Once your body started to fail, it seemed, there wasn't much to be done about it. Prevention was key. Good decision-making, too.

But Archie was as stubborn as ever. He kept going, the colder it got, toiling like an ox, and at some point, I pulled on his arm. As hard as I could.

"We'll come back," I shouted over the roar of the storm. "We've got to get back to the others. Otherwise we're going to die of exposure!"

He shook his head. "We're almost there!"

"You don't know that! We can't even see the trail anymore! We'll never make it!"

"Then go! I'll find my own way back."

"I'm not leaving you!"

"Why not? You said it yourself. You're going to die out here. You don't want that. So you should go. Here." Archie reached into his backpack and pulled out both sets of car keys. He handed them to me, his fingers dark with frostnip. "Now you don't have any reason to stay."

"Arch . . . ," I said.

"Go! Leave. I don't need you."

I stood firm. "I won't do that."

"Why the hell not?"

"Because I'm not your dad!"

Archie's eyes flared hot, mean. "You know, Gibby, I'd respect you a hell of a lot more if you were."

I threw the map at him.

The compass, too.

After that, there's a part of me that wishes I'd done what he told me to do. That I'd possessed enough instinct or will for survival to abandon Archie on that mountain for my own self-preservation. That I'd somehow been able to make the right choice at the right time. But you know me—not only do I not make the right choices, I so rarely make any.

So what's true is that he stayed on that mountaintop without me. That just as Captain Oates had stepped from tent to ice in one final act of self-determination, Archie turned and headed up that snow-covered trail, straight into the blustering storm. It was a death wish—no one could've survived those conditions, not dressed the way he was—and though I would've if I could've, I wasn't physically able to follow him. Instead, I watched him go, disappearing into the wind and the whiteness, to be swallowed up by his conviction—which was something he had in excess and which I had never found.

What's also true is that in the end, I didn't choose to leave Archie. What's true is that he left me.

38.

IT'S SAID THAT THE DEFINITION OF INSANITY IS ATTEMPTING TO DO the same thing over and over again, and expecting a different outcome. But if that's the case, then my attempt to get down that mountain safely in whiteout conditions during a freak blizzard wearing nothing but frozen track pants, a bloodstained T-shirt, and a leather jacket I'd stolen from a dead man must've been something far worse because I expected to die.

And I did it anyway.

I set myself to the task the way I approached every difficult or distasteful thing I'd ever done in my life—that is to say with a touch of avoidance and a whole hell of a lot of guilt. Clearly those were qualities I possessed in part from how I'd grown up, but I also think I was born that way. If my mother was flame, I'd always been ice, endowed not with a zest for expression or action but with a tendency toward stillness.

My father, my real father, as much as I knew of him, was similar—moody, sensitive, prone to shutting down. He'd met my mother after college while in the midst of an existential crisis. Not his first, I'm sure, or his last. His parents begged him to return to Rhode Island to attend medical school, but twenty-one-year-old Gus Gibson rebelled against their wishes, traveling instead to California where he wandered Kerouac-style up and down the Pacific Northwest with all his belongings shoved in a duffel bag. After a sun-soaked weekend spent at Reggae on the River, where he smoked hash, dropped acid, and fell in love with a dancing, green-eyed girl from Teyber, Humboldt became his natural resting place. He moved in with my mother, took up surfing, and wrote a lot of bad poetry, surviving, I guess, on what he made selling his driftwood furniture.

My mother likes to tell me he was prone to ennui. Or melancholy. Or any of those words that are meant to sound as if a person's more attuned to the world than the rest of us who don't go around feeling as awful as they do. I'd always taken that to mean he'd grown unhappy being tied down to an emotionally unstable woman and the screaming brat they'd produced. I also took it to mean he didn't want to settle, which I can sort of understand even if it's hard to sympathize with when you're the brat in question.

Either way, medical school must've started looking pretty good after a while. I was barely out of diapers by the time he took off, the prodigal son returning home to become an internist, leaving nothing behind but promises as empty as the way my mother must've felt, being stuck having to raise the son of the man she wasn't good enough for.

But in that way, I guess, I was nothing like my father. Because he'd given up and left, and I knew I never would.

When it rains it pours, and when it snows, everything turns to shit, I guess. God knows how long it took me, but I made it back down the waterfall somehow, only to slip on the icy steps at the very bottom and screw up my left shoulder. Something crumpled inside the joint, like a cardboard box that had been stepped on. Later I'd learn I'd blown out the cartilage, but at the time, it was just one more link of misery in a whole daisy chain of failure.

I waded back through the blizzard, the wind slashing my face hard enough to draw blood. After crossing the meadow, I searched for what I could find of our food and camping gear. There wasn't much. The snow was nearly a foot deep and everything left outside was buried in white, great swirling smears of it. I gathered what little remained, shoving it all into my bag.

Next, I staggered to the tent Rose and I had shared. My goal was to dismantle it, to bring it back to the others, but the metal stakes slipped from my grasp, too slick to pull from the ground. Unhooking the poles from the outer shell was equally futile, and my shoulder wasn't the only body part unwilling to do what was needed; my fingers had gone completely numb. I thought they might be dying and ended up wrapping socks around my hands for grip, but they were wet in seconds, and still, I couldn't grab anything or do anything so I just gave up and lit one of the camping stoves I'd found—a small single butane burner—and hunkered down with it in Mr. Howe's narrow tent. Thank God for boasting. Knowing he'd taken it up Denali made me feel a lot better about sheltering in there.

Once inside, I warmed my hands and boiled snow and gulped a packet of instant soup before realizing how badly I needed to lie down. I knew better than to take off my clothes, but made an exception for my wet shoes and socks. I also remembered to piss in a water bottle because the books I'd read told me that the effort to heat urine in one's own body was a waste of precious energy. Then I burrowed deep into Mr. Howe's sleeping bag and rolled onto my back. Stared at the roof of the tent.

The storm grabbed the structure on all sides and shook it, a howling roar. I lay stiff, my breath puffing above me, too terrified to move. I was Dorothy in her twister, waiting for liftoff. But as the tent walls rippled and pulsed like crashing waves, my mind drifted from Dorothy to another girl: Archie's lost aunt, little Laney, just eight years old, playing with her brother on the California coast only to be stolen from shore. My lungs choked, imagining her fear. Had she died with hope, with the belief that Archie's father would save her? Or had she known what was happening as he set her free in a world she couldn't navigate, turning back only to save himself?

Neither option brought comfort, but I knew I'd rather drown than know I was the cause of someone else's pain. That was noble, wasn't it? To think of others first? I'd always told myself that, but doubt chewed at the edges of my certainty. Maybe the truth was that I preferred death to guilt. It was hard to see anything noble in that.

The air grew colder and my mind sleepier. I placed my face as close to the stove as I dared, not caring what fumes I might inhale, so long as they were warm. I breathed and shivered and nothing changed. Every part of me ached. I wanted Rose. I wanted to tell her how sorry I was for everything I'd ever done wrong. And then I wanted to save her.

But even in my struggle to survive, my will to death was the greater pull, and I closed my eyes. Told myself to stop dreaming. I'd saved her before, yes, but mostly from herself, her own pain. I had no way of saving Rose from up here. Hell, I couldn't even save myself.

DAY FOUR

39

SOMEONE SHOOK ME. SLAPPED MY FACE.

I groaned. Opened my eyes to darkness and sucked in corpse-like air.

"Ben," a voice whispered. "Ben, wake up!"

"Is he okay?" someone else asked. "Tell me he's okay."

Hands were on my body, and I was pulled up to sitting. I cried out, my shoulder in agony, but my heart lurched, believing maybe I was being rescued or already had *been* rescued and just didn't realize it and wouldn't that be something? But no, it was only Avery and Clay, and they were filthy and freezing and they were somehow squeezed in the tent with me, only I didn't know how or why.

"What are you doing?" I gasped, then squeaked with pain.

"Where's Archie?" Avery asked. "We can't find him."

"Here." Clay shoved something into my good hand. A tin mug, filled with something hot. It burned my fingers but I didn't care. I inhaled deeply, letting the steam wet my face. The tent's opening flapped and fluttered, and I caught a glimpse of dwindling daylight among the snow and wind.

I wheezed and sipped from the mug: instant cocoa mixed with instant coffee. Bitter, but necessary. I sipped more. Clay and Avery were sorting through the supplies I'd packed before falling asleep, gathering what else they wanted to take. Avery smiled when she saw the camera I'd kept for her, then crawled from the tent to check the others.

"Can you walk?" Clay asked me.

My head felt grainy, but I nodded. "I think so."

"Good," he said. "The storm's eased off for now. It might start up again but the wind's not as crazy at the moment, so we should get going as soon as we can. We're sorry for leaving you here so long, man. It's just, there was no warning, and with the snow and the cold—"

"I get it," I said.

"—we weren't able to get out until sunrise. Ave and I left when we could, though. I swear."

I blinked. "What did you say?"

"I said we couldn't get up here any earlier. I'm sorry. This whole thing, it's so fucking shitty. The other three still have the fire going, but it's pretty—"

"Did you say you left at *sunrise*?"

"Yeah."

"What day is it?"

Clay cocked his head. "It's Monday. What day did you think it was?"

"Monday? I thought it was Sunday still. Maybe early evening." My hands shook, sloshing the drink on my lap. I'd slept all night apparently. "Holy shit."

"I'm sorry," he repeated.

"Don't be. It's just . . . *shit*."

Avery ducked back in. She looked from me to Clay.

"Where's Archie?" she asked again.

"Gone," I said.

"What do you mean *gone*?"

The fear was already there, in her eyes. Avery knew, I think, before I said anything, but I told them what happened. How it had happened. That Archie was lost to us. That he'd lost himself because I sure as hell hadn't chosen to give up on him. *Because he wouldn't stop looking for the money* didn't feel like the right explanation, but in the end, it was all I had.

"He's Archie," I said weakly. "He knows how to take care of himself. If anyone can survive up there . . ."

"It's not him," finished Avery. "We all know that."

She was right, of course. I wanted to tell her I was sorry. I knew she cared for him, but I couldn't do it. I finished the drink Clay gave me and ate a protein bar, before scavenging Mr. Howe's belongings for dry clothes, including his hiking boots and a pair of dry socks. He'd apparently run all the way down the mountain to save us in his water shoes. Clay had to help me change, which I didn't bother to be embarrassed about. The boots were too big, but in truth, they felt amazing—warm and sturdy. I slid my jacket back on, and we crawled from the tent to help Avery.

Daylight or not, stepping into the open air nearly knocked me on my ass. The wind might have died down, but the air was sharp enough to water my eyes and frost my lungs. I followed the lead of the other two, although with one arm I was only half as useful. We wrapped sleeping bags around our bodies for warmth, hauling what supplies we could on our backs before tethering ourselves together with rope.

"It can be hard to see where you're going," Clay told me. Ice already dotted his brows, the tip of his nose. "But just follow me."

I nodded. I was at the end of the rope, and the realization that Archie wasn't there to make some sort of *Human Centipede* joke at my expense hurt worse than anything.

We shuffled off. I had a moment of flustered panic, believing I'd somehow forgotten the keys. Or the map. Or something else I'd meant to bring back. Something that mattered.

But I hadn't.

"Hey," I called out to the other two, as we resumed our shuffling, heading toward the main trail that would lead us down the mountain. "Hey!"

They both turned to look at me.

"How's Rose?" I asked, and the strange thing was, I didn't know why I hadn't asked about her earlier. I hadn't even thought to ask. I couldn't explain it. My head was in a fog.

Clay glanced at Avery.

"What is it?" I asked.

"She's with her brother," Avery said.

"That's all you're going to say?"

"That's all I know."

"Fine," I said. "Whatever. Then let's keep walking."

So that's what we did.

Ours was a slow, mostly silent descent. I gazed at the landscape in awe—icicles dangling from tree branches, the deathly stillness of the white. The mountain was perhaps more wondrous than ever, now that I knew its full power. In less than twenty-four hours, more than two feet of wet snow had fallen, casting the Trinity Alps straight from fire season into the frigid depths of winter—a remarkable display no matter how you looked at it. And I had more than enough time to look—the hike down the icy mountain was endless. My admiration for the others swelled the steeper the snowy trail angled downward; I couldn't imagine climbing up it.

Avery and Clay talked more as we neared the gorge, entering into the now-white canyon. They told me how they'd been able to keep the fire going overnight, but that we were stuck on the mountain for the time being. The earlier rain had caused a landslide, a massive wave of fallen trees and earth, effectively cutting off the access trail we'd come in on, and Tomás had said we couldn't walk out from the south yet, because the drifts were too deep and he was worried about an avalanche. But now that the storm had stopped, Clay told me eagerly, there was hope that people would be looking for us.

"Who?" I asked. "What people?"

He glanced back at me. "Search and rescue. Or whoever it is that does that. They know we're missing. We were supposed to be back last night."

"But how will they know where to find us?"

"I don't *know*. Don't they just fly around in helicopters and look for people who get trapped or lost? I mean, Shelby's been trying to get a second fire going in the gorge, out of the tree cover, so maybe they'll see that. But didn't Howe tell the ranger where we were? They know we're here, right?"

I paused. "Yes, he told them where we were going."

Clay shot me a lazy grin. "Well, then that's good, right?"

"It would be if we were where we said we'd be."

"What do you mean?"

"We said we'd be camping near the summit. In the meadow by the waterfall. If they look for us anywhere, that's where they're going to go."

Clay was still confused. "You mean . . ."

"Yes," Avery cut in tersely. "That's exactly what he means. They're going to be looking for us back where we just came from. Not where we actually are."

40.

TOMÁS WAS THE FIRST TO GREET US AS WE HOBBLED OUR WAY INTO
the Preacher's campsite. With the last of Maggie's tartan blankets slung
over his shoulders, he rose from his seat by the fire and hurried in our
direction. Spotting his gaunt cheeks and dark owl eyes—Rose's eyes—
pricked with me a rush of despair.

Avery, Clay, and I had untethered ourselves prior to crossing the
China Spring to avoid all three of us falling into the icy water. Veering
from the others, I went to stand by the fire ring and its smoking ashes,
where I dropped the sleeping bag and backpack I'd been carrying. Then
I took in everything around me.

Familiarity came on fast: There was the tattered tent, windblown
but still standing, the rickety card table, pulled beneath a tree and piled
high with wood, and the row of canvas chairs, all damp with snow. I
recognized everything and still my mouth soured at the sight.

"How's Rose?" I asked Tomás, when I'd caught my breath.

He had eyes only for Clay. "She's resting. Shel's with her now."

"But she's okay?"

"No, she's not *okay.*"

"But . . ."

Tomás scowled but seemed to understand that the urgency in my
voice meant I needed affirmation that Rose was still alive. "She's in pain,"
he added. "A lot of pain. The pills are helping, but they're not enough."

"What can we do?"

"Get her the hell out of here."

"How?"

"I don't know," he admitted.

Clay sighed. "Ben says search and rescue won't look for us here."

"Why's that?"

"They think we're up by the meadow."

"Then we'll find a way out on our own," Avery said, and there was strength in her voice I'd never heard before. True authority. Decisiveness.

"Where's Archie?" Tomás asked. "Isn't he with you?"

No one answered.

"Come on," he pressed. "What is it? Did he do something stupid?"

I swallowed before answering. "He's still out there."

"Out where?"

"On the mountain. Up near the peak. Last I saw him, we were past Grizzly Lake, over the waterfall. That was yesterday. The snow started while we were up there. We could barely move in that wind, but he wouldn't come back with me. I guess . . . I guess he really wanted that money. Or something."

Tomás blanched at this news. "You're saying he's lost? In the snow?"

"Yes."

"By himself?"

I nodded.

"Is he alive?"

As always, I went for hope, not truth. "I don't know."

"You don't *know*? You mean he could be—"

"Yes."

"Oh, shit. *Shit*."

Things got weird at this point. Tomás, who had reason to hate Archie more than any of us, seemed to be on the verge of hyperventilating or passing out. He moaned and staggered back, grabbing for his chest like he was having a coronary. Clay, who gave me a dirty look like I had something to do with it, ended up taking Tomás by the arm and drag-ging him into the woods, beneath the tree cover.

"What was that about?" Avery asked when they were gone. She was crouched on the ground, starting to organize the items we'd brought back, laying them out in the snow. Her dark hair was pulled back, up off her neck, and the gold chain of her fox necklace glinted in the light, an alluring sight against her warm brown skin. A part of me longed to touch her, to run my fingers along the nape of her neck. But I didn't.

"I don't know," I said softly.

"And you?" She twisted her head to look up at me. "You're doing okay? You scared us, you know."

My cheeks burned. "I'm okay. But I don't know what would've happened if you guys hadn't shown up, Ave. Grateful doesn't begin to cover it."

"You would've been fine."

"You think?"

"I know." She held up her camera. "Thanks for finding this, by the way."

"No problem," I said. Then: "Hey, did the Preacher really sit for you by the river?"

She nodded. "He knew a lot about photography."

"Don't you think that's strange, though? That he'd let you do that? I mean, he's a fugitive."

Avery shrugged. "I don't think it's strange. It's not like I would've taken the photos to the cops or anything—I didn't know who he was then. And unlike you, he liked having his picture taken."

I snorted. "The narcissistic bank robber."

She reached for my hand, a point of connection. "Most people want to be remembered, Ben."

"Hey, where's Abel?" I pulled my hand back and turned away from her. It dawned on me that he was no longer tied to the tree by the card table. Considering the extent of his injuries, I assumed he hadn't walked off under his own power to race Archie up the mountain or to try to slip out of the country unnoticed. It was possible he'd been sandbagging so that he could make a run for it, but the sound I'd heard when Archie struck him with the gun wasn't anything that could be faked. But maybe he'd been moved somewhere due to his injuries. That was a thought that turned my insides weak. The idea he might be in the tent with Rose set off all sorts of alarm bells.

"He's dead," Avery said, effectively ending that line of thought. "He died during the night. He froze."

"Oh," I said.

And that was that.

Entering the tent, I found Shelby holding Rose in her arms. A gamey reek hung in the frigid air and every surface I touched felt grimy, filthy even, as I crawled toward where they lay huddled beneath a pile of blankets, Shelby's chin rested on Rose's head, her chest against her back. She also had the small Bible gripped in one hand, as she read by lantern light, whispering the words aloud.

"Hey," I said.

"Ben." Shelby pushed up on her elbow, matted hair falling past her shoulders. "You're here."

"Yeah."

"We're stuck, you know. We can't get out."

"I know. You should get some food, though. We brought some back."

She nodded, setting the Bible down before zipping her hoodie, and grabbing for her shoes. When she'd left, I took her place to lay beside Rose. Even with the lantern, it was hard to see much beyond shadows, and I put my ear to her heart to be lulled by its tender throb. I inhaled her scent, mostly sweat and pain, then kissed her cheek.

"Ben," she whispered, her lips sticky and pale. "I was worried about you. I didn't know if you were coming back. I didn't know if you'd be okay in the storm."

"I'm sorry I left."

"I told you to go."

"How's your side? How're you feeling?"

"Not good," she said.

"It hurts?"

"Everything hurts."

"Can I see?"

"You sure?"

"Yeah." I brought the lantern closer and lifted the blankets. Everything about her was small, knotted tight. Rose had one hip twisted over the other, and she winced as I pushed her shirt up.

"You okay?" I asked.

She nodded.

I ran the light across her skin. Lines of scabbed welts dotted her torso, covered the soft folds of her belly. I reached to touch one. "What are these?"

"Bug bites. Shel thinks there're bedbugs in here. They itch like crazy."

"Oh, Rose." My heart broke to hear this, and no, I don't know why my girlfriend being bitten by bedbugs was any more tragic than her getting shot in the stomach. But it was. Or maybe what was most tragic was that she was going to have to stay in those bug-infested blankets until help came. I had no way of making her current situation better. And her situation, as it was, really sucked.

Bringing the lantern closer, I inspected the front side of her wound first. The dressing that had been used made my mouth go watery. Tomás and Shelby must've done it; it was fresh still, not yet soaked with blood, but a torn piece of a cotton T-shirt was wadded against Rose's skin, held in place by *duct tape*. The shirt looked like it was the cleanest they could have found, but that wasn't saying much. I hesitated, not wanting to hurt her by messing with it.

"Go on," she said weakly. "Tell me how it's doing."

With the edge of my thumb, I worried the tape back, peeling it off with as much care as I could before lifting the T-shirt. I bit down on my lip. The entry wound was smaller than I would've thought, a neat hole crusted with dried blood and a bit of purple bruising around the edges. The area was puffy, too, but not alarmingly so. It was as if Rose's own softness had expanded to keep her whole.

"How's it look?" she asked.

"Pretty good, considering."

"The other side hurts more." She rolled forward while I lifted her shirt up in the back, and this time I had to use both hands to pull off the tape. I inhaled sharply. It wasn't at all what I expected—or hoped—to find. Just the opposite. The exit wound wasn't neat or tidy; it was horrible, a brutal mess of flesh resembling nothing more than ground meat. Worse still, the swelling on that side wasn't just puffy, but red, inflamed. Oozy, too. I cupped my hand against the small of her back, close to the wound, and felt the heat pulsing from within. Rose whimpered. I pulled her shirt down.

My heart was pounding.

"Ben?" she said.

"Huh?"

"How's Archie? Did he come back with you?"

I hesitated. "No."

"Where is he?"

"You really want to know?"

"Yes," she said.

So I told her the truth. I owed her that. I'm not sure what I expected after her brother's reaction. Grief, perhaps. Or sorrow. Maybe even guilt.

But I was a poor predictor of emotions. Because when I told Rose about how Archie had chosen to face certain death walking into a blizzard rather than give up his search for a fortune that was never his to begin with, she didn't shed a tear. She didn't even look sad—walking the walk, I suppose, on her assertion that death wasn't something to feel all that terrible about.

"I don't think he could've survived out there in the snow. Not overnight," I said, wanting her to know for sure how final his decision had been.

"But he was still looking for the money, wasn't he? He never gave up?"

"No, he never gave up."

Rose, ill as she was, remained content at my reassurance. Not happy or joyful, but there was satisfaction in her eyes, a certain strength against the pain. I wanted to ask why, what it was she knew about Archie that made her feel that way. And I also wanted to ask why *she'd* confided in him—but not me—about *our* relationship.

But I didn't.

Instead I pressed my lips together and set to work cleaning and changing her wounds with the first aid kit I'd brought down from the meadow. Whatever had been used already had set loose an infection inside of Rose, all that heat and ooze. Holding the bottle of antiseptic over her back, I knew it would sting, worse than when I'd cleaned her finger, and I didn't want to do it. I didn't want to pour it on her and be the one to hurt her. But I had no choice. So rather than telling her what I was going to do, I just dumped it on her ruined flesh as fast as I could.

Rose shrieked and leapt, and the wounded look she gave me wasn't one of betrayal but disbelief. I didn't stop, though, not even when tears welled in her eyes and rolled down her cheeks. Not even when she shrieked again as I ripped off the remaining duct tape and hurried to pack the wounds with fresh gauze and ointment. I said nothing to acknowledge the pain I was causing her, because it was for her own good and because I didn't want to worry her about it ahead of time.

When I was finished, she lay back to stare up at the ceiling and refused to look at me. Rose's tears continued to fall, hot and silent, and that was the moment I should've apologized—not for doing what needed to be done, but for being so cowardly about it. For letting fear guide my actions over love. But I didn't. I didn't say a word to comfort her or reassure her or let her know my love was unconditional, no matter what she'd done or why. I said nothing. And looking back, if there's one thing I truly am sorry for, well then, I guess that would be it.

41.

SHELBY ACCOSTED ME THE MINUTE I STEPPED OUT OF THE TENT, turning sick and dizzy in the chilled air. Flurries were coming down again. Light ones, but still.

"Can we talk?" she asked me.

"I'm getting Rose something to eat."

"This is about Rose." She waved me with her, walking farther into the forest, her shoes crunching on snow. I followed as best I could, the blond bounce of her hair, but not only were Shelby's legs somehow longer than mine, my joints had stiffened up while I'd been in the tent and my shoulder ached with every motion. My steps were halting, fawn weak and wobbly.

"Hey, slow down." I gasped.

A frown etched Shelby's face as she looked back at me.

"Sorry," I said. "My shoulder's busted. I don't feel too good."

She nodded and turned around. Waited for me to prop myself against a tree and catch my breath. "Well, I wanted to show you this."

"Show me what?"

Shelby pulled the bottle of Maggie's Percocet from her windbreaker pocket. Held it in her scratched-up hands.

I furrowed my brow. "Why do you have those? Isn't Rose taking them?"

"Yeah, she is."

"They help with her pain, right? She's in a lot of pain."

"They do help. But . . ."

"But what?"

"The bottle says to take one or two every six to eight hours."

"Right."

Shelby gave me a pointed look. "This morning she took four."

"All at once?"

She nodded. "I left the bottle in there with her after I'd already given her one. There were twelve more at that point. I know that. I was counting to see how many days they'd last, just in case we're stuck here for a while. Then Tomás started calling for me because he needed help keeping the fire going while trying to dry all those wet clothes. He's not very organized, by the way. Anyway, when I went back in she'd passed out with the bottle in her hand so I counted again. There were only nine."

"But she's okay? It was just an accident?"

Shelby licked her chapped lips. "I don't know what it was. I just know she's really hurting. Worse than she'll say. But I've been holding on to the pills ever since. Unless you want to."

"Sure." I took them from her, slid them into my pants. "Thanks, Shelby."

"Yeah."

"You know, I brought back all the medication Mr. Howe was keeping for us. There's a prescription of yours in there. If you need it or anything." I watched her closely, wondering if she'd share with me what the pills were for, if I'd earned that bit of intimacy.

But Shelby just lifted her chin. Let her eyes grow distant. "Cool," was all she said.

We spent the next few hours engaged in activities that, in retrospect, seem stupid and uninformed. But I guess when you want so badly to be doing *something*, you'll take almost anything. This involved not only collecting wood to keep the fire going and setting up the second tent, but we also got it in our minds that we needed to continue building a second bonfire closer to the water in a more visible spot. If a helicopter were to come by, went our logic, it would be easier to see.

We also talked about walking out to the south, the long way, but the storm started up again, first dusting us with more snow and hail, and then the wind really went wild, shaking the trees and dropping daggers of ice everywhere. We scattered then, crawling into our tents to huddle in safety, if not the illusion of.

I joined Rose, of course, but Avery came in with us, too, and you know, that might sound weird or whatever, but in the moment, it wasn't. Rose needed another Percocet, so I gave one to her. Avery curled up on the opposite side of her, burrowing between a sleeping bag and the frozen ground. I didn't mention the bedbugs. There wasn't anything to be done about them, and pretending the problem didn't exist felt like the most generous act.

My stomach growled. I couldn't sleep but laid my head on a pair of wadded-up sweatpants and let my mind dream of food my mouth longed to eat. Cooking was a skill I'd picked up as a kid. When my mom was up for it, it was actually one of few activities she genuinely enjoyed. She was good at it, too. Neither of us were adventurous eaters, but she taught me how to roast a whole chicken and bake oven fries salted with garlic and how to flip an omelet in a way that looked fancy. That last she'd learned from her line-cook days. Rose, on the other hand, always wanted me to branch out with my culinary interests, growing impatient when I didn't want to try things like ceviche or tripe or even our own local Humboldt Bay oysters topped with horseradish. "You have no *culture*," she'd say, exasperated, and while I saw her point, I also thought she was wrong. I was the product of my culture, same as her, and I didn't have to like or respect it any more than she did to know it was still a large part of who I was.

As I lay there, eyes closed, I overheard Avery talking to Rose. It was a quiet conversation, punctuated by the crack of falling branches and the sound of snow turning to rain to the strike the roof above us. I couldn't hear it all, what they were saying, and I suppose I wasn't meant to. Rose's voice, in particular, was softer, barely there, but I took in what I could.

"You're brave, Rosa," I heard Avery whisper. "I mean it. You're going to be okay."

There was a long pause as Rose said something I couldn't hear.

"No. It won't be like that . . . Yes, I promise."

Another pause.

"To the best of us," Avery said softly. Then: "Yeah, I miss him. I didn't . . . I thought this weekend was going to be different. I know you thought that, too. Maybe that was stupid, some of the things he said. But I know you tried. We all did."

Rose's answer still wasn't audible, but I knew she said something and I knew Avery heard her, because she said one last thing to Rose.

"It's how we should all go. I mean it. You gave him that. It was a gift. *Your* gift. We should all be so blessed."

Although the temperature rose enough to cause rain, the storm lasted most of the afternoon, sending sheets of water down from the sky; and it was hard not to picture Archie up there throwing buckets on us with glee. Lying awake while the girls slept, I endured a stretch of panic, en-visioning us being washed away by a flash flood. Nothing came of it, though. The rain tapered off by dusk and we crawled from our tents to survey the landscape.

Clay got the fire going again by some sort of alchemy. A lot of the snow was gone, but everything was soaked, pooling with rainwater, in-cluding much of our firewood. I was sent to check on the second bon-fire, which was likewise ruined. Shelby and Avery gathered all the food they could find and set it on the card table for an inventory. It wasn't much. Even with what we'd brought back from the upper campsite, we had only three packets of instant cocoa, a half-empty bottle of vodka, a package of beef jerky, two dehydrated camping meals, some trail mix, and a bag of cheese puffs.

"This is depressing," Clay said. "No one's coming for us."

"What're we going to do?" Shelby asked.

"We need to walk out," Avery said. "We should try the access road first."

Clay looked at her. "Tomás says it's impossible. The whole trail collapsed."

"That doesn't mean we shouldn't try."

"What about the long way?" I asked. "We could go out through Canyon Creek."

"It's ten *miles*," Shelby said.

I did the math in my head. It had taken us at least two hours to travel four miles that morning. And that had been downhill. "Then let's try the access road first. It can't hurt. Maybe there's a way around."

"Now?" Clay asked.

"No . . . it's getting dark. We'll have to wait until morning."

Shelby nodded. Rubbed her hands together. "Can we eat something already? I'm starving."

"I don't know," I said. "There's not a lot left . . ."

She groaned. "I'm hungry, Ben. I don't think I can stand spending the night like this. And if we don't get out of here tomorrow, then it won't matter anyway because we'll all be—"

"Fine." I cut that thought off. "Let's eat the jerky and the cheese puffs. We'll save the rest for the morning. How's that sound?"

"Sure." Shelby reached for the food. "I can live with that."

42.

THE CURTAIN OF NIGHT CAME DOWN, BLANKETING OUR WORLD WITH
darkness. The temperature sank below freezing again, turning everything icy and slick, a morbid chill.

We hadn't decided who was going, but I knew that I wasn't going to be
the one to hike out for help in the morning. Not with my busted shoulder.
To atone for my frailty, I volunteered to stay up that night and keep watch.

"Keep watch from what?" Tomás asked me, as the others trailed off
to their respective tents. He'd been in with Rose for the past hour or
so, which meant he'd missed the earlier conversation about the food
rationing and what we planned to do.

"I don't know," I said. "Anything. I'll keep the fire going."

He dropped his body into the damp chair beside me, pulled it close
to the flames. "Mind if I keep you company?"

I looked at him.

"I can't sleep," he explained. "It's kind of a long-term problem."

"I see."

"And I'm worried about Rose."

"Yeah, I am, too."

His fingers pulled at a string dangling from his sweatshirt sleeve.
"She can't keep anything down. She's getting weaker. She's sleeping
now—Shel's with her—but it's not good."

I nodded. I was too scared to say anything else.

After a few minutes, Tomás got up and retrieved the bottle of vodka
from the card table. "You want some?"

"Yeah."

We passed it back and forth, foolish maybe, but it was the only warmth available.

"So is it true what they say about twins?" I asked, after a moment.

"Is what true?"

"That you can feel each other's pain."

Tomás snorted. "Hell, I'm always in pain, man. How would I know which was hers?"

I didn't have an answer for that but that Chatterton poem he'd always been so enamored with floated through my mind. So I spoke the words aloud:

"But ah! my breast is human still;
The rising sigh, the falling tear,
My languid vitals' feeble rill,
The sickness of my soul declare."

Tomás gave me a funny look, but then dipped his head, seemingly appreciative of the effort if not the delivery.

"Can't believe you remember all that," he said. "I thought you hated that poem."

"I do. That's why I remember it."

He laughed, and I continued to drink and he drank more. I was buzzed in no time—there was nothing in my stomach—which turned out to be a good thing. It kept my mind off Rose and fear and loss and a martyr's march into the quiet death of snow. Not to mention the unfortunate fact that my arms and legs were itching like crazy.

"Hey, Ben?" Tomás asked.

"Hey, Tomás?"

"Can I tell you something?"

"Anything you want."

"Hold on." He held up the vodka bottle while rummaging around in his sweatshirt pocket. Finally he pulled out a pack of American Spirits and a Zippo. "Want one?"

"Sure." I wasn't a fan but was in no position to deny myself heat. "What'd you want to tell me?"

Tomás lit his own cigarette before handing me the lighter. "Shit."

"What?"

"It's not going to be easy."

"Telling me something's not going to be easy?"

"Confessing," he said. "I need to confess something to you."

I burst out coughing, the cigarette more harsh than smooth. "I hate to break it to you, but confessing's not supposed to be easy."

"Why's that?" he asked.

"Because it's meant to make you feel better after you've done it. You're not supposed to enjoy for its own sake. That's why it's a virtue."

"Confessing's a virtue?"

"Honesty is."

He blew smoke from his nose, letting it mingle with his frosted breath. "You really think that's true?"

"I'm probably the wrong person to ask."

"Yeah, you are, aren't you?"

I was silent for a minute, thinking of all the sins I'd confessed to in my lifetime and all the ones I hadn't. "You know what I do believe, though?"

"What?"

"Confession only makes you feel better under one condition."

"What's that?"

"That you're sorry."

At this, Tomás leapt to his feet with a shudder. After another swig of vodka, he began to circle the fire, walking around and around—a restless route, his shoes squelch-skidding in the icy slush as he paced. He wouldn't look at me, but more than once I watched as his gaze darted to where Abel's rifle hung from a tree branch above us.

"Ben, you've killed someone, right?" he asked. "I mean, we've never talked about it, but everyone knows. You shot your stepfather when you were ten. It was an accident, I know, but still . . . you killed him."

"Yeah," I said flatly. "I killed him."

"So how do you live with yourself?"

"Jesus, Tomás, I don't know. I try and forget about it most of the time."

"Can you really forget about it?"

"Sure. In a way. But I don't feel sorry for what I did. I hated him."

"Did he hit you or something?"

"No, not really. A few times, sure. I mostly stayed out of his way. He hit my mom a lot, though. When he thought she wasn't respecting him. And he did . . . other stuff to her. All the time. And the worst of it was, I couldn't do anything to stop him, because no matter how much he hurt her, she . . ."

"She what?"

I stared hard at the fire. "She believed she deserved it. She *wanted* him to care enough to hurt her. That's really fucked, isn't it?"

"I killed Archie," Tomás said. "And I almost killed you. That's what I needed to confess."

My mind didn't comprehend the words he'd just said. "You what?"

"I killed him. I mean, he's dead, right? You were there. He stayed on that mountain in the middle of a blizzard with no shelter or warm clothes or food, looking for some hidden money he thought was up there. So he's dead. He has to be."

"I believe so, yes. But, Tomás, you didn't—"

"I *did!*"

I drank more of the vodka, burning my throat. I didn't know what to say.

Tomás kept pacing. "You really want to know where I was that night? While Mr. H. and Dunc were getting shot? While everything was going to shit?"

My eyebrows went up. "Uh, yeah, I do."

"Well, after we left you up in the meadow, we all walked down here, just trashed off our asses, and I knew it was stupid. I knew the whole time. I mean, yeah, I care about Clay's sister, but that's no excuse. Or maybe it is. I don't know! But I wanted to somehow stop them before we actually did anything, only I couldn't. Even Rose wouldn't hear of it, which really pissed me off. Because it wasn't like coming down here was a decision any of them would've made on their own, you know? They could've only made it together. With Archie. There's a word for that, isn't there? Being stupid as a group, but not as an individual. What is it?"

"Groupthink?" I offered. "Risky shift?"

"Yeah, maybe. One of those. I mean, that night when it came to risk, all bets were off. I kept telling Archie we didn't know for sure who these guys were. I mean, we really didn't. We were basing it all off a hunch that I think you told us, you know?"

A swirl of dread went through me. "Wait, are you saying—"

"Let me finish, okay?"

"Yeah, sure."

"Well, I had my phone with me, only there's no reception out here. And we were nearly to the junction when Archie told me if I was so worried about what we were doing, that I should run down to the staging area and see if I could get a signal there. Then I could look up these fugitives online and see what they looked like. That would tell us. I agreed, of course, and Archie said he'd wait for me to get back."

"He said that?"

"Yeah."

"So that's what you did? You walked all the way down to the parking lot? That's like two miles."

"I know."

My heart sank. "Shit, Tomás. You could've gotten help. You could've left and—"

"I know. I mean, I didn't have the keys and I didn't know what had happened. But . . . yeah."

"Archie didn't wait for you, did he?"

"Of course not."

"What an asshole."

Tomás stopped walking to light another cigarette, a flame in the darkness. "We all were."

"What'd you find out?"

"It wasn't them."

I froze. "What?"

He gave me a sick grin. "That's what I found out. Those inmates, the ones from Napa, they were caught near Sacramento early Saturday morning. Before we even got here. And by the way, they hadn't robbed any bank, so I don't even know where the rumor about the money came from in the first place."

My mind turned slowly. "Wait, so you knew it wasn't them . . ."

"But I didn't get back here until *after* Rose was shot, and Dunc and Mr. H. were killed. I couldn't have stopped that. But I was so mad at Archie for what he'd done, for leading everyone into danger and for *nothing*. He got them killed. And he risked Rose's life because he didn't care enough to wait for me to find out the truth. That there wasn't any money to begin with."

"No money," I echoed.

"No."

"But Rose said . . ."

Tomás waved a hand. "I know what Rose said. That guy, Abel, I think he must've been fucking with her when he told her that. He probably heard you guys talking about the money and decided to screw with us. But the thing is, I *knew* when you and Archie left that you were going after something that didn't exist. I knew and I didn't say anything. I didn't try and stop you. I let you both go. In part because I blamed Archie for everything, but also, because I really fucking hated that guy."

"Oh." My mind continued to spin. There were other implications in what he was telling me—something wasn't right—but I was too drunk to see the whole picture, to put all the pieces together in a way that made sense.

"I'm really sorry, Ben," he said. "I thought you'd just come back with the keys and leave him. But then the storm . . . I didn't know—"

"It's okay," I said quickly.

He stopped walking. "No, it's really not okay. Don't say that. That's what you always tell Rose."

I tilted my head. "What do I always tell Rose?"

"That everything she does is okay. It's not good for her, you know. Or you."

I didn't respond. It wasn't that he was wrong, it just didn't seem very important at the moment.

"Then who *were* those people?" I asked. "The Preacher, he kept saying I knew who he was. They were hiding something, for sure."

Tomás turned toward the flames before answering, letting the smoke blow in his face. "You want to know what I think?"

"What?"

"I think they were transporting drugs. The guy who died last night, Abel or whatever, I was the one who had to move his body when we found him this morning. He had a bunch of meth or something on him, these bags were taped to his chest. They must've thought we were on to them about that, but I don't know where they were going with it or why they were here."

"Eureka," I said.

"Eureka?"

"That's where they were going." I pulled the paper I'd found earlier from the pocket of the Preacher's jacket. Pointed to the letters EUR AMTK. "I think they were probably meeting someone there. At the train station, I guess?"

Tomás stared at the paper for a long time. "This is all kinds of fucked up, you know? I mean, in a way, they were just camping like we were. But with drugs. And guns."

"Yeah." I didn't bother mentioning that we'd brought our own drugs and guns. "So do you feel better after confessing that to me?"

"A little, maybe. I'm not sure. How do you feel?"

"About that?" I asked. "Okay, I guess. I already knew you didn't like me."

"That's not true," he said.

"It's not?"

"No. I mean, I get that I can be a dick to you. But it's more that I don't think you're good for Rose. Or really, I don't think Rose is good for you. You remind me of me, actually, Ben. Or you did when you two first got together. I knew my sister wanted to fix you the way she used to want to fix me."

"Fix you how?"

"Rose never told you?"

"No."

He shrugged. "I kind of had a breakdown, I guess, when I was in eighth grade. Got really depressed and ended up in the hospital for a couple of weeks. It was part of why we moved. Rose tried to do everything for me after that and tell me what to think so that I'd feel good about myself or whatever, but it got annoying. She resented me for needing help, but it wasn't help I'd asked for in the first place."

"And that reminds you of me?"

"Yeah."

"Oh," I said. Then I scratched at my legs.

Tomás looked over. "What's wrong?"

"Bug bites."

"I got those, too. They're everywhere."

"They're bedbugs."

"Christ." He rolled his eyes. "Of course they are."

I asked him for another cigarette. Better to keep my hands busy than pick off scabs. After handing one over, Tomás ended up flopped beside me again in the camping chair. He threw his head back. And sighed.

I lit the cigarette and smoked silently. Part of me wondered if I should feel angry with Tomás—or even Rose—but I didn't. Nicotine pooled through my veins, my heart, and yes, there were shadows in the trees and a cruel bite to the air, but from where I sat, there was also a view of the moon rising high in the sky, pleasing in its fullness and the way it lit our small clearing. There was the scent of pine and the crackling of a fire and the promise of things that were good even as we sat in the depths of our very own tragedy. I had no idea how any of that could be, and yet there I was.

I breathed it in. Deeply.

Tried to hold on tight.

43.

THE WORLD CONTINUED TO FREEZE AROUND US, AND STRANGE
thoughts continued tumbling through my mind, ones about Archie and
Rose and all the others. What was it the Preacher had said? *We're very
private people.* That had been the first lie he'd told us. After hearing that,
I'd admired Avery for snapping a photo of him. The girl after the wolf.
But then he'd invited her scrutiny. Her probing lens.

Everything afterward, it seemed, had also been lies—who he was
and what he wanted. Although perhaps my imagination was limited by
the things I believed in. Perhaps the man we'd met had genuinely been
both a preacher *and* a drug smuggler. I had no proof to the contrary and
I was most certainly biased by my past experiences with a man who'd
claimed to speak on God's authority. Even so, when I thought about it
more, I decided that the Preacher's first lie to us had actually been, *We
won't bite.*

The vodka caught up with me, and I soon struggled to keep my eyes
open. The effort must've come through on my face, because eventually
Tomás told me, "Go be with Rose."

I rolled my head in his direction. "Huh?"

"She needs you."

"But I thought—"

"Forget what you thought," he said. "Go on. You don't need to stay
up. It's too cold."

"What're you going to do?"

"Me? I'm going to sleep, too. After this." He pulled out a final cigarette and gave me a weak smile.

I smiled back as best I could. Then I left him there, smoking, by the fire.

Rose stirred as I lay beside her.

"Shhh," I told her.

"Ben," she said.

"Go to sleep," I whispered. "That's what I'm doing."

Her nose wrinkled. "You've been drinking, haven't you? And smoking."

"How can you tell?"

"You reek."

"Sorry. I was just having a drink with Tomás. We were trying to stay warm."

Her eyes glittered in the darkness. "Tomás?"

"Yeah."

"Where is he?"

"By the fire."

"He's okay?"

"He's fine."

"But you don't like him."

"I *do* like him. We had a good talk tonight."

"You did?"

"Yeah."

Rose smiled. "I'm glad."

"How's your pain?" I whispered. "Is it getting worse?"

"It's not getting better."

"Can I check the bandages?"

She yawned. "Not now. In the morning, okay?"

"Okay," I said because I was tired, too, and as I settled beside her, the plaintive hoot of an owl floated down from the trees, breaking the night's silence. A second owl hooted in response—a warbling duet—and I kissed Rose. Closed my eyes.

Dreamed.

DAY FIVE

44.

WE WOKE TO SUN AND WARMTH, WHICH IS TO SAY HOPE, AND IT wasn't just owls now, there were more birds singing, chirping, chattering, alive. That, combined with the *drip-drip-drip* of melting snow, was a stark reminder that what had fallen was never meant to stay.

I let Rose sleep but joined the others by the fire as we discussed our plans, what we needed to do. Shelby and Clay agreed to attempt the hike up and around the landslide that had washed out the access trail, in order to make their way down to the staging area, where the cars were parked. I handed the keys over to them, but it was a real possibility, we realized, that the cars would be buried under snow and ice or wedged in mud, and therefore impossible to move.

"Then try your phones," Tomás told them. "There's a charger in the Pathfinder."

"If that still doesn't work, keep walking to the main road and flag drivers down for help," Avery added.

The rest of us planned to stay at the campsite and do what we could to make ourselves visible. Blue sky and bright sun and no wind infused us with energy. Our rescue was imminent. It had to be. There were no excuses for helicopters not to look for us, and even if they went to the top of the mountain first, surely they'd continue looking elsewhere. Surely they would make it to the other side of the mountain, to peer into this lonely gorge.

"We can try the bonfire again," I suggested. It was an optimistic plan, given that I could barely move my left arm—it was swollen stiff;

my damaged shoulder a rainbow of bruising—but in planning there was action. Avery smiled and said she'd help. I smiled back and let myself feel good that we could still be friends given all that had happened between us. But that was what death did. It put things in perspective. Reminded you what was important.

I also watched Tomás kiss Clay good-bye—first pulling him close, then nuzzling his neck before making his way up to his mouth. I looked away at that point, but it felt good to see that, too. And while I'm well aware *I* wasn't meant to feel anything about what they were doing, what I mean is that it felt good to know that passion had endured in those woods. Respect and admiration, as well. And, I could only imagine, trust.

Then Clay and Shelby took off. The melting snow sparkled jewel bright, and I walked with Avery to find more wood for the bonfire. We were going to spell out SOS if we could find enough branches to burn or just a single big X if we couldn't. The first place we looked was in the gully where we'd dumped the Preacher and his girlfriend, although we skirted past the burial site and headed for higher ground, crawling up the back side of the mountain.

Walking side by side, we hoofed through virgin brush, where the untouched trees grew close and tight, creating thick cover for the lower branches, leaving them relatively dry. Avery, who'd brought her camera along, stopped to snap a few photographs of the trees. When she was done with that, she stood on her toes and broke off the branches within her reach—something I couldn't do with my bad shoulder, so I stood beside her and cradled the wood in my good arm. A lot of it was too green to burn, but I didn't say anything. A squirrel ran above, at one point tossing a pinecone at my head, which made me laugh.

Avery gave me an odd look. "You're in a good mood."

"Not good," I said. "But better."

"Sun does that."

"Indeed."

"Back home, they're having classes right now. Can you imagine?"

I shook my head. If conceiving of anywhere overseas was the equivalent of visiting a modern-day dinosaur park, then envisioning myself dozing in second-period English while Ms. Johnson droned on about Dürrenmatt's *The Visit*, a decent play made boring by her endless lecturing on the distinction between comedy and tragedy, felt about as surreal as discovering the fountain of youth or believing in my mother's eternal happiness.

"Think things will be different when we get back?" Avery asked.

"How could they not?"

"I just mean, it's unbelievable, everything that's happened."

"I know," I said.

"I can't believe they're gone."

"I can't, either."

She pulled at another branch. "I haven't even cried over Archie yet, you know? It's weird. I loved him, awful as he was."

"I'm sorry."

"Don't be."

I paused, unsure of how to ask Avery what it was I wanted to know. "Hey, what were you and Rose talking about yesterday?"

The branch she was tugging on snapped. She passed it to me then wiped her hands. "When?"

"In the tent. When it was raining. You were talking to her about Archie. You said you both thought this weekend would be different. And that Rose had given him a gift."

"Oh," she said. "That."

"Yeah, that. What was the gift?"

"Reason." Avery brushed her hair back, pushing it from her face. "And hope."

"That's it?"

"At the time, it was everything."

"But I don't understand. Why would she do that? Why would Rose want to give Archie *anything*?"

Avery took a step toward me, closing the distance between us, and when she took my hand this time, she held tight. She didn't let me pull away. "Ben," she said.

"What?"

"Haven't you asked yourself the same thing about me?"

Avery and I walked from the gully to dump the wood on the wet shore of the China Spring. The snow had melted from most of the larger rocks and we sat together in the sunlight while dragonflies dipped and buzzed near the surface of the water. That was where she told me the things she wanted me to know and which she'd never meant to say.

With her legs crossed, her dark hair blowing in the breeze, she told me the story of two girls: one who wanted to save a boy but couldn't, and one who wanted a boy to save himself but who wouldn't. These girls, who met as lab partners in their senior-year science class, decided to help each other, in the way girls are wont to do. I pictured it happening like in Hitchcock's *Strangers on a Train*. Only instead of murder, these girls charted their course to freedom through kindness. Reason, too. And so one was tasked with teaching the other's boy how to hold on, while the second intended to help the first's learn to let go.

"What did Archie need to hold on to?" I asked her.

"His life," she said. "Didn't you know?"

Of course, I didn't. I knew nothing about Archie because I didn't like him and I didn't think he was funny or interesting or even very smart. But I guess Archie and I were of the same mind regarding the worth of his character, because according to Avery he'd been doing everything he could to destroy himself for the past two years. It was the reason he took so many risks. Why he stopped carrying his asthma medicine. And threw knives at his feet. He was waiting to succeed at failing.

Hoping, really.

"He was twelve the first time he was hospitalized for alcohol poisoning," she told me. "I don't know if he did that on purpose or not, but it doesn't matter. He also overdosed on pills last fall—that *was* on purpose, although he'd never say so. And he stole shit. Drove when he was wasted. Got into fights. He tried to die or get himself killed in pretty much every way possible, which meant he hated himself the more he lived because being alive only proved he was a failure. But I loved him, and I worried about him because he wouldn't talk to me or to anyone about any of that stuff. He knew I wouldn't be able to stand it if he actually took his own life. But telling him that, all it did was make him feel worse. And I don't know, it's strange how loving someone can make them feel worthless, but that's what sickness does. Abuse, too. But when Rose got a hold of him, it seemed like he was doing better. Because she's not me. She didn't waste her time telling him how great he was."

I was baffled. "What did she do?"

"She made him want things."

"What things? How?"

Avery sighed. "Ask her. I don't know, really, other than getting him to join the orienteering club. But they share a certain kind of pessimism, those two. It's like they're both determined to see the world for what it is, not what they've been promised—even if it hurts. Or *because* it hurts. I don't know that Rose even liked Archie. I'm pretty sure she didn't, but she helped him anyway because they connected over the ways they'd failed the people who tried to love them. Every time I thought he was going to end it all—he started carrying that dumb gun around once he found out he wasn't going to graduate—Rose gave him a reason to live. Even if it was just for one day, or one hour, it was something. Although, you know"—Avery blushed—"the ironic thing is that it was Archie who got Rose and me talking in the first place. I'd told him about you coming to see me at my dad's shop this summer, and he could tell I liked you, I always have, I guess. But when Arch saw that Rose and I were partners, he told her how I felt. He was just being a dick, but the thing was . . ."

". . . it's what made you and Rose friends," I said, without finishing the last of my thought: *Because Rose wanted you to have me.*

Avery nodded.

"So I was the boy meant to let go?"

"Yes."

"Of Rose."

"That's right."

"Why?"

"That's between you and Rose. But I think . . . but I think she doesn't want to hurt you. And more than that, she wants you to know how to walk away from pain. How to choose what you need, not what you think you have to give."

My head was spinning. "And us? What about us?"

Avery shrugged, at the same time reaching to slide off her camera's lens cap. "There is no *us*, Ben. That's just it. Don't you see? There's you and there's me. But those"—she added with that easy smile of hers— "are both very good things."

She lifted her camera then and snapped the picture you've all seen by now on the news, the one that's come to define me and my motives. I don't know how she did it, but Avery managed to capture everything about that moment: me, hunched on a rock in a small patch of sunlight, knees pulled tight to my chest, and there's the most love-lost look on my face—an expression of heartbreak, bewilderment, and utter, utter despair.

45.

WE GOT TO WORK ON THE BONFIRE AFTER THAT, BECAUSE THERE
wasn't much left to say. Avery and I arranged the wood we'd gathered,
first clearing the ground of snow, as much as we could, sweeping it off
with our feet and with branches too wet to burn. When the pebbly
shore below was visible, we positioned the dry wood we'd found into
a shape that was ultimately my suggestion—and a petty one, at that: a
pair of twin Xs.

The double cross.

It's hard to remember what I was feeling in those moments. A lot
of things, I'm sure. But as crushed as I was, what I kept coming back to,
over and over, wasn't Rose or Avery. Or even myself.

It was Dunc's goofy smile and all the lonely suffering it hid.

It was Archie's final march into the snow, which had seemed like
suicide, but had also been an act that saved me.

It was, above all else, Mr. Howe's undying determination, in the face
of a future marred by disappointment and dreams unfulfilled, to stay at
peace with nature, never at war. It was his boundless joy and unfailing
wonder at every mountain climbed, every vista reached, every turn in
every goddamn trail.

In truth, I'd envied so much of what he'd chased and found, but
when I thought about it more, I realized Avery might've gotten the
whole desire and want thing mixed up. Maybe desire wasn't just about
going after what made you feel good; maybe it was also about finding a
way to feel good about yourself in the first place.

My skin tingled at the thought, the possibility. Could life really be that simple? It was a novel idea, to consider I might make my own joy, rather than waiting for the things I loved to be taken from me. To believe contentment wasn't something to pursue, but something I could *be*.

A state of mind.

Yes, I told myself. *But of course.*

"Hey," Avery said sharply.

I glanced up, a faint smile on my lips, but she was looking somewhere behind me. I turned to see Tomás running toward us, waving his arms frantically. He was calling for help, and I knew exactly what he'd say before he even said it. How could it have been anything else?

"It's Rose," he gasped as he reached us. "Something's wrong!"

We raced back to the campsite. *Wrong* was an understatement. I fell to my knees next to Rose, where she lay on the tent floor in a puddle of sweat. Everything around her looked strange. Eerie. It was the sunlight, I realized. It filtered through the worn beige nylon to cast Rose's skin with a golden glow. But where she'd always been bright, vibrant, lit from within, she was now pale and panting and shivering all at once. I put my hand to her forehead. Felt the fever roaring inside of her.

Tomás bumped up beside me. "What's wrong with her?"

"Rose," I whispered. "Can you hear me?"

Her teeth chattered and she wheezed with each breath, but nodded. I wrapped her shoulders in as many blankets as I could find. Avery crouched on the other side of her and held her close, whispered in her ear, while I switched on the lantern and ducked down low to inspect her injuries.

Pushing her shirt up, I winced at the sight of her skin. Not only were the bug bites everywhere, but they'd grown bloodied from her scratching and it seemed hives had risen up in solidarity; she was covered in blotchy wheals. I let my fingers stroke her skin before pulling back the tape and gauze to inspect the entry wound. My throat felt thick, but the wound looked fine. Clean, at least, and my mind rattled with thoughts of hantavirus or Zika or plague or even some horrific unknown disease that was transmitted primarily through bedbugs.

Next I rolled her forward so that I could see her back, easing the tape and gauze off slowly. Tomás pushed in closer, then groaned. Put a hand to his mouth. Crouched beside him, I didn't make a sound, but I knew how he felt because I could see what he saw and smell what he smelled. Not only was the area on Rose's lower back hot and pus filled, it reeked of horror, like meat left in the sun. The wound had grown, spreading into a wet gaping circle edged by black-crusted skin. Worst of all, things were moving in her flesh, filling my mind with images of fly-strike—blowfly swarms that gathered to lay eggs in the wounds of sick animals, allowing their maggots to feast and grow on what was un-likely to survive.

What it looked like, more than anything, was death.

46.

I DIDN'T LET MYSELF PANIC. I COULDN'T. TOMÁS WAS ALREADY FALL-
ing apart, slipping into a shuddering mess. Rose had been fine earlier,
he told us, with tears pouring down his face. Yes, she'd been tired and
foggy and not wanting to eat. But she'd had water and hadn't said anything about feeling this sick. And then he'd found her like that less than
an hour later.

Terror bubbled inside me. Part of me wanted to snap at Tomás, to
tell him that while he shouldn't take responsibility for what had happened to Archie, he and Shelby sure as hell should feel bad about putting that dirty T-shirt on Rose's wound when she'd first been shot. But it
wouldn't have been fair to say that. It also wouldn't have helped.

Avery took charge, spurring us into action. She ordered me to boil
water and sterilize tweezers and find a towel so that she could try and
drain the wound.

"Damp heat can pull the infection to the surface," she explained.
"It's worth a try."

"What are the tweezers for?"

"Don't ask," she said. "What about medication? Do we have more?
She's in a lot of pain."

"I have Tylenol 3. It should help her fever."

"How much can she take?"

"No more than two. You can't . . . you can't overload on Tylenol. It's
toxic."

"I don't think we can worry about that right now," Avery said.

I nodded. Told her where to get the pills.

Then we did those things. We boiled the water. We cleaned her wound. We gave her more pills. The sun rose higher in the sky and we were desperate and scared, but there was nothing to do but wait for the others to return or for help to arrive. So we waited.

And we waited.

Rose alternated between sleeping and moaning in pain. Tomás, Avery, and I took turns sitting with her, but our uselessness soon grew unbearable. So did the thought of failure.

"We don't know where the hell they are," Tomás said, referring to Shelby and Clay. "We don't even know if they got back to the cars. What if they took a different route and got lost? Or if they're injured somewhere?"

"What do you want to do?" I asked him.

"I want to get help. She needs a hospital."

"So then let's walk out," Avery said. "We'll go the long way to Junction City. The snow's mostly gone. It won't take more than three hours if we hurry."

"But we can't all go. We can't leave her."

"I'll stay," I said.

Tomás looked at me. "You sure?"

"Yeah. My shoulder's too screwed up. You'll be faster without me."

He nodded, growing restless now that there was a plan. I got the map out and showed them exactly where they'd be going. It was a straight line once they got past Papoose Lake. They just needed to head due south, connecting up with the Canyon Creek Trail and keeping the ridge of mountains to their right. I helped them pack clean water and salt pills and gave them the last of the food.

Tomás ducked into the tent to kiss Rose good-bye and returned with his eyes brimming with tears. Avery hugged me hard.

"We'll be back soon," she said. "It'll be okay."

"Thank you," I told her.

Then they were gone. Opting to let the fire burn out rather than tend it, I crawled into the tent to stay with Rose. I lay beside her. I stroked her hair. Held a wet towel to her burning cheeks.

I wouldn't leave her, I promised myself.

Not until she was safe.

Not until we were saved.

47.

ROSE WOKE EVENTUALLY.

"Ben," she said weakly.

"Shhh." I felt her forehead. It was as hot as ever. "You're okay."

"What's wrong with me?"

"The gunshot. It's infected. Maybe gangrenous. It's making you sick."

She began panting again. "That's bad, isn't it? Like, really bad."

"It'll be okay. Help is coming."

"What help?"

"The storm's over. It's sunny. Everyone's walking out. Someone'll be here soon. I promise. A doctor. Real help."

"Everyone?"

"But me."

"Why didn't you go with them?" she asked.

"I couldn't leave you, Rose. I won't. I'll be right here."

She nodded. Her eyes fluttered closed. I watched her sleep.

She began twitching, her shoulders and legs. I panicked, thinking she was having a seizure, and tried holding her down with my good arm. Rose thrashed against me, then twitched again, quicker this time, and she made a gurgling sound, deep in her throat.

"Rose!" I hissed. "Rose, wake up!"

"Gah," she said, before turning her head, throwing one arm across her face.

"Rose!"

"Stop it," she mumbled, and she pushed my hand away. "Just leave me alone."

I sat back, temporarily relieved. She wasn't seizing, just fitful. She was asleep, it seemed, hovering in that space between rest and REM. She settled eventually and the thrashing slowed, although her limbs continued to twitch and jump, like a dog that was dreaming of running past its fence.

48.

DAY DRIFTED INTO AFTERNOON.

No one returned to say they couldn't make it through the melting snow.

No one came back with help.

No search-and-rescue team found us on their own.

Nothing.

It was just me and her.

But, I whispered in her ear, it was also us.

Rose's fever climbed. She woke again but didn't recognize me. Her cheeks, which had been so pale and sunken, were now flushed bright like she'd been slapped, and she was breathing hard. Too hard. Steam train fast. Puff-puff-puff.

I'd tied open the tent door earlier to let the air circulate, and I glanced out at the trees. At the growing patches of wet earth and budding moss. The shadows looked longer. The sun lower. Or maybe that was my imagination? I had no clue when night would fall but Rose couldn't wait until then.

I couldn't, either.

"Please," I prayed out loud to no one in particular—or to everyone, really; my desperation was nonspecific. "Please come. Please, please save us."

Rose needed more Tylenol, but before she could swallow it I had to boil more water. Spring or no spring, I couldn't risk getting her sick from giardia, which was everywhere around here. That meant starting up the fire again—the propane was long gone, as were the water purification pills. I flirted with the idea of jogging back up to the upper campsite and foraging there for supplies but couldn't bring myself to do it. A fire wasn't hard. I'd watched Clay every time he'd started ours.

"The flame is like your voice," he told me, back on our first night by the river, after he'd hauled in all those fish. Then he'd glanced over at me, tomcat scowl etched across his skinny face. "That's not, like, a shitty metaphor or anything. Acoustics and fire behave really similar to one another. It's all energy, okay? It's waves. And if you need more of something you don't have, you bring in a second energy source to amplify the first. Like this."

I'd leaned in close as he crafted a nest of dry grass kindling beneath the larger logs he was trying to light. As the kindling caught, its flames flickered short of goal, unable to reach the thicker wood. Its heat quickly dimmed, but before going out completely, Clay crawled forward on his knees and blew beneath the ashes. Oxygen flooded in and the kindling erupted again, its flames shooting higher this time, sending lit sparks spiraling upward to set the logs ablaze.

He sat back on his knees in a haze of satisfaction.

"And that," he said, "is how you do it."

Unable to rely on my own skill or experience, I worked hard to re-create just what he'd done: stacking the wood I found into a triangular shape. Finding kindling was more difficult. There was no dry grass or bark—everything was wet and mushy—and as the wind picked up again, whistling through the gorge, I did the only thing I could think of: I pulled the cash I'd found in the Preacher's jacket from the inside pocket and began to shred it, stuffing the torn bills beneath the branches.

When I'd stuffed enough in there, I set it all ablaze with a match.

Only unlike Clay's fire, there was too much of a breeze for my kindling. It threw the flames in every direction, and I had to cup my hands around the burning money to contain all that energy. Finally, the flames shot straight up and took. I frantically stuffed more cash in to keep it going, and when the wood began to crackle and the heat felt constant, far out of my control, I stuck the water kettle directly on the flames. Once rolling, it would have to boil for three minutes for purification purposes, but the time until then was anyone's guess.

Rose began to scream.

"*Shit.*" I slipped and fell trying to run to her, landing on my bad shoulder with a howl. I got up again, quick as I could, and when I got to her, all I could tell was that she'd gotten sick on herself and the blankets. She screamed more when I touched her, tried to help her, and flailed her body.

"Rose, Rose, Rose," I said. "Please, baby, it's okay. I'm making water for you. I've got more pills. They'll help."

Her screaming trailed into hacking coughs and sobbing, only her tears were dry, and that was a bad sign. It meant she was dehydrated and I had no fluids to give her. I put one of the Tylenols in her mouth and tried to get her to swallow it, but she ended up choking. Spitting it out. Sobbing more.

The tent reeked of vomit. I brushed flies from her body, but they kept coming back. I couldn't stop shaking. I couldn't stop telling Rose I loved her, that help was coming and that she would be okay. The pain would stop, I said. She just had to hold on. Her heart jittered against my chest, a wild double-time beat it couldn't possibly sustain, and while my tears were as dry as they always were, it wasn't long before I heard my own sobs mix with hers. A hoarse sound both ragged and rare, but not wholly forgotten.

She jerked hard and fell against me. I threw my good hand out to steady myself, letting it land first on the squishy air pillow Rose had been using. I knocked it aside only to set my hand on cold metal. Startled, I looked down to see Archie's loaded handgun, the one he'd brought on the trip to ward off any apex predators. It lay there on the tent floor, where it must have been, all this time—hidden not close to Rose's heart, but mere inches from her head.

My stomach soured. The first thrum of a migraine began worming its way into my skull as I took in what I was seeing and what it meant. Rose had stolen that gun from Archie on purpose. I knew she had. She must've lifted it from his backpack before sending the two of us up on that mountain together. Or else she'd had Avery do it. Either way, knowing me well—and not knowing about the storm—Rose had trusted me not to leave him. Not even to save her.

But she'd done more than that, I realized. Far more. I was *sure* of it. Because Abel was no bank robber—Tomás had told me that. And while he'd been far from innocent, I didn't believe he'd told Rose a story about any fake money, not even out of spite or malice. He'd been too close to death for dissembling. Not to mention, it couldn't have been him who'd spun the bank robbery story in the first place. That had happened back up on the mountain. All of which pointed to the fact that Rose had been telling the truth when she said that everything that had happened was *her* fault. Because the gift Rose had given Archie was a lie.

A hopeful one.

I picked up the gun.

No, Rose didn't want me. She hadn't since the day she'd returned from Peru with her skin tan and her heart ripe with remorse. But in that moment, my love for her burned more fiercely than it ever had. I loved her for caring enough to push me away. For trying to teach me that abandonment didn't have to be my destiny. For not giving me any easy outs and for insisting that some choices were the kind I had to navigate alone.

My hand shook, but I held her close. I cooed my love song in her ear, no longer a duet, but no less loving, and I told her about the beauty around us: the sunlight dancing on the water; the mountains kissed with snow; the tender spaces hollowed between the trees that were built to bear witness to secrets always to be kept and promises never broken. Rose gasped and struggled to breathe, her hands clawing at her throat, her back arched in constant pain.

I held her closer, and I told her about the gun. How I'd come to realize that like freedom, salvation could look different to different people, depending on where you were and what it was you needed. How I knew now that who we were was more often defined by what we'd done than what it was we one day hoped to achieve. And how I'd learned, more than anything, that survival so often meant letting go. I knew she understood that. We'd talked about it the night we'd lain half naked beneath the stars. It was the reason Rose had told Archie the things she did, offering him purpose even in the hell of his mind's own winter. Hope soared over surrender, and reason triumphed over despair. Even in death.

That had been *her* gift, I whispered, pushing her soft hair back as I brought the gun to her head. Hope and reason. Now freedom would be mine. And for my beautiful, wilting Rose, who was stuck in her own agony, just like my mother before her, it was one I gave willingly.

Only this time, it was with my eyes wide open.

AFTER

49.

WHAT MORE CAN I TELL YOU?

What else is there, really, to say?

50.

WELL, THERE IS MORE TO SAY, OF COURSE.

Only I don't know where to start. Or even how to begin. In reaching the end of her story, all that remains is now mine alone, and I never wanted that. Other people are born to be the protagonist, the main character, the brightest star in their galaxy.

But not me.

I could tell you, I suppose, about the snow falling outside my window as I write this, a near-poetic dusting of the dawn. It isn't easy to see through the bars, but if I close my eyes, I can picture the way the flakes might gather on the ground, sticking together to become something greater than themselves.

Speaking of poetic, it's not Chatterton, but William Bryant who haunts my conscience these days, his ode to impermanence capable of savaging my soul.

> Loveliest of lovely things are they
> on earth that soonest pass away.
> The rose that lives its little hour
> is prized beyond the sculptured flower.

Do you see? Do you see how those words might ruin me?

As well they should.

I could also tell you it's been two months since the trip to Thompson

Peak, which means it's been two months that I've been housed here in Trinity County's juvenile detention facility, waiting to stand trial for the murder of Rosemarie Augustine. I left my Humboldt home back in October and have yet to return, which I guess makes this place a purgatory of sorts.

No one from that trip has come to see me, in case you're wondering about that. They also haven't called. Or written. Or communicated with me in any way. None of this is a surprise, but it still hurts. From what I hear, though, they're alive and healing, so I suppose that what I ought to feel is gratitude.

There *are* people who visit me, and they like to ask all sorts of questions. About Rose. About Archie. About Rose and Archie. About everything that happened, and why, when search and rescue finally showed up on that mountain, I was found alone in a tent, with my dead girlfriend in my arms and the gun I'd used to shoot her lying on the ground beside me.

My court-appointed lawyer doesn't let me answer any of these questions. I understand why, but even when we're alone, he never wants to hear what I have to say—unless it's that I'll take a plea deal, which I won't because I'm not guilty of what I'm being accused of. So it turns out the only person around here I'm allowed to talk to with any degree of honesty is the county doctor they send me to who helps me with my migraines.

He also asks about my shoulder, that doctor. It worries him, I guess, that I still have so much pain. That's what we talk about mostly. Pain. How bad it is and what I think I can live with. He wants to refer me to someone else in case surgery is necessary, but I don't want to do that, to be cut open. I can live with the pain, I tell him. I'm pretty sure I can live with anything.

Hearing this always makes him frown. Pain isn't meant to be

punishment, he says. It's a signal to tell you when something's wrong. Well, I've heard this before and I know what he means, but I'm not sure I agree. My mother's only spoken to me once since I've been here, and that was to tell me she's through with me and my problems— forever. That she can't handle what I've done, no matter with what love I might've done it.

Not this time.

Not ever again.

51.

THE SNOW'S CONTINUED TO FALL OFF AND ON OVER THE PAST FEW days, and I think it might be getting to me. I started feeling bad after lunch today and ended up in the bathroom for a long time and then I ended up sort of wanting to die. That's an awful thing to say, I know, but it's an awful way to feel and it can overwhelm me at times, everything that's happened. All that's been lost. Doing the right thing doesn't preclude regret, I've found. Or self-loathing. These are truths I have to learn to live with, and I suppose the good news is I managed to get myself out of there without doing anything stupid.

My little hour, such as it is, marches on.

But fate works in strange ways. After leaving the bathroom, I made my way down to the main common area. They've got a television in there, mounted high on the wall, and if I'm lucky, I can sometimes catch a glimpse of myself on the news and catch up with what's happening back in Teyber. Lucky for me, there's been a lot more coverage of my case lately, now that it's been determined I'll be tried as an adult. I sort of live to see the storm clouds on Tomás's face. Not for the storm itself, but because I see Rose in him. She lives there, beneath his thorns, and she's as beautiful as ever.

I'm always eager to spot the rest of them, too, the ones who made it back from Trinity. Grim-faced Avery, who's too wise for what she's going through, aloof Shelby, and gloomy, grieving Clay. Although, from what I gather, Clay's grief has far more to do with his little sister not getting her transplant in time than anything that I did.

Today, unfortunately, I didn't get to see any of them. Football was on and most of the guys were sprawled on the floor watching the game. They cheered with gusto; the Raiders were pummeling the Broncos, and that being a good thing was one of the few agreements I've seen within these walls. It still made me a little sad, though, to hear their shouts and see their pumped fists. To know those moments of vicarious victory might be the sole sparks of joy in all their week.

It was around the end of the fourth quarter that someone came and told me I had a visitor. That was weird because it wasn't visiting hours, but they said it was a doctor who'd come to see me, and that confused me even more. Was it about my shoulder? I left the common area and walked back to the deserted cellblock, which is where I sleep, only to find the door to my room wide open.

I stepped inside and saw that the doctor waiting for me was a woman, one with long dark hair that fell all the way down her back. It took a moment to register that I was looking at Lucy. Mr. Howe's Lucy. And then I froze, right in my tracks, because she was the last person I expected to see. In fact, I stayed like that for a while because not only was Lucy sitting on my bed, awaiting my return, but she was reading this notebook. She had it open on her lap, seemingly engrossed, as she slowly turned the pages.

I watched but said nothing. She kept reading, and eventually I sat in my desk chair and picked up a book I'd borrowed from the library so that I could pretend I was reading, too. But I grew restless the more time passed, the more pages she turned. Finally, I just held the book in my hands and spun the chair I was in, propelling myself around and around, as the mottled mix of shadow and light fell through the window to stripe my arms, my legs.

Lucy read for a long time. I waited, as the day stretched toward evening, transforming the light and shadows in the way all endings do—moving up the wall and beyond my reach. Moving on without me. Rose once said I heard the world in a minor key, and it's in these moments before the darkness, when my despair is at its greatest, that I can see that she was right; I *am* sentimental. Maybe a little bitter, too, because in finding my conviction, I've also found myself alone.

I flipped on the overhead light, so Lucy could continue to see. She nodded her thanks, but she was crying by that point. She was reading about the death of her husband, after all. And while she must've known the details of how he'd died and the hero he'd been, she was reading for the first time about those pieces of him I'd found on the mountain— those small ways he'd loved her and yearned to keep her close. I guess what I didn't expect was how much she'd cry when she'd *finished* reading what I'd written. And Lucy's tears, it seemed, weren't only for Rose or her husband or even for herself, because she threw her arms around me and held me to her.

"Oh, Ben, Ben," she wept. "I'm so, so sorry."

Sorry for what? I wanted to ask, but didn't. Her tears were soaking through my jumpsuit, and it felt good to be held, to be what she needed. I didn't want to do anything to change that.

After a few minutes, Lucy sat back, wiped her tears, and pulled herself together. She told me she was there in an official capacity; it turns out she's a consultant for the county and after the medical doctor reported I was depressed, she got permission to come and see me. I felt bad about that, her worrying about my well-being, but Lucy wanted to know if I was getting the care I needed. I told her I was, and then she asked if she might come back another time, to talk to me more and to read what I'd written again. She also said it might be a good idea for other people to read my notebook, although I don't know who would want to do that or to what end.

Still, I nodded yes to everything she said—not because I want people to read my words but because I want Lucy to have a reason to come back. I know I'm not enough of a reason on my own, so I'll do whatever she asks. I'll do anything. And maybe that sounds weak or whatever, in light of all that's happened, but the way I'm trapped now is different from before. I'm no longer ice drawn to flame; I'm captured beneath glass, far more sculptured than alive, and there's nothing about my current situation that's going to change—no matter how much I believe in myself. No matter what choices I make.

But necessity is the mother of invention, as they say, and maybe I'll find that hope is, too. So I guess what I really want is for Lucy to feel good about me. That means a lot somehow.

In a way, it sort of means everything.

ACKNOWLEDGMENTS

MANY, MANY HEARTFELT THANKS TO EVERYONE WHO HELPED BRING
this book to life: Michael Bourret and Andrew Karre; Anna Booth,
Theresa Evangelista, Melissa Faulner, Rosanne Lauer, Julie Strauss-
Gabel, Natalie Vielkind, and the whole Dutton crew; copyeditor Anne
Heausler; and dear friends Brandy Colbert, Phoebe North, Stephanie
Sinkhorn, Kody Keplinger, Courtney Summers, and Kate Hart.

Thank you also to my children for their title help; to Will, for
forever dragging me into the California wilderness; to David Friedman,
for sharing his love of rock climbing; and to the kind nurses and doctors
at the Weaverville ER, because research can be dangerous.